EVE OF THE FAE

Eve of the Fae

MODERN FAE BOOK 1

E. MENOZZI

For my family, blood and found.

1

MY eyes were playing tricks on me. That was the only rational explanation. I'd been traveling all day—a car, two planes, and now this taxi. At this point, I was so tired that I was starting to imagine things lurking in the darkness beyond the cab window. I focused on the back of the passenger headrest in front of me. There was no way that foggy blur on the horizon had actually been a group of armored men on horseback racing across the moonlit English countryside. I rubbed my eyes and leaned back against the sticky leather seat.

My fingers itched to reach for my phone and text my best friend, Angie, but I hesitated, remembering her parting words on the drive to the airport this morning. *I hope it's worth it.* Not exactly the most encouraging send-off, but she didn't understand how much Lydbury meant to me. She already thought I was crazy, running away from my perfectly acceptable life in the Bay Area to follow a dream. A dream job or a dream school would be one thing, but following a literal dream about a woman in a tapestry, half a world away in England, was a little too far out there for my business-minded bestie. Honestly, it was a little too far out there for me, as well. But I couldn't get that lady out of my head, and once I'd figured out where I'd seen her before, it all came together. I just knew what I had to do.

When I opened my eyes, my weary reflection stared back at me from the cab window. Reaching up, I smoothed a hand over my ponytail, twisting the thick dark hair around my palm. We had to be close now. I pressed my face toward the window, careful to keep from touching the glass, and scanned the dark, rolling hills. No sign of metal armor flashing in the moonlight. I breathed a sigh of relief. Not crazy. Just tired. Then I caught my first glimpse of the peaked roof of Lydbury Manor rising up from the horizon, silhouetted against the night sky. Excitement thrummed in my veins, and I scooted to the edge of my seat.

The taxi slowed, and the crunch of tires on gravel signaled that we'd turned onto my aunt and uncle's private drive. Tall stone pillars framed the gated entrance. At the top of each, a bronze dragon curved around an iron ball, its mouth open and its forked tongue flicking out. Moonlight filtered down on them through the bare winter tree branches, and they appeared to slither and twist as we drove past. A chill ran down my spine like I'd been soaked with a bucket of ice water, and I shivered.

I tried to shake that eerie feeling as the driver guided the car down the long, tree-lined drive. He parked at the bottom of the wide stone steps leading up to the mansion entrance. Evergreen hedges garnished with strings of sparkling white lights bracketed an enormous oak door. All the windows remained dark, and other than those few strands of Christmas lights, the place looked abandoned—but I knew better.

"Are you quite sure you have the right address, miss?" asked the driver.

I confirmed this was, indeed, the right address, then double-checked the fare and handed over my carefully counted bills. I grinned as I stepped out of the taxi and stared up at the doorstep of the ancient mansion. I loved this creepy old place and all its bizarre history so much. I'd spent every spare minute for the past few months reading and studying the legends and relevant bits of information I could get my hands on. Hopefully, my preparation would be enough to convince Uncle Oscar to take me on as his assistant. Once I'd accomplished that, the rest would fall into place. I was sure of it.

The driver set my suitcase and duffle on the bottom step and gave me one last questioning look before returning to his cab and disappearing into the darkness. I pulled my coat closed against the brisk winter wind and swung the strap of my duffle over my shoulder. At the top of the steps, I reached for the iron knocker and rapped several times.

The last time I'd been here, I hadn't been able to reach the knocker. My father had lifted me, and even then, I hadn't been able to make enough noise to rouse my aunt and uncle from their library at the back of the house. Most likely that's where they were now, tucked into their favorite chairs, reading and working in front of the roaring fire. I waited for my aunt to make the long walk through the dark hall, past enormous rooms filled with antique furniture, which I'd been forbidden to play in as a child.

The door creaked open and my aunt's face peeked out. When she saw me, she smiled and opened the door wide. "Come in, come in. Have you been waiting long? You must be freezing. Let me get your bag. Come, come. In you go."

She shut the door behind me, then pulled me to her. I bent to return her hug, and all the worry drained from me. This was exactly where I needed to be.

She pushed me away and held me at arm's length. "Let me get a look at you. Our beautiful Eve... You've grown so tall, just like your father. Oh, how I hated that he got all the height in the family. But listen to me, carrying on. How was your trip? Made it here okay, then?"

"Yes, Auntie. Thank you so much for letting me stay for the holidays. Your house is just as big and spooky as I remember."

"Oh, well, you know Oscar. He won't change a thing. It's a wonder I got him to agree to 'The Great Purge,' as I've dubbed it." She shook her head but smiled and squeezed my hands. "But enough of my prattling on. Let me show you to your rooms so you can get some rest. Unless you want to stay up with us old folk?" She paused to study my face but didn't give me time to respond before she continued. "Look at you. You're exhausted. Come now, up this way. We'll get you settled and catch up over breakfast in the morning. Yes?"

Aunt Vivian took my duffle from me and headed up the curving staircase. Even though we talked every week over video chat, her warm smile was even better in person. As much as I wanted to prove to her husband that I was ready to assist him with his museum project, I'd be much more convincing after a good night's sleep.

I pushed away my anxious thoughts and followed my aunt up the stairs. Now that I was here, I wanted to absorb every detail of my uncle's historic home, starting with the woodwork that I'd been too young to appreciate on my previous visit. I ran my fingers over the carvings in the banister as we climbed, tracing the patterns of leaves and marveling at the woodland creatures sculpted into the vertical supports. At the first landing, I paused in front of the tapestry hanging on the wall. A woman with flowing golden hair billowing around her pale face sat on a throne, surrounded by lush green flora and delicate flowers.

"She's still here." I shuddered as I stared into the woven eyes of the golden-haired woman I'd seen in my dream.

"Who, dear?" Aunt Vivian paused partway up the next flight of stairs and turned to look over her shoulder. "Oh! The Faerie Queen. Of course. You were quite taken with that tapestry when you were a child. You used to play with your dolls right there on the landing, making up stories about their adventures."

"That's meant to be her, right? Lord Edric's wife?" Once I'd recognized the woman in my dream, I'd dug up everything I could find about Oscar's ancestor Edric and his wife, Godda. If this tapestry was any indication, she certainly was beautiful enough to be a storybook faerie queen, as claimed by the local legends.

"Oh, yes. The Queen of the Faeries. Though, why she ever agreed to marry Oscar's ancestor after he kidnapped her and brought her here, I'll never understand." She shook her head at the tapestry. "Do you remember playing here?"

"I remember so much about this house, but it's funny...I don't remember playing here." Goose bumps prickled across my skin. I had some new theories about that story, based on my research, and none of them involved Godda being a Faerie Queen. After all, faeries weren't real, and my uncle was an historian, not a storybook writer. I was convinced he'd appreciate my careful analysis and ideas.

"Hmm." She squinted at me. "I think it was just after that visit you exchanged dolls for sneakers and books. After that, you were either running too fast for anyone to catch you or hiding with your nose in a book." Her eyes glazed over for a moment. Then she blinked, turned her head away, and continued climbing.

I took one more long look at the tapestry, then forced myself to follow Aunt Vivian up the stairs.

She paused at the second-floor landing, then turned to say, "I'm glad you decided to take a vacation and let me spoil you rotten." Before I could respond, she disappeared to the left and started down the hall to the guest wing. My stomach clenched as I remembered that I was going to have to tell her I hadn't been completely honest. I wasn't here for a relaxing Christmas holiday, at least not if I could get Uncle Oscar to agree to let me help him with the exhibit. Now that I'd arrived, I started to question my decision to withhold the true purpose of my visit, no longer sure why I'd worried that they would try to talk me out of it. Not that it mattered. It was too late to turn back now. I'd already quit my job, and I didn't even have a return ticket.

When I reached the landing, a movement at the end of the main hall caught my eye. I squinted into the darkness, but there was nothing in the hallway or on the back stairs that led up to the attic bedroom. I shook my head. That was it. I was exhausted and definitely imagining things. Still, a wave of nostalgia washed over me at the thought of that attic bedroom. That was where my brothers and I had slept when we'd last visited. I'd kind of hoped I'd get to sleep up there again. But my aunt had started walking down the hallway, so it looked like she had given me one of the guest rooms instead.

I turned and followed her down the hall, still carrying my suitcase. I didn't want to ruin the beautiful hardwood floors or dirty the long, plush carpet that ran down the center of the hallway with the scratched and grimy wheels of my luggage.

Wainscoting covered the lower portion of the walls in a stain that matched the wood on the floors. The upper portion had been painted with a deep wine color and washed in light from electric candles with leaded glass shades mounted along the hall every few feet. I followed my aunt past several closed doors before she finally stopped and placed her hand on one of the doorknobs.

"Here you are, right in here." She twisted the knob and pushed the door open to reveal an enormous bedroom. "Your own bathroom." She pointed to a door in one wall. "And we started a fire in the hearth for you. Gets a bit drafty in this old place. If you like, I could bring you up a hot cocoa. Are you hungry at all? The cook's gone home, but there might be something left from dinner that I could warm up for you."

I shook my head no as I placed my suitcase inside the room and then threw my arms around Aunt Vivian.

"What's that for, dear?" she asked.

"Thank you, Auntie. I like it when you spoil me."

She leaned back and placed a hand on my cheek. "Make yourself at home. If you need anything, we're down in the library. Your uncle will likely be up all night working. I'll probably fall asleep reading in my chair. Some things never change." She laughed and gave me a quick kiss on the cheek before leaving me alone in the room.

I shut the door behind her and pulled my phone out of my pocket on reflex. A quick glance at the screen confirmed I had no new messages. I turned off the screen and slid the phone onto the dresser, then tossed my duffle onto the bed and began unpacking my toiletries.

Once Uncle Oscar agreed to take me on as his assistant, I'd start by organizing and digitizing all his files. He probably still wasn't using a computer. Then I'd take over coordination of his project with the local history museum. He had classes to teach, and I had experience managing projects. It only made sense.

I changed into my pajamas and brushed my teeth, then peeled back the thick, soft duvet and crawled up onto the plush mattress. My mind continued to churn with plans long after I'd turned out the lamp. I stared at the ceiling in the darkness, listening to the crackle of the logs in the dying fire. Only then did I let myself think about the woman in the tapestry.

I closed my eyes, and a vision of Godda, seated on her throne, floated before my eyelids. Suddenly, I wasn't even remotely sleepy. Throwing off the covers, I decided to take Aunt Vivian up on the offer of a hot cocoa before bed. I pulled on my new, thick socks, grabbed my sweater off the chair, and padded down the hall toward the front staircase.

At the end of the hallway, I decided to take the back stairs that led straight to the kitchen instead of going down past the Faerie Queen tapestry. I turned left and started down the main hall, peeking into any open doorways I passed. A rustle and thunk from inside one of the dark rooms behind me made me stop and turn around.

I crept toward the open door, pausing outside to listen. Another thunk rattled the floor, followed by the unmistakable hiss of a cardboard box sliding across carpet. A dim light glowed from inside the room, one that was definitely not there a moment ago when I'd walked past.

"Uncle Oscar? Aunt Vivian? Is that you?" I called out.

A mumbled curse and a thud followed by a low growl was the only response I received.

I poked my head into the room, pausing in the entry to look around. "Uncle Oscar? Do you need help?"

A figure emerged from behind a stack of boxes. The light source seemed to be coming from behind him, but even in silhouette, I knew it wasn't my uncle.

I clutched my sweater in one fist and took a step backward, preparing to run. "Who are you? How did you get in here?"

"I could ask the same of you," he said. He stepped forward, wiping his hands against his pant legs. "Except, given your resemblance to Vivian, I take it you must be her niece, Evelyn, from California." His thick English accent curled around the words, making them sound a hundred times sexier than they should have.

I hesitated. I should have been running away from this intruder, not drawn in by his accent. "How do you know who I am?" My hand found the light switch just inside the door, and I flipped it on, flooding the room in bright light and causing us both to wince and blink. Once my eyes adjusted, I realized he was staring at me and remembered I'd left my room in my pajamas—tank top and shorts with no bra. I crossed my arms over my sweater, hugging it to my chest, and glared at him.

He grinned at me in response and took a few more steps to close the distance between us. Extending his hand, he said, "I'm Liam, your uncle's secretary."

Shock froze me in place for a moment before I extended my own hand to meet his, observing his warm, slightly rough but firm grip. "Since when does Uncle Oscar have a secretary?" I frowned at this new development.

"Since October," he said. "Your uncle is a very important man. Why shouldn't he have a secretary?"

I squinted at him. I'd been thinking the same thing earlier, only I'd imagined me filling that role, not this scruffy young man with his week-old, scrubby beard and his wavy brown mop of hair that probably hadn't seen a brush or a barber since Easter. "It's almost midnight. Shouldn't you have gone home by now?"

He shrugged. "No need. I'm living here. It's easier that way, given the hours your uncle keeps."

I stumbled backward a few steps into the hallway, and he reached out to steady me, wrapping his warm fingers around my bare arm. His fingers shocked me like he'd been scraping his socks against carpet, and I twisted out of his grip, still trying to process what he'd said. He lived with them. Certainly, Aunt Vivian would have mentioned if they had another houseguest.

"Come on," he said. "I'm about done up here. I'll take you down to the kitchen."

"I know where the kitchen is," I said, pulling my sweater over my head. The way he looked at me left me feeling very exposed.

"Right, then." He grinned. "After you." He waved a hand toward the back stairs.

I hurried ahead of him, only to remember that my pajama shorts barely covered my backside. Instead of stopping, I forged ahead. Let him stare. Once I'd convinced my uncle that I'd be more than happy to take over, he'd send this so-called secretary packing. If only I'd announced my plan when I'd booked my ticket, maybe he would never have hired this guy in the first place.

I pushed open the door to the kitchen. Then I stopped as I realized that I had no idea where to find anything. When I spun around, I found myself face-to-face with Liam, who was well inside my personal space. "Oh."

"All right?" he asked. He stood only a few inches taller than me. Our eyes were nearly level and entirely too close for my comfort.

I took a step backward. "Do you know where they keep the cocoa?"

"I'll make some for us. Go ahead and sit down. It'll just take a few minutes." He stepped around me and headed for the refrigerator.

I plopped down onto one of the benches at the farm-house-style table and watched him pour milk from a glass jug into a pot. He pushed up the sleeves on his baggy, misshapen wool sweater before setting the pot on the stove to heat.

"So, what were you doing before you started working for my uncle?" I asked.

He shrugged. "This and that." He lifted a tin of cocoa powder out of one of the cabinets and returned to the stove to stir the milk.

"Well, where'd you go to school, then?" I squinted at him. He looked too old to be a university student. I'd pegged him as late twenties, probably about my age, but maybe I'd misjudged. It was hard to tell with that day-old scruff on his chin and his hair constantly flopping down and obscuring his face. "If you're working with my uncle, you must have graduated from some world-class university."

He glanced over his shoulder at me, lips twitching into a lopsided grin. "Not exactly. I didn't graduate because I didn't go."

"And my uncle hired you?" I leaned forward and stared at him. This whole secretary thing was getting stranger by the minute.

"Of course." He shrugged. "You don't need to go to uni to learn history. All you need are books. I can read." He lifted two mugs off their hooks and placed them on the counter next to the stove.

"You taught yourself enough history that my uncle hired

you to be his secretary." I shook my head. A much more likely scenario came to mind. Perhaps he'd heard about my uncle's upcoming exhibit and decided to weasel his way into Lydbury and attempt to make off with some of the family treasures. "I don't believe it."

"Believe it," boomed a voice from the kitchen door.

I jumped up and ran over to give Uncle Oscar a hug. "Uncle!" I stood on my tiptoes to throw my arms around his neck. He smelled like cedar and library books.

"I thought I heard talking in here." Uncle Oscar slung his arm across my shoulders as he led me back to the table. "Didn't expect you to be up at this hour, though."

"I couldn't sleep. Then I ran into Liam upstairs." I glanced at Liam out of the corner of my eye. "Aunt Vivian didn't tell me that you'd hired a secretary."

"Ah! Well, I'm sure it just slipped her mind," he said. "Liam's been a great help."

I nodded, forcing my face into a smile to hide my frustration and disappointment.

He gave my shoulder a squeeze before releasing me. "And how's the job?" His bushy eyebrows climbed toward his hairline as he waited for my response.

"Fine." Not that it mattered since I'd already turned in my resignation. The job I'd been secretly hoping for was helping him with his museum project. Instead, he'd already hired a potential thief with no credentials. "Actually, I've been doing some research on Edric and wanted to talk to you about the legend of the Faerie Queen."

"Of course. But, perhaps we can talk in the morning." He glanced across the table at Liam. "Unfortunately, I came to steal Liam. I need his help with something."

Liam had been watching while he finished stirring the cocoa and then poured the mixture into the waiting mugs. He tilted his head like he wanted to ask me something, but I ignored him.

"I can help," I offered, turning my back on Liam to focus on my uncle.

"No, no. It's late. Get some rest. I'm sure you're exhausted from your travels." He kissed the top of my head. "Liam? Shall we?"

Liam nodded. "Of course, sir. I'll be right there."

Uncle Oscar turned to me. "Sleep well. I'll see you in the morning." He squeezed my hand before walking toward the door.

Liam handed me one of the mugs, now steaming and full of chocolaty goodness. "If you want—"

"It's fine," I said, interrupting him. I didn't need pity from this interloper. Besides, now that I knew he had no credentials, I was even more convinced he had to go. "I'll talk with my uncle in the morning." I brought the mug to my lips.

"All right." He slid his hands around his own mug. "Guess I'll see you around, then."

"Thanks for the cocoa." I watched his back as he disappeared into the hallway and only felt a little bad that I'd be taking his place in a few days. He may have been able to charm my aunt and uncle, but I wasn't about to let his scruffy good looks and sexy accent fool me.

———

He'd mentioned she was bright. He hadn't said she was also beautiful. I bent over the files and tried to focus on my work, but I couldn't stop thinking of Evelyn in her pajamas, scowling at me with her straight dark hair pulled up into a messy bun, trying to figure out how I could be smart and not have gone to university. I laughed.

"What's that, Liam?" The professor's voice cut through my thoughts, and I remembered I wasn't alone.

"Nothing, sir." I bit the inside of my cheek and turned my back to the old man so he wouldn't catch me smiling. I had to snap out of it. I had work to do, and the last thing I needed was the added distraction of the professor's lethally tempting niece. Besides, I was fairly certain he wouldn't be terribly keen on me flirting with her.

"Liam, bring me the file on Sir William, will you?"

I reached for a file among the several scattered across the table and brought it over to the professor's desk.

"Ah, yes," he said, glancing up over the top of his reading glasses at the label on the folder. "That's the one." He set down the journal he'd been reviewing and lifted the file from my hands. I turned and started back across the room, but he called me back.

"Liam, my boy," he said, "there's a note here about an artifact? What's this?" I turned back and found him holding up a scrap of paper by one corner.

"Yes, well, sorry, sir. I meant to tell you, I've started cataloging the artifacts in the attic room upstairs. I created an index and have been cross-referencing the index with notes in the relevant files."

"Dead useful, that."

"Yes, well, I thought it might help a bit." I had my own reasons for creating the system, but he didn't need to know about that.

Oscar shook his head and placed the paper back into the file. "With your help, we'll be done with this in no time."

"Well, sir, at the very least, I expect you'll spend quite a bit less time banging your shins on crates while hunting about in the clutter upstairs." Which was precisely what I'd been doing when Evelyn appeared. Not that it could be helped; nearly every room in the house was packed with artifacts covered in a thick layer of dust.

"Quite." He pushed his glasses up on the bridge of his nose and bent his head over the file.

I started back toward the filing cabinet. Cute niece or no, I had a mountain of artifacts to sift through and less time than Oscar realized to complete it in. The museum exhibit was the least of my concerns.

"Liam," he said.

I stopped walking. "Yes, sir?"

"About my niece..."

I sighed. *Here it comes*, I thought. The speech about keeping my hands off his precious, brilliant, and beautiful niece. I turned to face him and pasted an innocent look on my face, as though I hadn't been imagining her tight body under that tank top and shorts.

"Yes, sir?" I asked.

"I know I've been keeping you busy these past months with all this cataloging." He removed his reading glasses and tapped them against the file folder.

"Yes, sir." I nodded and kept my face blank.

"And I do so value your help," he said.

And now the lecture.

"But I think I can spare you for a few days if you'd be so kind as to show my niece about town."

I had just opened my mouth to reassure him that I'd keep my hands to myself. But, as my brain made sense of what he'd said, I quickly shut my mouth and raised my eyebrows. "Sir?"

"I'd like her to enjoy her holiday, and I'm fairly certain

she'd enjoy spending time with someone closer to her own age. Vivian and I are too old to know what you young people do for fun these days. If she had to spend all her time with us, I'm sure she'd be bored, and Vivian is quite concerned that Evelyn enjoy her stay."

"Oh. Well. I see." This was certainly not what I had been expecting.

"I'm sure it won't be much trouble." He adjusted his reading glasses and looked back down at the file.

"Of course, sir. If you think she'd enjoy that." I did my best not to sound too eager.

"I do." The corner of his mouth twitched, but he didn't look up from the file.

I took a few tentative steps backward in case he decided he had more to add.

"That will be all for now, Liam. Best get some sleep." He shooed me with his hand but didn't look up again.

"Yes, sir," I said. "I'll just tidy up the kitchen, then be off to bed."

The professor didn't respond, so I took that as agreement and collected my empty mug, which gave me a plausible excuse to return to the kitchen. My luck couldn't possibly be so good as to find her still sitting there. My heart beat faster as I pushed the door open, but the kitchen was empty.

I set the mug in the sink and glanced out the window as I washed up. The gardens were barely visible in the moonlight. They contained the usual for an historic manor. Manicured hedges. Rosebushes. Gravel paths dividing patches of grass where Vivian's chickens would be pecking about come morning. Not bad for a country estate. It didn't hold a candle to Mum's garden at home, but it wasn't shabby.

Thinking of home made my heart ache and reminded me

why I'd agreed to take this job in the first place. Evelyn was an ill-timed distraction from my mission. A delicious and potentially delightful distraction, but a distraction all the same. The professor thought he could spare me for a few days, but he didn't really understand what was at stake. I clenched my fists. My cataloging project gave me an excuse to examine every piece of the collection up close. But if I were right, and what I'd been searching for was here, I couldn't waste any time.

I only had a few more days before the solstice. Time was running out. I needed to speed up the work without breaking my promise to my family and blowing my cover. Now that the professor had asked, if I didn't spend time with Evelyn, I might get sacked before I found the artifact I'd been sent to retrieve.

Sod it. I'd find a way to make it work. I wanted to spend more time with Evelyn. I'd find a way to do both. Without magic.

2

WHEN I returned from my run the next morning, I found Aunt Vivian outside, bundled up and enjoying a cup of tea. She had given me a tour of the gardens as I cooled off, telling me about the improvements she'd been making. As we returned to the flagstone path that would lead us back to the mudroom, she decided it would be a good time to catch up on my love life.

"Your father said you broke up with that boyfriend of yours."

"Connor," I reminded her, scrubbing the post-run dried sweat off my face. "Months ago. But technically, we're still friends." I stepped closer to her and linked my arm through hers, hoping my running shirt didn't smell. I didn't want to talk about Connor. What I wanted was an opening to confess why I was really here. "Is that all Dad told you?"

"Why, is there something else I should know?" She gave my arm a squeeze.

I took a breath. Now was my chance. "I quit my job." I'd

begged my father to keep quiet, and I had to admit, I was a little surprised that he'd resisted the opportunity to complain to his sister and request she use her influence with me to convince me to change my mind.

"That bad?" She arched an eyebrow at me.

I sighed. She was taking this well, as I expected she would. "It was horrible." I wasn't ready to talk about how horrible it had been, and I knew she wouldn't press me. "I think I might go back to school."

"Is that why you wanted to spend Christmas with us this year?" she asked.

I nodded. "I needed to get away."

"Your father's not thrilled, I take it?" she asked.

"Definitely not thrilled." I frowned, remembering the argument we'd had over the phone before I left for England. "He supports the graduate-school part but thinks I should have waited until just before school starts to quit."

"Better to take some time off." She patted my arm with her free hand. "What do you want to study?"

"History." I bit my lip, nervous about her reaction. "It's always been the part of my job I like the best. Who knows? Maybe I could be a professor like Uncle Oscar. Or go back to working in a museum, but as an historian instead of an admin assistant."

She grinned. "He'll be thrilled to hear that, you know."

"Really? Do you think so? I've been nervous about saying anything. I've applied to a few programs and been accepted to Berkeley, but I haven't heard back from Oxford yet." Uncle Oscar taught at one of the local universities, but he had connections to Oxford. If he really did support me, and if I had some experience working with him, I was certain I'd have a better chance at getting accepted into their program.

Aunt Vivian glanced at me. "You've been quite busy, haven't you? Why haven't you said anything?"

I shrugged. "It's not practical. I was a business major. If Connor's old coach hadn't hired me, I wouldn't know the first thing about history. I thought everyone would laugh at me."

"Well, that's your father talking, there," she said. "Between this and your breakup, you've probably been getting an earful. But you know you can talk to me, don't you?"

"I do. I just wanted to tell you in person." I'd hoped that, if anyone might understand, it would be Aunt Vivian. My parents had invested too much in my education and my relationship to understand why neither of those was ever going to work. But I remember, when I was little, I heard my mother tell someone that Aunt Vivian had left her fiancé at the altar. At the time, I didn't understand what that meant, but now I knew Aunt Vivian's decision to move to England and marry Uncle Oscar had been quite the family scandal. To this day, no one talked about it. So I knew she wasn't likely to tell me to do the responsible thing.

Since I'd gone this far, I decided I might as well casually steer the conversation toward my plan to work with Uncle Oscar. "Let's talk about something else. How about you and Uncle Oscar? How's the museum exhibit coming along?"

"Not bad. I'm so glad he agreed to bring on that boy, Liam, to help him. Now that the historical society has asked him to give a series of lectures in Scotland in the spring, he's got that to sort out as well. Oscar's never been the most organized man, and Liam's been so much help. He keeps me sane, not having to talk Oscar through every crisis. You met him?"

"Yes." I flashed back to Liam's floppy hair and baggy sweater, and his lack of credentials. "That was a surprise. Why didn't you tell me that Uncle Oscar had hired a secretary?"

"I'm sorry about that. It must have slipped my mind. I've been so busy with the fund-raiser for the university. Then, supervising the greenhouse construction. They finished it just in time, too. It's going to be lovely to have a vegetable garden again." She sighed.

On any other day, I'd have been happy to talk about Aunt Vivian's projects and vegetables, but today I wanted answers about what in the world they were thinking letting that guy into their house. "Liam said he's been living here? Since October?" It was bad enough that he wasn't even qualified to work with Uncle Oscar, but letting a random stranger move in with them was completely bizarre. Besides, it was the holidays. Didn't he have family to go stay with? What was he doing here?

"We gave him the old attic room. You remember? You and your brothers stayed up there the last time you came to visit? He's very quiet, though. You won't even notice he's in the house. And since I don't have to help Oscar with his work, I'll have more time to spend with you." She patted my hand and smiled.

My stomach clenched at her mention of the attic room—of my attic room. So that's why I'd been put in the guest room. A childish anger filled my chest, but I squashed it down.

"Uncle Oscar seems pleased with Liam's work," I said, forcing my voice into a pleasant tone that concealed both my annoyance and my frustration that this underqualified outsider had trespassed on my plans.

"Oh, he's quite bright. And such a nice, thoughtful young man. He's working out quite well." Aunt Vivian snapped a dead twig off a hedge as we walked past and spun it between her fingers.

"But how did you find him?" I asked. I still didn't understand why my uncle would have chosen to hire someone who hadn't even attended university when there had to have been any number of more qualified candidates. Like me.

Aunt Vivian cocked her head at me. "Are you concerned, dear? You needn't worry about us. Or, perhaps... Are you interested in him? He is rather attractive, I suppose."

"No," I said, more forcefully than I'd intended. "I mean, it's just strange, that's all. Uncle Oscar's never had a secretary before. And I guess I thought it would be just the three of us for the holidays." I mentally kicked myself. Why was I hesitating? I couldn't make myself say that I wanted Liam's job.

"Well, the more the merrier, no? It is the Christmas season, after all." We walked a few more steps in silence. "Do you want me to find out if he has a girlfriend?"

"Auntie! No!"

She tossed her head back and laughed.

"He's not my type," I said, not that it mattered. Once I figured out what he was up to, he'd be sent packing. No point in getting attached.

"And what type is your type, my dear? That Connor of yours, I presume?" She opened the door to the mudroom and wiped her boots on the mat.

"Not Connor." I grimaced. "I don't know...I suppose someone smart...driven...athletic..." Someone who would stand up for me and believe in me. Someone who had my back, unlike my ex-boyfriend, who, when I'd told him about the things my boss had been suggesting I assist him with, things that were definitely not part of the job description, dismissed the whole thing as *no big deal*.

"Hmm," Aunt Vivian replied, interrupting my thoughts. "Liam is smart, and driven, and fairly athletic. He's taken to chopping all our wood."

I shook my head. Chopping wood was not an Olympic sport. "Maybe he is smart, but he said himself he didn't go to university."

"Ah! You sound just like your father. So Liam didn't go to university. Neither did I. You'd think the world didn't function before they invented universities."

"I'm sorry. I didn't mean it like that." She was right. I did sound like my father. This so-called secretary had gotten under my skin. "I'm just worried he's taking advantage of you and Uncle Oscar."

Aunt Vivian slipped her arm around my waist and gave me a warm squeeze. "It's all right, dear. Liam's harmless. You'll see." She waved me into the kitchen. "Now go on up and shower. Your uncle will be ready for a break in another hour or so. We'll have some lunch and you can tell him about your plans."

I kicked off my running shoes and sprinted through the kitchen and up the back stairs. If Uncle Oscar didn't mind having an assistant with no credentials, it should at least be someone who had his best interests at heart. Someone like me. I inserted a new step in my plan. First, I'd figure out what Liam was really up to and get rid of him before he could do any harm to my family. Then I'd take over as Uncle Oscar's assistant. And maybe get my attic room back in the process.

As I passed the room Liam had been poking around in last night, I slowed to a stop. An hour gave me plenty of time to have a look around before I showered. Maybe I could find something to help me out with step one.

———

A sound in the hall pulled my attention away from cataloging. I bent my head around the wardrobe door so I could see into the hallway, only to find Evelyn standing in the doorway in full running kit minus the shoes.

I stepped out from behind the boxes that blocked me from her view. "Looking for something?"

She froze when she saw me. My predatory instincts kicked in when I sensed the surprise and fear rolling off her, but years of living among humans had conditioned me well. I'd squashed any flicker in my glamour with a thought while she pulled herself together and adopted a more casual posture.

"I thought I heard something digging around in here," she said. "I'm glad it's you and not some rodent."

I grinned. She was a terrible liar, but I could play along. "Nice to see you again, as well." I stepped away from the wardrobe and closed the door on the boxes I'd been sorting through. Cataloging could wait.

"What are you doing in here anyway?" She leaned against the doorframe and placed a hand on her hip, exposing a tiny slice of skin between the hem of her running shirt and the waist of her tights. Lust fanned the embers of the predatory instincts I'd managed to rein in.

"Working." I ran a hand through my hair and reminded myself of my promise to my family. "Your uncle has quite the collection. I'm just getting it sorted."

"You are, huh?" She pushed off the wall and stepped into the room. "Find anything interesting?"

My brain had decided to clear out at the worst possible moment. "A few things. I could show you, if you want." Her uncle's request surfaced in my mind. "Or...I was thinking about going into town later. If you wanted to join me."

She cocked her head, exposing that graceful neck. "I think I'll find my own way around, thanks." She started to turn away, and I scrambled for a response.

"Sure. But it might be more fun with a friend," I offered. Friends seemed like an acceptable place to start with a beautiful, brilliant woman who seemed completely unimpressed with me, since charming her into my bed was out of the question.

"A friend?" Her arched eyebrows signaled her skepticism.

"Yes. They do have those in America, don't they?" I smiled my most innocent smile.

She grinned. "Yeah." She set her hand on a stone statue that I'd placed on the table just inside the doorway. When she didn't notice what she was leaning on, I grinned.

"As your friend, I feel I should warn you that he might bite," I said, jutting my chin in the direction of the statue.

She glanced down and jumped, snapping her hand back and hugging it to her chest. "What is that?" she asked, taking a step closer and bending her head until she was eye level with its snarling snout.

I laughed. "It's a Gargoyle."

"But what is it doing here?" She craned her neck to peer at it from each side.

"I think it looks quite nice there." I'd set it on the dressing table temporarily while tidying up, but something about it made me feel like I had a friend keeping me company while I worked. Today, I'd tucked a stack of leather-bound books under the bat-like wings that hovered in their frozen, half-extended pose.

She reached out a finger to touch the point of one of its fangs. "Sharp," she said, holding her finger up to see if she'd punctured the skin.

"It was a wedding present," I said.

"For my aunt and uncle?" She glanced at me with a horrified look on her face.

I shook my head. "No. For your uncle's, let's see, great-great-great-, oh, never mind. I'm going to lose count that way. One of your uncle's ancestors. I found it up in the attic. There's another around here somewhere." Actually, I knew exactly where it was, but I decided now was not the time for an explanation of my system for cataloging artifacts. "I'm fairly certain they were mounted on the house at one point and then removed by a later generation."

"You found them in the attic?"

"Yes, why?" I asked.

"Oh. Nothing." She shrugged and tucked a strand of hair behind her ear. "It's just...I don't remember ever seeing anything like this in the attic. I think I would remember."

"When was the last time you were up there?"

"I was just a little girl. I think I was maybe eight when we came to visit last. But I stayed up in the attic, with my brothers. I'm sure if there was anything like this up there, my brothers would have found it and wasted no time using it to scare me silly." She wrapped her hands around her waist and stared past me.

"Well, lucky for you, your brothers never found these. Instead, I discovered them on a shelf behind a cabinet. The other one is still up there."

"You really are making yourself at home, aren't you?" She didn't appear particularly happy about the idea. I still couldn't decide if it was the living arrangement or my job that had ruffled her feathers. I tried to keep it light.

"Just making sure we've cataloged and cross-referenced everything. Never know when you might need a few gargoyles. Couple of these in the front of the lecture hall, and no one would dare fall asleep."

"I suppose." She laid her hand on top of the gargoyle's head, between its pointed ears, like it was a favorite dog. "I wonder if I have anything interesting hiding in my room."

"I'd be happy to help you look." I grinned at her, unable to resist the opening she'd given me.

She glared at me out of the corner of her eyes.

I held up both hands and smiled. "Purely in a friend-like capacity." Years of living among humans had not given me nearly enough practice with this thing they called flirting. Without using my powers, I'd have to rely on their primitive method of charming others if I hoped to win over Oscar's niece.

"Friends," she said.

"Friends," I said. It was a start. She relaxed a bit and stopped glaring at me. "So, I can wrap up here if you want to head into town." A flash of light near the ceiling caught my eye, and I sucked in a breath. My eyes darted between Evelyn's profile and the ceiling, but she didn't turn her head. Good, she hadn't noticed.

"I don't think I have time. I was planning to have lunch with my uncle," she said.

"Maybe later, then?" As much as I wanted to attempt to change her mind, that flash of light meant I needed to get rid of her, fast.

"Sounds good," she said.

I waited until she'd retreated down the hall toward the guest rooms before I shut the door and turned to lean against it, looking into the chaos of crates. "All right, Ari. Where'd you go?" I asked.

Arabella stepped out from behind a stack of boxes. She smirked at me. "How adorable," she said.

"What are you doing here?" I hated when she used her

powers to just drop in on me whenever and wherever she pleased. Especially when she knew magic use near Lydbury would leave a mark that my protection spells couldn't cover. She might as well set off a beacon and alert our enemies that we were snooping about Edric's manor. Her disregard for simple instructions put me and my defenseless hosts in danger.

"Don't worry. I'll cover my tracks." She paced around the clutter until she'd reached the one window in the room. "I told you I'd be back to check on you. Found a distraction, have you?"

"Get away from that window before someone sees you." I waited until she'd stepped away before answering her question. "She's Vivian's niece. Visiting for Christmas."

"Well, if you're planning on charming a human into your bed for a lark, it sounds like you don't have much time, then, cuz." She ran her finger over the frame of an oil painting I'd propped against the wall.

"Not to worry. I'm not charming anyone, anywhere."

"Yes, well, as long as we're clear on that," she said, smirking at me. Of course Arabella would find this amusing. That someone of our heritage—the son of the reigning Faerie Queen, no less—would resort to human-style flirting instead of exercising full-force Fae charm to seduce a lover must appear ludicrous to her. But magic use was magic use, and I couldn't risk it. Not that something like that had ever stopped Arabella when she was on the hunt.

She stalked across the room until she was standing in front of me. My cousin had the feline grace of a huntress, honed over the years she'd spent as second-in-command to our eldest cousin, Fiona, who was next in line to be queen. "You haven't found anything useful yet, have you? In this pile of junk?" She waved a hand toward the artifacts in the room.

"No. But I will. Just give me more time."

"We're running out of time. The solstice is in a few days. If we don't figure out how to stop them, the Hunters will return, and we can't afford to lose any more Fae to the Hunt."

I resisted the urge to snap at her and instead ground my teeth in frustration. Being hunted each solstice for centuries by Edric and his gang of underworld spirits had reduced our folk to near extinction. We wouldn't last much longer if we didn't find a way to stop Edric and keep the Hunt from returning.

"I know," I said. "I searched all the files in his office. I can't find anything on Lord Edric."

"Well, look again. Use your powers if you have to. There has to be something. An object, a note, something that is helping hold him to this world. You"—she took a step closer to me and jabbed her finger into my chest—"just need to find it." She punctuated those final two words with additional jabs.

"Arabella," I said as sweetly as I could, "for the last time, Oscar is Godda's descendent as much as he is Edric's. That puts him under our protection. Magic use will lead the Hunt directly to Lydbury. Even if I didn't have to worry about Oscar and Vivian, I don't think we want Edric to know what we're up to here. Do you?"

"Fine. Don't use magic." She paced and pouted. "But you don't have time for distractions. So keep away from that human and stay focused on the mission."

"I'm afraid that's not possible, either. Evelyn's become part of the mission."

"What? How? She's not even related to Godda and Edric."

"Oscar's asked me to entertain her. I can't decline without blowing my cover."

"Then just tell him who you are and what you're after."

"And then what? Kill him? He's human. It's against Fae law, even if he is descended from Godda. Not to mention the fact that it's highly unlikely he'd let us just destroy one of his precious artifacts."

"You have an answer for everything. How would he even know anything's gone missing in this place?" She gestured to the dusty boxes crowding us into the corner of the room.

"Why don't you leave this to me? I'm sure you have something better to do." I pulled myself up to my full height and allowed some of my power to leak through and radiate off my skin. "After all, as you like to remind me, we're running out of time." I smiled at her and put a hint of dazzle into it out of habit. Not enough to leave a marker but enough to remind her with whom she dealt.

"You know your charm doesn't work on me, cuz." She pinched my chin. "Faerie immunity." She met my eyes and flashed her own dazzling grin back at me. "Now get back to work and make your queen proud." She snapped her fingers and disappeared in a flash of light.

As much as I hated to admit it, Arabella was right. I needed to find the artifact linked to Edric, fast. But first, I needed to convince Oscar to skip lunch so Evelyn would be free. If I couldn't manage to improve Evelyn's opinion of me, she might convince Oscar to give me the sack.

3

*A*FTER my shower, I reached for the phone on my dresser, only to discover a dozen missed messages. I skimmed through them. One was from my mother. Two were from my brothers. I'd read those later. I scrolled through the rest, stopping when I realized that most of the messages were from friends I hadn't seen or talked to in months. College friends that Connor was probably hanging out with right now.

I opened the first message. Lacie: *It's not the same without you. Call me if you want to chat.*

I scrolled to the next message. Serena: *R U ok? Here for you.*

One of Connor's East Coast friends' family had a vacation home in Vermont. Ever since junior year in college, when Connor and I started dating, we'd flown out from the Bay Area for what started as a post-finals, pre-Christmas party weekend before splitting up and returning to spend Christmas with our respective families. The tradition continued after graduation. This was the first year that I'd skipped it. I missed our friends, but they had more history with Connor, so I'd assumed he'd get to keep them after we broke up. It seemed odd that they'd all start texting me at the same time, expressing concern.

I skimmed through the names, stopping when I found a message from Connor. I read it quickly. Then I read it again.

Hey. Ignore Jace. He's a jerk. Talk later?

My heart sped up. Something had definitely happened. I had no message from Jace, one of Connor's best friends from his East Coast prep school rowing days. So, I opened an app to check our friends' profiles. There were some new pictures from a party last night, but nothing unusual. I skimmed through the photos again. At the edge of one of the photos, a little blurry and partly in shadow, was someone of Connor's approximate shape and size, wearing a Berkeley rowing sweatshirt, holding hands with a girl who didn't quite make it into the photo. Interesting. But Jace hadn't posted that one. So, I kept scrolling. That's when I saw it. "Beloved History Professor Suspended," read the title above a photo of my former boss.

I opened Lacie's message again, and my thumbs hovered over my screen as I considered my reply. I typed: *Miss you, too!*

I stared at the words for a minute, and then hit send. After, I flipped back and started to read through the article, but a notification popped up almost immediately. Lacie. I opened it.

Can't believe you missed B's engagement party last night. Connor said you were in London. What r u doing in London?!

Technically, I was miles from London, but I supposed, from Vermont, it seemed close enough. I replied: *Visiting family. How's B?*

I wanted to ask what else Connor had told her, but I hadn't spoken with Lacie or Becca in months. As much as I didn't want to chat about how everyone was doing, or talk about my trip, I also didn't want to look too desperate for information, just in case Connor hadn't told her anything. Just in case that article Jace posted had nothing to do with me after all. I tapped my finger against the edge of my phone while I waited for a response.

Lacie: *Fine. Wish I were there! Is that why you and C broke up?*

My thumbs froze an inch above the screen. Connor and I had broken up months ago. I wondered what Connor been telling them at the party. As I considered my response, another message popped onto my screen.

Lacie: *Didn't ask him for details. Taking your side. Esp after watching him drool all over Haley last night. Yuck.*

Haley. So, the girl in the photo was his little sister's best friend, Haley? I wasn't really surprised, but I did wonder if this was new or if it had been going on for a while now and he'd been keeping it from me. More important, though, I wanted to know what she meant by "taking your side." I suspected it may have something to do with the article and my ex-boyfriend's inability to keep his mouth shut about my business.

Thanks, I sent. Before she could reply I added: *GG. Talk later?*

She replied. *Ltr <3*

I checked the time. If I didn't hurry, I'd miss my chance to have lunch with my uncle. I sent a short message to Connor: *What time?* Then I shoved my phone in my pocket and headed down the hall to the top of the stairs.

Halfway down the hall, my phone buzzed. I reached into

my pocket and glanced down at the screen. But before I could check my message, I crashed into another body. I looked up and found myself staring into a pair of brown eyes, framed by floppy brown waves of hair. Strong hands squeezed my upper arms. Liam.

"Sorry," he said. His hands held me in place, about a foot away from his chest.

"I should be the one apologizing. I wasn't looking where I was going." This close, I realized that he smelled like fresh snow, or maybe my mind was still stuck in Vermont. I slipped my phone into my pocket and resisted the urge to step closer.

"You all right?" His lips had suddenly become very distracting.

I nodded, not trusting myself to speak.

"I was just coming to tell you that your uncle said he's really busy and wanted to have tea with you this afternoon, instead," he said. "Since we have time, Vivian asked if we might pick up some things for her in town. Interested?"

I squinted at him. This seemed entirely too convenient given our earlier discussion. Still, I could use this change of plans to my advantage and try to pry some information out of him. "Sure," I said. "Just let me get my jacket, and I'll meet you downstairs."

I jogged back to my room to grab my jacket and wallet. Then I hurried down the stairs, past the Faerie Queen tapestry, to the entryway. When I got there, Liam was leaning against the front door like he owned the place.

"Ready?" he asked.

I nodded, instantly regretting that I'd agreed to spend any time with him at all. Silently raging at his smug grin, I fought to shove my arms into my jacket sleeves, which had become a tangled mess, making me look like an uncoordinated idiot.

Just about the point where I wanted to throw the thing on the ground and stomp on it, Liam reached down and lifted the jacket from my hands, holding it so I could slip my arms into the sleeves. As he settled the coat on my shoulders, he let his hands linger for a moment before I turned to face him.

"Thanks."

He lifted an old leather jacket off a peg and shrugged into it before opening the front door. "After you," he said, stepping aside so I could pass.

I shivered when the brisk wind hit me, just outside the door.

"You need a hat," he said.

"I didn't bring one. I didn't realize it would be so cold here." I tugged the collar of my coat closed and held it in place with one hand before stuffing the other deep into my pocket.

He shook his head. "We'll find you one in town." He stepped up next to me and offered me his arm. "Shall we?"

I looked at his arm and then up at him. "Are we walking?" Based on what I'd seen from the taxi when I'd arrived, we were miles from anything resembling a town, and there were no cars anywhere in sight.

He smiled. That smile of his tugged at something in my chest, something I pushed way back down under a pile of *nope, not gonna go there.* He gave up waiting for me to take his arm and gestured for me to follow.

"Not far," he said. "Just to our ride." I let him lead me around the side of the house.

Just before we turned the corner, I remembered. The old carriage house. Set back from the front facade of the main house, a separate building, covered in climbing vines and surrounded by manicured hedges and rosebushes, the old building now housed the family cars. On the rooftop, a bronze dragon rotated on a post, its tongue flicking out of its open mouth, pointing into the direction of the wind. We walked toward the twin tall oak doors. Liam lifted the crossbeam and swung one open.

The scent of leather and oil hit me as I stepped into the darkness. Light filtered in from a few high windows, tinged green by the vines climbing up the exterior walls. Dust swirled in the sunbeams and a layer of sandy dirt covered the concrete floor.

"Which one's our ride?" I asked, glancing back and forth between the two vehicles parked inside. One was a sleek black sedan, and the other a dusty, muddy, older-model Land Rover.

"Neither," he said, walking between the two cars toward the back wall of the carriage house. I followed him, wondering if there was enough room back there for another, maybe smaller, car to be hiding. Instead, I rounded the back of the Land Rover and found him standing next to a sporty motorcycle with knobby tires. He had a helmet in each hand, and was holding one out to me and smiling.

"No," I said, shaking my head. The last thing I wanted to do was climb onto the back of a motorcycle with a guy I barely knew. Those things were death traps.

He squinted at me. "What's the problem?"

"Can't we just take one of the cars? I can go ask my aunt. I'm sure she'll let me borrow one." I took a step backward and reached for the back of the Land Rover.

He took a step closer to me, the offered helmet suspended between us. "Are you scared?" His smile was gone, and he gazed down at me with a look of serious concern.

"No." I stood up straighter, looked past him, and stuck out my chin at the offending beast. I wasn't scared, I was sane.

And sane people didn't ride motorcycles.

"Well, what's the problem, then?" He shook his shaggy hair out of his eyes and leaned his head into my field of vision until I was forced to meet his eyes again.

"It's just..." I scowled and glanced at the back wall. Motorcycles were dangerous. I'd seen those crazy riders zipping between cars on the highway back home. "I like my body parts where they are, thank you very much."

He snorted. "I agree." He raised an eyebrow and smiled. "And I have no intention of harming any of your body parts." He cocked his head to one side and offered me the helmet again. "I'll go slow. Promise."

I wondered if maybe we were no longer referring to this motorcycle ride. But I pushed that thought out of my head and placed my hands on the helmet. "Slow," I said. Was I really agreeing to this? What was I thinking?

"Promise," he said. I took the helmet from him and held it. When I didn't move to put it on right away, he narrowed his eyes and added, "You have been on one of these before, yes?"

I shook my head.

"I see." He rubbed the scruffy hairs on his chin. "We can take the car if you want."

I shook my head again. "No. I trust you." As the words escaped my mouth, I realized that I had no idea where they'd come from. I didn't trust him. I didn't even know him, and he was clearly up to something that had nothing to do with helping my aunt and uncle. Still, this was why I'd come here, to escape the mess I'd made of my perfect life and try something new.

"Let's do this," I said.

"Okay, then. Meet me outside."

I turned and walked with the helmet back toward the

doors. The short journey gave me way too much time to think about what I'd just agreed to do. I swallowed my fear and stepped out into the surprisingly bright sunlight filtering through the overcast skies. I blinked down at the helmet in my hands until my eyes readjusted. Then I fiddled with the straps and visor while I waited for Liam.

I didn't look up until I heard the crunch of tires on the gravel. Then, before I could change my mind and chicken out, I pulled the helmet over my head and busied myself with fastening the straps.

Liam leaned the motorcycle on its kickstand and placed his helmet on the seat. "Here," he said, walking over to me. "Let me help you with that." He tested the straps, then placed his hands on the helmet, one on either side of my head, and tried to move it, but my head moved instead. "Good," he said. "It's not too loose." He smiled at me and lifted the visor. "Okay in there?" he asked.

I nodded.

"All right, then." He placed his hands on my shoulders and steered me over to the motorcycle. "See this peg?" He pointed at a piece of metal and rubber sticking out from the side of the motorcycle. I nodded. "I'm going to get on first. Then you put your foot there and climb on behind me. Got it?"

"I'm not an idiot." I crossed my arms over my chest. "I've ridden a bike before. Same concept."

"Hey." He held up his hands. "I'm just trying to make sure you feel safe."

"Thanks," I muttered. The helmet muffled my voice, but he nodded once like he'd heard me.

He pulled his helmet over his head and buckled the strap with practiced ease before swinging his leg over the seat to stand, straddling the motorcycle. When he turned the key, the motorcycle rumbled to life.

I gulped and took a step forward. Liam held out a hand to me, but I ignored it and set my foot on the peg without assistance. Resting my hands lightly on his shoulders, I pressed up and swung my leg over, then collapsed onto the seat. My legs shook as I pressed my damp palms against my thighs.

The motorcycle started to shift under us as Liam searched his pockets for something. I sucked in a breath and grabbed for the back of his jacket, afraid we'd topple over. But, a moment after I touched him, the bike stopped moving and he turned toward me, holding out a pair of fleece gloves. I exhaled in a sigh and tried to relax. The gloves were huge, but my fingers felt much warmer once I'd slipped them on. I stuffed the baggy ends into my jacket cuffs so they wouldn't fall off, then returned my hands to rest on my thighs.

He'd been watching with his head turned, looking back over his shoulder at me. I couldn't see more than a corner of his face, but I could tell he was smiling. My stomach flipped. *Just nerves*, I thought.

He sat down, and his warm body settled between my legs. He lifted one hand off the handlebars and reached backward. His gloved fingers closed around the fleece covering mine, and he lifted my hand and placed it on his waist. I sighed and lifted my other hand and placed it on the other side of his waist, but I maintained a wall of air between our bodies.

Liam patted my leg, revved the engine, and shifted the motorcycle into gear. The wheels started to roll, slowly, down the drive, and I tilted my head up to watch the trees arching over our heads. The bare branches against the gray sky mesmerized me. Liam pressed on the brake at the end of the drive, and my body came crashing forward, pressing me against his back. Before I could shift backward, he reached for my arm and held me in place.

Fine. I held tight and leaned against him as he accelerated onto the country road, but only because I'd convinced myself it would be safer that way. Not because I had changed my mind about hooking up with my uncle's secretary. And definitely not because I liked the feel of Liam's body against mine.

———

When we pulled into town, I had an enormous grin on my face. I hadn't been able to stop smiling since the moment Evelyn gave in to physics and leaned against me. I told her I'd take it slow, but I don't think she realized I'd need to lean into the curves, and there were quite a few nice bends in the road on the way to town. The first time I leaned the bike, she grabbed my jacket in her hands and scooted even closer to me. I kept the speed low and the ride smooth, but I loved the way she clutched at me when we leaned.

I almost didn't want to park the bike, but I did want to check on her and make sure she was okay. She'd barely said two words since agreeing to this ride. I found an open spot and parked the bike with the back wheel against the curb. I cut the engine and placed one of my hands over hers, but she'd already started to lean away from me. My smile faded. Of course she'd let go as soon as we stopped. What was I expecting? She'd already as good as told me she wasn't interested.

"Can I get down?" she asked.

I pulled my helmet off and ran a hand through my hair. "Sure. I'll hold her steady for you."

She touched my shoulders briefly. Then she was gone. She'd already pulled off the gloves I'd given her and started fiddling with the helmet straps by the time I'd dismounted and had the kickstand down.

"All right?" I asked.

She tugged at the straps and grumbled. I pulled off my gloves and reached over to help. My fingers grazed the soft, tender skin under her chin and her eyes met mine.

"We made it," I said. "And you're still all in one piece." That was an easy promise for me to keep. I always had my magic to fall back on if we encountered anything truly dangerous.

"Thanks." She tugged the helmet off and handed it to me. "It wasn't that bad."

"Not bad?" I raised an eyebrow.

"Okay," she said, sweeping her hair back and twisting it up. "It was fun." She frowned as she secured the elastic around her hair. "But not fun enough to make me want to run out and buy one of these when I get home." She slipped the gloves back on her hands and tucked the ends into her jacket sleeves.

"I could teach you to ride, if you wanted to learn." I patted the seat and smiled.

"No." She shivered. "Thanks, but I think I'll stick to cars. Or walking."

"You're cold." I didn't feel cold, but then again, I wasn't human, or from California.

She rubbed her hands on her upper arms and nodded.

"Let's go get something warm to drink and find you a hat," I said, leading her across the street to the cafe.

I held the door open for her and followed her inside. "This is it for coffee around here," I said. "It's a pretty small town and there's only the one cafe."

"Do you even drink coffee? I thought all English people preferred tea." She glanced around inside the coffee shop, which did in fact feature more tea than coffee.

"I do prefer tea, mostly because I'm hopeless at making coffee. But I'll drink it, if someone else makes it."

"What's your drink?" she asked.

"Espresso."

"That's it? Just an espresso?" She held up her hand and curled her fingers above her thumb as though she were holding a tiny espresso cup between them.

I shrugged. "I can drink tea all day long, but I don't like the taste of coffee enough to drink a whole pot. Or one of those supersize cups you Americans prefer."

She laughed. I liked making her laugh.

"What about you? What's your drink?" I asked.

"That depends," she said. "But right now I think I'd like a mocha. Something about mochas remind me of the holidays. Especially if they put a little peppermint in it. Mmm..."

I ordered our drinks and she tried to give me money to pay for hers, but I waved it away. "My treat," I said. "To celebrate your first ride." We moved to the end of the counter to wait.

"Hey," she said. "That reminds me. I saw some stone ruins on the way here. Do you know what they were?"

"The ones off in the middle of the field?" I pulled out a chair and sat down at one of the tables.

"We passed a lot of fields. But yeah. The one that had stones instead of sheep." She slid into the chair across from me and slipped her long, thin hands out of the fleece gloves I'd lent her.

"They're the remains of an ancient temple. Your uncle published a paper on it. Fascinating stuff. But most tourists don't know any of that history. They just read the bit in the guidebook and come snap a few photos before having a lark about town and driving home."

"Huh. I'd love to go check them out, after I read my uncle's paper, of course," she said. I realized that I'd never asked her field of study or what she did for work. I tended to forget how invested humans were in that sort of thing. If I intended to win her over, I would have to do better.

"Sure. I can get that paper for you and take you out there when you're ready," I said. "Of course, you should also check out the guidebooks if you want to learn about the local legends and superstitions. They're not the best source for information on that type of thing, but they do a good summary."

"What kind of legends?" she asked.

I shrugged. The barista called my name to pick up our order, and I returned to the counter to retrieve our drinks. I handed Evelyn her mocha and waited for her to take a sip. She tipped the cup against her lips and closed her eyes.

"Wow! You guys take mochas to a whole new level!" She licked a bit of foam off her lip, drawing my focused attention to her bow-shaped mouth.

"It's the chocolate," I said, finding my words.

She took another sip and nodded. "Definitely the chocolate. But the milk, too. It all tastes so fresh!" She appeared to be completely ignorant of my struggle to maintain a platonic conversation and not lean across the table and lick the foam from her lips myself.

"Well, some of those cows we rode past probably contributed to the effort." I took a sip of my espresso and pictured those very unsexy cows, hoping that might help cool me off.

She nodded. "Yeah, I suppose that makes sense." She took another sip. "So tell me about these legends and what they have to do with my uncle."

I sighed in relief. Perfect way to distract me. Talk about history. "Well, they're mostly ghost stories. Certain times of year when people claim that you can go there and speak with the souls that have crossed over. That sort of thing."

"Why would people think that?" She wrinkled her nose and frowned. If she hadn't just been telling me how great her drink was, I'd have thought she'd tasted something sour.

I hesitated before responding, just long enough to give my brain a chance to sort the human stories from my family history. I couldn't lie to her, but it would be safer if I stuck to telling only the things other humans knew.

"Hunting has always been important in this area, at first for survival, and then, later, for sport." Arabella, as captain of the Queen's Guard, had earned the title of Huntress among the Fae. Humans might consider her a goddess, I supposed. Any who still believed, anyway. But I pushed those details to the background and focused on what Evelyn's uncle would tell her. "Most historians, your uncle included, believe that it was a temple dedicated to the Goddess of the Hunt."

"You mean, Diana?"

"Similar. Each culture appears to have put their own twist on the God or Goddess of the Hunt in their mythologies. Around here, the Goddess of the Hunt was believed to be one of the Fae." I needed to tread carefully here. Strictly speaking, the historians didn't officially agree on this conclusion. But I knew the truth.

"Are you telling me that my uncle actually wrote an academic paper saying the Goddess of the Hunt was a faerie?" She said this like I'd just told her that her uncle had exposed himself in public.

Of course Oscar had not written that, precisely, because he couldn't, and not for the reasons she thought. I struggled to find an acceptable response that wouldn't involve lying. "This is the land of the Fae, Evelyn," I said. As long as I stuck to human facts and beliefs, no one could accuse me of break-

EVE OF THE FAE

ing our laws.

Oscar knew about the Fae. Years ago, he'd encountered the Hunt and been granted an exception as a descendent of Edric and Godda. But he'd been sworn to secrecy because no humans could know of the Fae. The price for revealing our secrets or learning of our existence was death. I was fairly certain he hadn't guessed my true identity, but I couldn't be certain without breaking any number of rules.

"But those are just stories they tell children." Something in her tone told me that she wouldn't be swooning from excitement if she found out about my heritage. The thought made me smile. It would be nice to find someone who liked me for me and not because I was the son of the Faerie Queen. But I would never know how she really felt about it because telling her would mean signing her death sentence. I pushed the thought away and refocused on the conversation.

"It's also history because it influenced what the people who lived here before us believed. It affected how they lived their lives." She seemed like someone who would appreciate this more rational argument.

She took another sip of her mocha and looked thoughtfully out the window. "I suppose," she said.

"So do you still want me to tell you about the legends?" I almost hoped she'd say no. This conversation was reminding me that I should be back at the house, searching for an artifact, not sitting here trying to impress a human woman and fool myself into thinking I was only doing this because Oscar had asked me to.

"Sorry," she said. "Go on." She finished the last sip of her mocha and licked her lips before dabbing them with a napkin.

"All right. I'll tell you while we walk." I needed to remember she was off-limits and I had a job to do. "Let's go find you a hat, shall we?" I stood and placed our cups on the counter.

Outside, the bite of cold stung my cheeks. "Even though historians believe it was a temple to the Goddess of the Hunt, the legends claim the Hunters also went there to honor the death of the animal they'd killed. To gain a measure of forgiveness for taking a life. And for this reason, spirits who are unable to cross over, spirits they believe have unfinished business, linger near the temple ruins. Or at least, they linger there at certain times of the year."

"Like the Day of the Dead?"

"Around here, it's All Saints' Day." Those were just human celebrations. "There are other days of power. The solstice, for example."

"Do you believe this?" She turned to look at me. Her lips pressed together and her forehead creased as she studied my face, waiting for my response.

Of course I believed this. It was part of my life, my world—a world I could not share with her, but one that was very real. I knew Edric's spirit grew stronger as the days grew shorter, and come the solstice, he'd lead his band of vengeful spirits on their Wild Hunt. If I didn't find and destroy the object he'd chosen as an anchor, allowing him a foothold in the living world, he would continue to hunt my kin in his pointless search for Godda.

This knowledge was off-limits for Evelyn. Instead, I limited my response to human-appropriate facts. "I've studied the stories collected from people who profess to have experienced these sightings. But I don't see any reason to believe temple ruins like this one are any more likely than any other place for sightings."

"You sound like you believe these sightings are real."

I shrugged. "There's no proof that they aren't."

She shook her head and frowned. "There's no such thing as ghosts."

"How do you know?" I grinned at her. "Just because you've never seen one?" I nudged her shoulder with mine.

She snorted. "You're impossible."

"I prefer 'open-minded.'" Brightly colored yarn caught my eye, and I stopped in front of a store window. "Ah, here we are. I think they'll have something suitable." I stepped over to the door and held it open for her. She slipped past me and disappeared into the shop.

The inside of the shop smelled like felines and herbs. An old woman with a weatherworn face appeared from behind a display of wool sweaters. "Can I help you?" she asked. Her gaze lingered on me a bit longer than I'd expected and made me wonder if she might be a seer. Some humans were born with the ability to see past a glamour to the true Fae form beneath. I could only hope she wasn't one of them.

"I'm looking for a warm hat," Evelyn said.

The woman grinned, creasing the wrinkles around her eyes. "Well, you've come to the right place," she said. "Follow me."

She led us over to an assortment of winter hats on display. Most were knitted wool in a variety of colors. Some had long tails or tassels. Some had yarn balls at the top. Evelyn gravitated toward the standard beanies in neutral shades of gray, black, and cream. She ran her hand over the cashmere knits and ultimately selected a speckled gray beanie made from a cashmere and wool blend. Boring and practical. I scanned the display while she checked her reflection. A red-and-green-striped hat caught my eye. I reached for it and smiled when I realized it had ear flaps.

"Try this one," I said.

Evelyn turned from the mirror to look at me. "What's wrong with this one?" she asked, glaring out of the corner of her eyes at the hat I had balled up in my hand.

"Nothing. It's fine. Just try this one." Everything she'd said, everything she'd done, every word she'd spoken, had left me with the impression that she was the type to play it safe. But the world was a colorful place. If I couldn't show her my world, I could at least bring some color to hers.

She pulled the gray hat off her head and smoothed down her hair. Then she reached for the one I held out to her. As she unfolded it, she began to frown and her forehead wrinkled.

"Go on," I said. "Try it."

"You're trying to make me look ridiculous, aren't you?"

"I think it will look brilliant. It has personality."

She squinted at me and turned toward the mirror before pulling the hat down over her head. I watched her reflection as she blinked at herself in the mirror. Then the corners of her mouth twitched and slowly turned upward into a smile. Grinning, she tugged at the strings that dangled from the ear flaps.

Our eyes locked in the mirror, and I returned her smile. "You like it, don't you?"

"It's all right," she said. But her smile grew, and she bounced a bit on her toes.

"Turn around," I said.

She turned to look at me and stretched her arms out at her sides. "Ta-da," she said.

"Much better."

"It's very festive. Did you pick Christmas colors on purpose?" she asked.

"Not exactly," I said. I'd been so focused on the solstice, human religious holidays hadn't registered. "Maybe I just thought you'd look good in red."

"You don't think it will be too warm?" she asked, running her fingers over the soft wool knit that hung down to cover her ears.

"Definitely not. It's perfect."

"Okay," she said. She turned and started walking to the register.

"Evelyn?" I called after her.

"Hmm?" she turned toward me.

"You might also want to get some gloves."

"Oh!" She held her hands up, the fleece baggy around her fingers. "Good idea."

She picked out a pair of red mittens that matched the hat and carried everything over to the shop lady to pay. I kept my distance from the old woman to avoid further scrutiny.

When Evelyn finished, she walked over to me and returned the gloves I'd lent her. "I guess I should give these back to you."

I put the gloves in my pocket. I had no need for gloves, but they helped to keep up the appearance of being human. It was nice to see them actually get some use. "Let's see the new ones."

She held up her hands, and I admired the mittens. "Those fit much better," I said.

Her phone buzzed in her pocket, and she jumped. She started to reach for it, then stopped so she could yank off her mittens. She stuffed them into her jacket pocket as she glanced at the screen of her phone.

"Everything okay?" I asked.

She looked up at me. "I should get back."

"All right," I said. "We just need to get a few things for Vivian and then we can go."

She nodded. That glimpse of sunny, carefree joy disappeared, replaced by a shadow of dread that appeared to loom over her while we shopped. I'd thought I'd made some progress winning her over, but now nothing I said could snap her out of her foul mood.

4

LIAM parked the motorcycle in the drive but left the engine running. He turned his head and flipped his visor up. "Go ahead and jump off."

I dismounted and managed to get the helmet off without much trouble. "Sorry I had to cut our trip short."

He shrugged. "It's okay. Some other time."

I handed him the helmet. "Thanks."

"Put your hat on before you freeze," he said.

I pulled my new hat on. "Better?"

"Much." He didn't smile. He only stared at me with those eyes that seemed to see right through me.

I shivered and broke eye contact with him. "See you later." I waved as I jogged toward the front steps. I had a moment of worry, wondering if my aunt and uncle had locked their front door. But the handle turned freely and the door opened. I shut it behind me and fled up the stairs and down the hall to my room. Inside, I threw my coat onto the bed and reached for my laptop. The screen took a moment to come on, and

I waited, worrying I'd missed him. As soon as I logged in, I opened the chat application and clicked on Connor's picture.

Home now. Can you talk?

I tapped my fingers on the keyboard while I waited for a reply. The video chat notification started ringing and my heart started to race. I hated confrontation, and I had a feeling I knew what was coming as soon as Connor's face popped into view. He was wearing his Berkeley rowing hoodie and his short hair was sticking up in different directions.

"Hey," he said.

"Hi," I replied.

"Is that your room?" he asked.

If he wanted to do small talk first, I could do small talk. "Yeah." I spun the computer around to give him a better view of my bedroom. "I thought I'd be staying in the attic bedroom." I caught myself just as I was about to mention Liam, and changed my mind. "But this is so much better. I have my own bathroom and a fireplace and everything."

"Your aunt and uncle's place sounds great."

"How's Vermont?" My stomach had already tied itself into knots, and I could feel my heart racing, but I kept my tone casual.

He shrugged. "Colder than California. But I guess it's cold there, too, huh?" He pointed at me. I'd forgotten to take off my hat in my rush to talk to him. I tugged it from my head and clutched it in my hands as my cheeks grew warm.

"Yeah. I bought it today. I didn't realize it would be so cold here."

"It's cute." His eyes sparkled when he grinned at me, and I realized I'd had enough.

"Thanks," I said. "So, what's this thing with Jace?"

He leaned back in his chair, scratching at the nape of his

neck. "I, uh, just thought we should talk."

"What happened?" My heart started hammering again.

"Lots of folks were asking about you at Becca's party last night." He leaned back in his chair, like this was all no big deal.

"So what did you tell them?" I smiled and played along, even though I desperately wanted him to cut to the chase and get this over with.

He shrugged. "Not much, but then Jace got to talking about what happened to Coach, and..." He shrugged again, but shifted in his seat this time.

"And what?" I asked. Just spit it out, Connor.

He frowned. "I, uh...you know. I mentioned that you'd been working for him."

"And that's it?" I leaned toward the screen.

Connor shook his head. "Well, no, but he kinda guessed some stuff from that article he'd read, and he asked about it. I mean, we've been friends forever. I'm not gonna lie to him."

"And what about *our* friendship? I trusted you. I asked you not to say anything. That means you don't talk about it with other people. Even your friends." I gripped the edges of my laptop so hard my fingers started to sweat.

Connor cocked his head to one side. "Come on. It's cool, Evie. You know Jace. He won't tell anyone."

"I don't know that." Staying friends with Connor had been a bad idea. But I hadn't realized until that moment that maybe, just maybe, I'd been staying friends with Connor as some sort of misguided attempt to prevent exactly this from happening. Like, if we stayed friends he'd maintain some sort of loyalty to me. So much for that idea. "Were you two alone when you were talking about this?"

"Well...not exactly." Connor's microphone picked up

the scratch of stubble against skin as he scrubbed his palm against his chin.

I sighed. "So who else heard?"

"Um...I don't know. There were a lot of people around. It was pretty loud, though. So maybe only Haley." He paused and scratched his head. "Did I tell you Haley and I are dating? I wanted to tell you, you know...so you'd hear it from me first."

I resisted the urge to roll my eyes. Did he seriously think our friends wouldn't have said anything? Or that I cared? "We've been broken up for months. You don't owe me an explanation." I honestly didn't care that he was moving on. I did care that he'd confirmed to our friends that I was probably the main reason their beloved prep school coach had been suspended.

"We're still friends, right?" His question hung in the air while he stared at me with those brown puppy-dog eyes.

"I don't know, Connor." I shook my head, forcing the words out that would end this for good. "I don't think I can trust you. So, no. I don't think we can be friends."

"Aw, come on, Evie. It's no big deal. This whole thing with Coach will blow over. In a few months, no one will even remember what happened."

"That's exactly the point. You don't get it. Your coach is a sexist jerk who doesn't understand the word 'no' just like you don't seem to understand what 'private' means."

"That's not fair," he said. "Why are you being so sensitive about this?"

"Of course." I snorted. Classic Connor response. "Thanks for telling me what happened. I think it would be better if we didn't talk for a while. Please tell your family Merry Christmas from me."

"Fine. Whatever. Merry Christmas, I guess."

"Bye, Connor."

"Yeah." He frowned. "Later."

I clicked the button to end the call, and Connor's face disappeared from my screen. I shut my laptop and tossed it onto the bed next to me. Then I buried my face in my hands, which were still holding on to my new hat like a security blanket. The rough wool scratched at my cheeks but absorbed my tears.

I sat like that for a while, not entirely sure why I was crying. Ever since I'd reported my boss to HR, I'd been dealing with people suggesting I'd misunderstood or was making a big deal about nothing. When I told Connor what had been happening, he insisted that my boss had just been joking, and I just didn't understand his humor. I'd broken up with Connor. I'd quit when it became clear HR wasn't going to do anything. I'd tried to put all this behind me. The last thing I wanted was for this drama to follow me to England.

"Eve? Are you up here, dear?" Aunt Vivian knocked on my door.

"In here." I wiped my eyes and tried to rub the dried tears off my face.

The door swung open, and Aunt Vivian stopped inside my room. "Ah! There you are, dear! I was looking for you."

"I was just about to come down for tea," I said.

"Yes, well, about that... It turns out that your uncle has some faculty holiday tea that he forgot to tell me about. So, we're on our way out. It's a long drive, and we need to get dressed and leave soon. I've asked Marge to make dinner for you before she goes home. But I'm afraid you'll be on your own this evening. I know it's your first evening here, and I feel terrible about it. Even Liam's gone. Oscar sent him out on some errand. And now we have to leave you by yourself. I could just strangle him for forgetting to tell me about this."

"It's okay, Auntie. Really. I'll be fine."

"Are you sure? You look like you've been crying."

I sniffed. "Maybe a little."

"Did you have another fight with your father?"

I shook my head. "No, it's fine. I'm okay."

She sat down on the bed next to me and smoothed my hair back from my face. "I'm going to tell Oscar he can go by himself. I'm staying home with you. I'll find us some ice cream and you can tell me everything."

"No, Auntie." I leaned toward her and gave her a hug. "Really. I'll be fine. You go to the party. I'll tell you all about it tomorrow. I don't want to talk right now, anyway."

Aunt Vivian squeezed me tight. "Well, all right, but I'm clearing my calendar for tomorrow. We can spend the whole day together. And I'm still going to make sure we have ice cream in the freezer. And chocolate. I think I have some stashed somewhere, in case of emergency, you know. I'll leave it for you." She leaned back and held me by my upper arms. "You're sure?"

I nodded. "I'm sure."

"All right, I'll see you in the morning." She kissed my cheek and turned to leave.

"Have fun!" I called after her.

I changed into my pajamas and splashed some cold water on my face, then stared at my reflection in the mirror. Angie had been right, of course. And she'd tell me so when I talked to her. I should have cut Connor out completely so I could have healed properly after our breakup. With Connor out of my life, no job to return home to, and Liam occupying the one job I wanted, for the first time in a long time, I had no idea what I was doing with my life. There was always grad school. I still wanted to follow in my uncle's footsteps. That's when I remembered what Liam had been saying about local legends.

I found my slippers, then padded down the hall, past the storage room with the gargoyle, and down the back stairs to the kitchen. Uncle Oscar's library held probably the best collection of books on local history for miles around. I'd start there. If Liam could learn history from books, then I could, too. Maybe in the process, I could finally figure out why he was really here.

———

The light was on in the library when I got home, but I knew the professor and his wife had gone out for the evening. I'd hoped to return early enough that I'd have time for another search of the house before they returned. Then I remembered Evelyn. When I peeked my head into the library, I found her curled up in an armchair, fast asleep.

I crossed the room and lifted the book out of her hands, glancing at the title before marking her place and setting it on the table. One of her uncle's books about local history. An empty wineglass. Her laptop. A crumpled foil wrapper. Fuzzy slippers and striped pajama pants. I smiled. She looked so peaceful, I didn't want to wake her up, but she'd be much more comfortable in her bed.

I rested a hand on her shoulder. "Evelyn," I whispered.

"Mmm..." She rolled her head to the side but didn't open her eyes.

"Eve," I tried again, a little louder this time.

Her eyes blinked open and she rubbed her hands over her face. "What time is it? I must have fallen asleep."

"It's late." I flopped into the chair across from her.

She stretched her arms and yawned. "Are Aunt Vivian and Uncle Oscar home yet?"

"I don't think so." I hid my own yawn behind my hand. Apparently, the things were contagious. Fae didn't yawn.

"What are you doing home? I thought they said you were gone for the evening."

"I just returned. Saw the light on and came in to see who was awake."

"Oh." She looked around the room and then down at her pajamas. "I should go to bed."

"Or stay up a bit longer. I'll throw another log on the fire and get some more wine." I should have been encouraging her to go to bed, but I didn't want to appear too eager to see her off.

"No. I should really go to bed." She started to get up from the chair.

"I saw you were reading about Lord Edric," I said, motioning to the book on the table between us. "If you want, I'll tell you what they left out of that story." Unfortunately, I couldn't tell her everything I knew. According to my family, the story she'd been reading wasn't even close to right. But my family did like to exaggerate that whole kidnapping-of-Godda thing. Not that I can blame them; Godda was my aunt. My mother had been there that night.

Evelyn cocked her head. "Why are you going out of your way to help me?"

"Would you rather I ignore you? Don't people have conversations with their housemates where you live?"

"I suppose. It's just, you're not really a housemate, you're..." Her voice trailed off, but I knew where she'd been going with that statement.

"Your uncle's secretary?" I offered. If only she knew.

"Well, yes." She frowned.

I tapped my fingers on the arm of the chair. "Right." She thought I was a joke, and I couldn't prove otherwise.

"I'm sorry. I didn't mean it like that." Her cheeks had begun to turn pink, but I didn't think it was from the warmth of the fire. It took some of the sting out, thinking that she might be embarrassed by her own snobbery.

"You didn't mean to imply that I'm hired help? That being someone's secretary is somehow beneath you?" I had to remind myself that she was human. Her worldview was so small. I tried not to let it bother me, but it did.

"No. I mean, everyone has to start somewhere." She winced, possibly realizing how awful that sounded.

I shook my head. "But what if this is where I want to be? What I want to be doing?"

Her eyes widened. "Well, I guess. If you're happy."

I groaned. "You think success is a graduate degree? Is that what's going to make you happy?"

She shifted in her chair until she was sitting up straight. "It's a start. Graduating from Oxford would make me happy. So would following in my uncle's footsteps and traveling as an expert guest lecturer to New York, or San Francisco, or London, or maybe Paris. Or maybe all of them. I don't know."

"So, because I don't have a degree, I couldn't possibly be successful, or happy, according to you." I flexed my hands. My magic surged inside, screaming to be let out, but I pushed it down.

Her eyes widened, and she sucked in a breath. "I...I didn't mean it that way—"

"I get to do something I love and live somewhere I love and spend time with people I admire and respect. What difference does it make where I did or didn't go to university or what my title is?"

"It doesn't." She buried her head in her hands. "I'm sorry. I'm kind of having a bad day."

"What happened?" I asked. My annoyance melted in the face of her misery.

"It's nothing," she said. "I just...I just had this plan, you know? I had it all figured out and now nothing seems to be going right. I think I made a huge mistake coming here."

"To Lydbury?" I was completely confused. What could possibly have been so bad about visiting her aunt and uncle for Christmas?

"No," she said. She shook her head. "Or maybe. I don't know. I should have just told Aunt Vivian." Her face twisted like she was in pain, and she pulled the sleeves of her sweater over her hands and clutched the fabric.

"Told her what?" I scooted to the edge of my seat and placed a hand on the arm of her chair.

"Never mind. You wouldn't understand," she said.

My frustration flared in response to her dismissal. Was she saying this because she didn't respect me?

"Try me," I said. A tiny bit of anger might have leaked into my voice because she looked up at me with wide eyes.

"Well, for starters, I should have told her I wanted to work with Uncle Oscar," she said, glaring at me.

"What?" That wasn't what I'd been expecting.

"That was my plan. But now you're here. Doing what I wanted to be doing. And I think I may have ruined everything."

"Ruined how?" I asked. Dread flooded my chest as I waited for her response.

She stared at me for a moment, clearly evaluating me. Trying to decide if she could open up to me. For the first time, I suspected her annoyance with me had been because she'd seen me as competition.

"You can talk to me," I said. "I won't say a word unless you want me to."

"You promise?"

I nodded.

"Fine." She sighed and leaned back in the chair. "First, I quit a perfectly acceptable job, because my boss was a sleaze."

I leaned forward. "I'm sure there are other jobs—"

She cut me off with a glare. "You said you wouldn't say anything."

I pressed my lips together and pretended to zip them shut.

A small smile flashed across her face. Then she continued. "I don't want those jobs. I don't want to put myself in that position again. Powerless." She blinked and shook her head, but I'd already spotted the tears welling in her eyes.

I strained against the urge to speak but kept my lips glued together.

"I decided to apply to graduate schools. But I don't know the first thing about history. I was a business major. But I do have experience working in a museum. That's why I'd hoped I'd have a chance to work with my uncle." She gave me a pointed look.

I knew it. She'd been mad about me taking this job.

"I thought he'd understand. I thought he'd just know that was why I'd decided to spend the holidays here. I'd said I wanted to help. I guess I didn't make it clear enough what I really wanted. Now I think I ruined everything. I received this today." She reached for the history book, pulled out a folded printout, and handed it to me.

I unfolded the paper and scanned the page. The block of

text at the top made little sense to me. It appeared to be a letter, but not one sent by mail. The professor didn't use technology the way most humans did, but I'd snooped around his study enough that I'd seen printed messages like this lying about and recognized the correspondence as an email. The message was short, but a few key words jumped out at me. Oxford. Admissions. Waitlist. I glanced up from the paper and met her eyes. They were brimming with tears, threatening to overflow.

I slipped out of my chair and stood, dropping the paper on the table between us. Then I perched on the arm of her chair and wrapped my arm around her shoulder, careful not to speak and break my promise to her.

She sniffed. "I thought everything would just work out, and now I have nothing."

I touched her chin and tilted her face up toward me, wiping away a few tears with my thumb. I raised my eyebrows and hoped she'd get the hint and free me from my vow of silence.

She narrowed her eyes at me. "Fine," she said. "Go ahead. Say whatever you're going to say."

"It's not all ruined," I said. "You can still work with your uncle."

"But what about you?" she asked.

"What about me? You think there's not enough work here for two people?" I watched her face and searched for a reaction.

"Maybe," she said softly.

"Or you don't want to work with me because I don't have a fancy degree?" I arched an eyebrow.

"No. It's not that. It's just..."

I reached out and brushed another tear from the soft skin

of her cheek. She closed her eyes and leaned into my hand. I traced my fingers along her jaw and under her earlobe until they were wrapped around the back of her neck. I'd wanted to do this since I'd first set eyes on her.

She tilted her head back and looked up at me. She wasn't stopping me. She appeared to be waiting to see what I'd do next. I leaned down until my lips brushed against hers. Her eyes fluttered closed and our lips pressed together, our breath mingling. I pulled back to search her face and give her a chance to push me away. I knew this was a bad idea, but I couldn't resist. Instead of pushing me away, she wrapped her arms around my neck and tugged me back down.

A part of my brain worried her actions had more to do with her reaction to her bad day than they did with how she felt about me, but it was probably better that way. We could never be together. Feelings would just complicate things.

I leaned on the arm of the chair to keep my balance as my fingers explored her skin and my lips met hers again and again. She tangled her fingers in my hair and placed a hand on my cheek as her lips parted, and I reached for her tongue with mine. I knew I was in trouble when she pulled me down and arched her body up. Wrapping an arm around her waist, I lifted her from the chair until we were standing with her body pressed against my chest.

A log shifted in the hearth and the fire collapsed in on itself. Evelyn jumped at the sound and took a step backward, out of my arms. I reached for her, but she shook her head and stepped away. "What am I doing?" she mumbled as she walked over to stand in front of the fire.

I started to reply, but a flash of light caught my attention. Damn. Arabella had the worst timing.

I ignored my cousin's signal and walked over to the hearth

to stand behind Evelyn. I slipped my hands around her waist and pulled her against me. Arabella could wait.

"I should go to bed," she said, but she leaned into me. I buried my face in her hair and inhaled the sweet tropical scent of her shampoo.

"What are you worried about?" I asked softly into her hair.

"We shouldn't do this," she whispered.

I swept her hair to one side and placed my lips against her neck. The beat of her pulse under my lips proved I had set her heart racing at least as hard as mine. I kissed my way down her long, elegant neck, taking my time, savoring the feel of her skin against my lips.

The creak of the front door opening and Vivian's persistent chatter echoed down the hallway. Evelyn froze and pulled away from me.

"I should go to bed," she said. She grabbed the book, her laptop, and the empty wineglass off the table. "Good night," she said. Then she hurried out of the room and turned toward the kitchen. I could hear Vivian and Oscar on the front stairs. They wouldn't come this way. They'd go straight up to bed. I considered going after Evelyn but remembered Arabella's signal.

Oh, well. Might as well see what she wants.

"Where'd you go?" I whispered to the empty room. I waited, but there was no response. "Getting a good laugh, are you?" I asked. Still no response. I walked in the direction I'd seen the flash, toward the table where I'd left my work earlier. I kept my senses alert, expecting Arabella to jump out at me at any moment. But I made it all the way to the table without her appearing. That's when I saw the note scratched on a piece of paper lying on my stack of books.

Forget the girl and come home. Flida fading. Asking for you.

I struggled to remember to breathe. Something had happened to Mother. I needed to go home.

After scrambling to find paper and a pen, I sat and scratched out a brief note to the professor. Then I jogged up the back stairs to the attic room to pack a few things for the journey. My family needed me.

5

I DIDN'T want to go down to breakfast. There was no way I could face Liam in front of my aunt and uncle in the light of day after kissing him last night. I mentally kicked myself as I unpacked everything I'd left in my suitcase into the empty dresser drawers. If I closed my eyes, I'd start to imagine Liam's lips on my neck, his arms around me. So, I just wouldn't close my eyes. Then maybe that fluttering feeling in my chest would go away.

I stared down at my empty suitcase. I'd have to face him sooner or later. Better to get this over with. It didn't mean anything. It was just a weak moment. I was confused after my confrontation with Connor and then discouraged by the email from Oxford. I was jet-lagged. I was half asleep. I'd been drinking. It was only one glass of wine, and I'd been asleep in that chair long enough for the effects to wear off. But still. All the excuses I could name hadn't managed to relieve the sinking feeling that I'd crossed some sort of line by making out with my uncle's secretary.

Then I remembered the look he'd given me just before he'd kissed me the first time, like he was waiting for permission. My heart sped up just thinking about it. I shook my head. No. This was not a good idea.

My stomach growled. I glanced at the clock. I couldn't delay this any longer. I checked my hair in the mirror and straightened my sweater. Then I realized what I was doing and stuck my tongue out at my reflection and walked out of my room.

When I reached the end of the hallway, I couldn't decide between going down the front stairs and having to walk past the library or going down the hall past what I'd begun to think of as "the gargoyle room" on my way to the back stairs. I stood still and listened. I didn't hear anyone down that hall, so I took a chance and hurried past all the rooms, not stopping until I'd reached the bottom of the stairs. I paused in the hall, then took a breath and pushed open the kitchen door.

"Morning," I said. My aunt and uncle were seated at the table, but there was no sign of Liam. My stomach dropped. I couldn't be sure if it was in disappointment or in relief.

"Good morning," my uncle said, glancing up at me over his paper.

"Help yourself to breakfast and join us." She motioned to the serving dishes already on the table. "I was worried you were going to sleep all morning."

"I would have been down earlier, but I decided to unpack a little."

"Oh! Did you have enough room in the dresser for your things? And the wardrobe? Did you find enough hangers? Do you need more?"

Her thoughtfulness and concern made me smile. "I found everything and there was more than enough room." I sat down and began heaping eggs and bacon on to my plate.

"Oh, good. It's so nice to have you here, dear. If you need anything, just let me know, all right?"

Uncle Oscar folded his paper and pushed his chair back from the table. "Well, I best get to work. Lots to do with Liam gone."

I froze with my fork partway to my lips. "What's that, Uncle Oscar? Did you say Liam's gone?" This had been what I'd wanted, only now it didn't feel right. Did they somehow know we'd kissed? Did Uncle Oscar fire him because of me?

"Not to worry. It's likely only for a few days. His mother's not well, you see. Had to go home for a bit to take care of her. I'm sure he'll have it all sorted soon enough." He gave me a kiss on my cheek and opened the door to the hallway. "Have a good day, you two." He slipped out into the hallway and the door swung closed behind him.

"Did you get enough?" Aunt Vivian asked, inspecting my plate. "There's more warming on the stove if you're hungry."

"This is plenty. Thank you." I scooted my chair a bit further under the table and let the morning's news sink in. Liam had left. He'd gone home and hadn't even bothered to tell me or say goodbye. I reminded myself that he didn't owe me anything. A few kisses in front of the fire didn't make him my boyfriend. Also, I was going to have to tell him it could never happen again, anyway. So what if he hadn't said goodbye.

"Are you all right, dear?" Aunt Vivian asked, snapping me out of my thoughts.

"What? Oh. Yes. I'm fine." I took a bite of scrambled eggs.

"You look flushed. Are you sure?"

"Yes," I said, swallowing. "Thank you for breakfast, Auntie. Everything is delicious."

"My pleasure, dear." She leaned across the table. "Now, we

must get out of the house today. With Liam gone, your uncle will probably want me to fetch his files. But I plan on spending the day with you. I was thinking we might do some sightseeing. So, I propose we get out of the house as soon as you've finished breakfast. After I show you around a bit, we can drive into town and maybe find some lunch and do some shopping. Then we'll be home in time for dinner. What do you think?"

I nodded but didn't respond because I'd just taken a bite of buttered toast.

She continued, "I haven't forgotten your promise, you know. You said you'd tell me what happened yesterday to make you so upset. But I can always make sure we have enough fun to take your mind off things, if you'd prefer. What do you say?"

"That sounds good." I didn't really want to talk about my conversation with Connor. I didn't want to think about any of that. And of course, I wasn't going to tell her about kissing Liam. My thoughts drifted back to last night while she continued telling me about the different places where we might stop for lunch. I wondered if Liam would return before my visit ended. It was nearly Christmas, and his mother was sick. He'd probably want to spend the holidays with his family. It was entirely possible that I might never see him again.

My stomach churned, and I lost my appetite. Somehow I kept getting mixed up with the wrong guys. I pushed the remaining scrambled eggs around on my plate while my aunt talked.

"You don't have to finish it, dear." My aunt took a sip of tea and set her mug down on the table.

I blinked. "What's that?"

"Your breakfast." She nodded at my plate. "If you're not

hungry, just throw it on the compost and let's go."

"Oh. Okay." I stood and walked over to the sink with my plate. Liam's absence might provide me an excellent opportunity to show Uncle Oscar how valuable I could be to him. A new plan started to take shape.

"Are you sure you're okay, dear? You're not getting sick, are you?" She followed me to the sink and held the bin open for me as I scraped my plate.

"No, Auntie. I'm fine. Just a little preoccupied this morning, that's all." It was time to snap out of this and get to work.

"Yes, well, I should say you have reason to be."

Her comment pulled me away from my train of thought. "What do you mean?" She couldn't possibly have guessed I'd been making out with Liam.

"Deciding where to go to graduate school is a big decision," she said. "And if you get into Oxford, moving to England, away from your family. It's a big change."

"Oh," I said. I set my plate in the sink and washed my hands. "I didn't get accepted to Oxford. I got the email last night. I'm on the waitlist."

"I'm sorry, dear. Have you talked with Oscar yet? Perhaps there's some way he can help."

I smiled. "Thanks. He's been so busy, we haven't had time to talk. But I'd like to talk to him when we get back." I turned to face her as I wiped my hands on the dish towel.

"Of course! I'm sure your uncle would be happy to tell his friends at Oxford about his fantastic, intelligent niece. Don't count yourself out yet. After all, I have a personal, selfish interest in you getting accepted." She placed her hand on her hip and grinned at me.

I laughed. "All right, then. Let's get going." I shook my head as I refolded the dish towel. "I was thinking, there are these stone ruins not that far from here. Liam said it used to be some sort of temple? Maybe we could go there?" If Edric had been a hunter, and everyone thought his wife was the Faerie Queen, maybe there was some connection between Edric and Godda and that temple. I hadn't been able to find anything in Uncle Oscar's books last night, but maybe a visit would give me a new lead.

Aunt Vivian nodded. "I think I know the ones you mean. That sounds like a good place to start our tour." She stood and walked over to stand next to me. "It's going to be fine, you know." She slipped her arm around my waist and gave me a hug.

"Thanks," I said. She gave me another squeeze.

"Go on now," she said. "Go upstairs and get your coat. Let's leave before your uncle starts calling for me."

I retreated up the back stairs to grab my coat and my new hat and gloves from my room. Before leaving, I reached for my phone and sent a quick note to my parents letting them know if they wanted to reach me to call me at Lydbury. Then I shut my phone off and stuffed it into my drawer. No more phone for a while. No more obsessing about the life I left behind or Liam. I needed to focus on my future.

By the time I'd reached the foyer, I was filled with excitement. I followed my aunt to her car and listened to her chatter as we rolled down the driveway under the arched trees. She'd handed me a stack of guidebooks before I'd climbed into the car, and I flipped through them as she talked. Every once in a while, I paused in my skimming to stare out the window and watch the fields fly past or answer one of her questions. By the time I spotted the temple ruins in the field, I'd already absorbed two different entries about the ancient temple and my aunt's gossip about the local squabbles over the surrounding land. Liam had been right, everything around here came down to some nonsense about faeries or ghosts, or both, at some point.

"When is the winter solstice?" I asked Aunt Vivian.

"The winter solstice? Let's see...I think that's two days from now. Why do you ask?" She slowed the car and turned down the gravel drive that led to a nearly empty parking lot near the cluster of stones.

"Some of these stories say that's the best time for spotting ghosts. Not that I believe that sort of thing." A few tourists wandered in the grass, laughing and snapping photos.

"Here we are!" Aunt Vivian smiled and reached for her purse.

Yes. I know. I clutched my hat and mittens. I hoped Liam wouldn't be too disappointed that Aunt Vivian had taken over as tour guide. But what Liam felt didn't matter. Surely, he wasn't thinking about what I thought or what I was feeling.

———

I stared out the window and wondered if Evelyn was awake yet. The train had slowed to pull into the station, and I watched the scenery, wishing I could have at least said goodbye even though there was no way I could have explained where I was going. Now all I could think about was what I would say to our queen when I returned.

Hi, Mum. Didn't find anything about Lord Edric yet, but I did make some progress winning over Oscar's niece. Yeah, that conversation wouldn't go well. Of course, Mother wouldn't scold me. She'd just remind me about my place in the Court and my sworn obligation to defend our future queen, my cousin, the dazzling and daring Fiona. Subtext: *Why can't you be more like your cousin Ari?* Arabella had accepted her place by Fiona's side as her future second-in-command as soon as she'd been old enough to wield a weapon. Mother probably would have been happier with a daughter. A daughter like Arabella. Or Fiona.

The brakes on the train screeched, and I gathered my things. My cousins would laugh at me if they knew I'd taken the train partway. But I hadn't been using my magic recently, and I worried I'd end up off my mark if I attempted to transport myself any great distance. After the train pulled to a halt, I made my way to the door and walked down the steps to the platform. There weren't that many travelers in the station, but there were still too many for me to disappear into thin air. I walked around the corner of the station until I'd slipped out of sight of other travelers. Then I let my magic course through me for the first time in months, and I thought of home.

When I opened my eyes again, I was standing outside Mother's cottage, deep in the woods, far from the station. I breathed a sigh of relief and knocked on the door. A movement in the window caught my eye, and a moment later the door swung open.

"About time," Arabella said, blocking the doorway. She glared at me, then turned and stomped away down the hall.

"How is she?" I asked, hurrying to catch up.

Arabella shook her head. "She's been asking for you."

"So you said." Was that really all she was going to tell me? I guessed that she'd be mad, but this was my mother we were talking about. The woman who raised us, me and my two cousins. Was Arabella really going to freeze me out now? Over a mortal?

She stopped and spun to face me.

"What were you thinking?" she asked, her voice low and threatening.

Instinctively, I took a step back. "I don't know what you mean."

"You know exactly what I mean." She stepped toward me. "What are you thinking, messing with that human?"

"Ari—" I started to explain, but she cut me off.

"You're Fae. She's mortal. Have you forgotten your promise to your family? The promise you made to your mother? The Oath you will swear to our future queen?"

"Of course I haven't forgotten." She might as well have punched me in the gut; her words had the same effect.

"Then why, when I come to tell you your mother is sick and asking for you, did I find you snogging that human? There's a time for that sort of thing, and that time is not now." She was in my face, poking at my chest, willing me to grovel or fight back.

"I know. I'll keep my promise. You know I will." I wrapped my hand around her finger and pressed her hand down and away. "I'm sorry."

"You're sorry." She spun around and stalked down the hall away from me. I followed, several paces behind, toward the faint candlelight coming from Mother's bedroom at the end of the hall.

"Aunt Flida, Liam's here," she called when she reached the open doorway.

"Liam? Liam, my love? Where are you? Come closer so I can see you." Mother shifted in her bed and reached an arm toward the door. My heart broke. Arabella was right. Nothing else mattered more than this.

I stepped closer to my mother's bedside and held her thin hand in my own. Her skin felt dry and stretched paper thin over her delicate bones. "I'm here, Mother."

"Liam. You came." She pulled my hand toward her face and pressed her lips against my skin.

"Of course I did. How are you feeling?" I smoothed her hair away from her face and bent to kiss her forehead. It was warm. Too warm.

"It won't be long now, my love," she whispered. I tensed and she squeezed my hand in response.

"Hold on, Mother. We need you." She wasn't just our current queen, Mother was one of the oldest, and most powerful, of our kind. I knew she wouldn't live forever, but we needed her magic to defend against Edric when he returned. Without her, without the artifact I had been unable to find, we'd be defenseless. He'd pick us off, one by one, capturing us, torturing us for information about my aunt Godda.

"Fiona will make an excellent queen. And you and Ari will be by her side to advise her, and protect her, and keep her safe," she said.

Even without the threat of Edric's return, I wasn't ready to let her go. "But what if I need you, Mother?"

"Oh, Liam, my love. I'm so proud of you."

I winced, knowing I'd done nothing yet to deserve her praise. I glanced over at Arabella, who just scowled at me in response. So, she hadn't told Mother about my failure, or my distraction.

"Rest, Mother. I'll stay here with you." I pulled a chair closer to her bed and sat. Then I took hold of her hand again and began to sing the songs she'd sung to me as a child, the ones that lulled me to sleep and made me feel loved and protected.

Arabella's face softened as she listened. I began to relax as Mother drifted into sleep. But an earthy and slightly floral scent followed by a knock at the door caught my attention and made me sit up straight. Arabella was already up and out of her chair, walking toward the door. When she returned, she brought Fiona with her.

Fiona stood tall and strong in the doorway. Her dark skin glowed in the candlelight, and the short, twisted hair that covered her head made her look like she was wearing a spikey crown.

"Liam," she said with a hushed voice so she wouldn't wake Mother.

I tucked Mother's hand under the covers and stood to face my future queen. "Fiona," I said, bowing my head to her.

"How is she?" Fiona's wide brown eyes shone with unshed tears.

"She's sleeping now. She says it won't be long." I turned my head and watched the shadows flicker on the walls.

"Liam, I'm so sorry." She lifted my hand and pressed it between her warm palms.

I turned to meet her gaze again. "At least I had a chance to know my mother, Fi. We will avenge yours. I promised you, and I will not break my vow."

She dropped her chin to her chest. Fiona's mother, Arabella's mother, and my mother were three of Godda's six sisters. My mother had been Godda's second-in-command, left to fill in as queen when Godda disappeared after Edric's betrayal. Their five younger sisters, Arabella's and Fiona's mothers among them, had been some of the first Fae to be hunted and killed by Edric. When their capture and torture didn't lead to Godda's return, Edric and his Hunters continued their quest. Thousands of Fae had perished over the past centuries at their hands. This was why we needed to stop him. If we didn't, this war would end with our extinction.

When my mother died, Fiona would become the next Faerie Queen because she was the eldest daughter of the seven sisters. At Fiona's coronation, I would be expected to swear my Oath, officially binding me to the Fae High Court as one of the Queen's Sworn. After that, I'd need to take my place at Fiona's side, helping her rule and, once we'd won this war, rebuild. No more masquerading as a human. My only other option would be to turn my back on my family, give up my powers, and become human. If I couldn't fulfill the promise I'd made to my cousins to help them avenge their mothers and kin, if I couldn't put an end to this centuries-old war with the Underworld, that was exactly what I planned to do.

Arabella was right. I'd let myself become distracted. Now I needed to get back to Lydbury and find every artifact that brute Edric had ever touched. My attraction to Evelyn could wait until after I found the artifact binding Edric's spirit to this world and destroyed it, banishing him and ending this brutal war.

6

AFTER exploring the temple ruins, Aunt Vivian insisted on taking me to town to pick up some things for tea. I left her to finish browsing in the cheese shop and wandered next door to the bookstore in search of more books on local history. A bell chimed as I opened the door, and I inhaled the scent of leather and dust. I wove around cases and displays, browsing the titles, so absorbed that I didn't see the young, well-dressed guy leaning against the end of one of the bookcases. As I turned the corner, I ran right into him and tripped. He grabbed my arm to steady me and set me back on both feet.

"I'm so sorry," I said. "I didn't see you there." I felt my cheeks growing warm as his form came into focus. He looked to be about my age or a little older. Tall and fit, with firm muscles hinted at under his crisp gray button-down shirt. The stylish black wool trousers he wore accentuated his thin waist. He'd draped his coat over one arm and appeared to have been flipping through a thick leather-bound book when I ran into him. He looked like he'd just stepped out of a Brooks Brothers catalog.

"I'm sorry," he said in a posh English accent. "I've chosen an awful place to lounge about. Are you all right?"

I straightened my jacket and reached up to smooth my hair. That's when I realized I was still wearing that ridiculous earflap hat. I slipped it off my head and into my pocket. "Oh," I said. "I'm fine. Are you okay? I think I stepped on your toes." I looked down at his refined black leather boots.

"I didn't feel a thing." He smiled. His teeth and his nose were both slightly crooked, but the overall effect was entirely charming. "I'm Nigel, by the way. And you must be new in town. I'm sure I would have noticed if you lived here."

"I'm Evelyn," I said. "I'm just visiting. Staying with my aunt and uncle for the holidays."

The door chimed and a gust of cold winter wind blew through the store.

"What a pity. I guess I'll have to make what time I have count, then, shan't I?"

Aunt Vivian appeared at my elbow. "Oh, here you are, dear!" She caught a glimpse of Nigel and stopped. "Pardon me, I didn't mean to interrupt. I'll just be over here while you finish chatting, dear." She started to turn and walk away, but I reached out and placed a hand on her forearm.

"Nonsense, Auntie, you're not interrupting. Let me introduce you to Nigel. We just met, and he's being very polite about the fact I nearly squashed his foot when I plowed into him. Nigel, this is my aunt, Vivian."

Nigel held out his hand to my aunt. "Pleased to meet you, ma'am. Your niece was just telling me about you. The family resemblance is striking, though I'd have pegged you for an older sister, not Evelyn's aunt."

Aunt Vivian shook Nigel's hand and blushed at the compliment.

"Do you live near town?" he asked. Other than his slightly crooked nose, he was absolutely perfect. I tried not to stare, but I couldn't help it.

"Yes, we live at Lydbury," Aunt Vivian said. I silently thanked her for saving me while I remembered how to speak.

"Ah, of course. The old manor house. I'm familiar with Lydbury. Old estates are such treasures." My lips twitched. Who even talked like that, anymore? Posh young English guys, apparently.

"Yes, it's been in my husband's family for years. Are you familiar with the Sauvage family?" Aunt Vivian had warmed to the conversation, and I could tell she'd completely take over in a minute if I didn't get my brain back.

He turned his focus toward her. "I am familiar with the name. Though, I can't say I know of your husband. What did you say his name is?"

"Oscar. Oscar Sauvage," she replied. I discreetly nudged her with my elbow. "But I'm afraid I've hijacked your conversation. I should let you two chat and go find that book I wanted." She arched her eyebrows at me and shot me a significant look before walking away.

"Your aunt is lovely."

"Yes, she is," I said. I wanted to slap myself. I finally had him alone again and that was the best I could manage for conversation. I'd clearly been out of the flirting game too long.

"So, what do you say, can I take you to dinner?"

I blinked at him. It was like he'd heard my thoughts. I couldn't believe this gorgeous, well-dressed, and, by the looks of it, well-educated young man had just asked me to dinner. I nodded as I struggled to find the right response.

"I'd be happy to drive out to Lydbury to pick you up. It would be no trouble. There are some lovely places out that way."

I swallowed and found my voice, finally. "Oh, you don't need to do that. I could just meet you in town and we could go to a pub."

"Nonsense. Besides, there's a much nicer pub near Lydbury. Let me take you."

I nodded. "Okay," I said.

"Brilliant. Shall I pick you up around seven?"

My eyes went wide. He wanted to take me out tonight. I blinked. Maybe I hadn't been dating much recently, but he seemed to be moving pretty fast. Still, what harm was there in having dinner with someone? Perhaps he could tell me more about the area. He seemed to already know something about Lydbury.

"Sure. I can be ready at seven. You know how to find my aunt and uncle's house?"

"Certainly. Lydbury is legendary around here."

"You're not asking me out just to get a closer look at their place, are you?" I crossed my arms over my chest and smirked at him.

He took a step closer to me and lifted my hand. "It appears only one of Lydbury's treasures has my full attention." He bent to place a light kiss on the back of my hand, and my heart raced. He glanced up at me as his lips brushed my skin and met my eyes. "See you tonight?"

My mouth had gone dry. I swallowed and nodded. "See you then."

He released my hand, and I smiled at him before walking over to join my aunt.

"So?" she whispered to me when I stepped alongside her.

"Oh. My. God," I said.

"Yes, he is godlike, isn't he?" she whispered.

I elbowed her in the ribs. "Let's go."

She paid for her selection, and I attempted to browse book covers until she returned. Unfortunately, their history section didn't hold much of interest. I resisted glancing over at Nigel until we were about to leave. When I did, he looked up from the book he was reading, met my eyes, and smiled. I waved and followed my aunt through the door.

"Well, that was productive," Aunt Vivian said. "I get my shopping done, and you manage to run into possibly the most attractive young man in the entire town. Did you get his number, or whatever it is you young people do these days?"

"He asked me to dinner." The cold air did nothing to chill my still warm cheeks. I tugged my hat over my head, hoping the earflaps might manage to hide some of my blushing.

"Well, then. A gentleman who knows what he wants and isn't afraid to ask for it. I like that. And you said yes, of course." When I didn't respond immediately, she clutched my arm with her free hand. "You did say yes, didn't you?"

"Yes." It thrilled me that Nigel had been so clearly interested. I pushed away the tiny thought that something wasn't quite right and blamed my hesitation on the fact that I'd had such bad luck with guys recently.

"Good. Once we find you a boyfriend here, you'll never want to leave." She grinned. "When's your date?"

"Tonight. And I'm not looking for a boyfriend. It's just one date." Nigel appeared to have everything I thought I wanted in a guy, but I was nowhere near ready to think of him as a potential boyfriend.

"Tonight? My. He certainly doesn't waste any time, does he?"

I shook my head. "My thoughts exactly."

"Did you see those biceps, though? And that hair?" My aunt sighed and fanned herself. "I wish my hair had half as much body as his does."

I giggled. He did have nice hair. Dark hair, cut in a sleek short and professional style, but thick on top and shiny. It made you want to run your fingers through it. Only, shiny probably meant product. Guys and hair product were not a good combination, in my experience.

"What time is he picking you up?"

"Seven."

"Good. We still have time to stop at a few more stores. Then I'll get you home so you'll have plenty of time to get ready."

"Will Uncle Oscar be upset that I'm not staying home with you two this evening?" I needed to be spending more time with him, not less. But one dinner out couldn't hurt, so long as I could convince him at tea to let me help him, at least while Liam was away.

"Oh, no, dear. He wants you to enjoy your visit. Besides, we'll be home in plenty of time for you to have tea with him and catch up. Now, this may be a small village, but we happen to have an amazing bakery." She started listing off more potential treats we might bring home for tea, but my thoughts drifted back to the temple ruins and the paper Liam had told me about. I was sure there must be a connection. Perhaps the legends had it all wrong and Godda had been some beautiful temple attendant whom Edric had met on one of his visits there. It was time to find out what my uncle had to say on the subject.

Thinking of Liam made me feel a little guilty about saying yes to dinner with Nigel. But I reminded myself that Liam had no claim on me. So what if I'd kissed my uncle's secretary? It didn't mean anything. He'd left without saying goodbye. And, besides, Nigel looked like he was more my type.

———

Mother felt stronger after resting most of the morning. I'd left her sitting up in bed, talking with Fiona, and stepped into the hall to find Arabella. Every minute I spent here was time I should be spending searching Oscar's artifacts for something that would help us. I needed to get back to Lydbury.

I found Arabella pacing outside Mother's cottage.

"Hey," I called.

Arabella stopped and turned to face me. "How is she?"

"A bit better." I sighed. "She insists that she won't last much longer. Fiona is talking with her now."

"We'll need her magic to destroy the artifact, once you find it. There has to be something that can help her keep her strength, even if it's just for a little longer." She crossed her arms and frowned.

I ran a hand through my hair. "I know. I need to get back to Lydbury, but I don't want to leave her."

"Go see your sire. Maybe he can help. If we can't find something to help her hold on, I'm going to need you here to help me protect Fi."

I nodded. "Fine. Where is he?"

Arabella shook her head. "I heard he's been spending time near the Falls. But he may be on one of his pilgrimages again."

"All right. I'll start at the Falls and see what I can find. I won't be gone long."

I walked to the edge of the trees and concentrated on pulling my magic up to the surface. There wasn't time to waste worrying about being out of practice, but knowing Arabella was watching made me nervous. I closed my eyes and imagined my sire as I'd last seen him, standing in front of the glassy pool at the foot of Faerie Falls. When I opened my eyes, I was standing in front of that pool, but there was no sign of him. The magic cloaking this place was thick and newly patched. Other than that, there were no obvious signs that he had been here recently.

Cahal, my sire, was possibly the most ancient Fae still alive. His magic linked him with water and healing, but his spirit was restless and he frequently traveled across England, drawing power from, and bringing life to, the country's bodies of water. The Falls were his sanctuary.

I stripped and waded into the cool, clear water until it lapped against my chest. Then I pushed off the rocky bottom and swam across the pool to the base of the falls, ducking under the wall of water. I surfaced on the other side and let my ears adjust to the crashing roar of tumbling water echoing against the rock before climbing up onto a ledge. It took only a thought to dry my skin and conjure my clothes back onto my body. Then I ducked into the cave entrance hidden by the waterfall.

The falls blocked most of the light, and within a few meters, the darkness had enveloped me. I cupped my hands in front of me and conjured a ball of light. Then, with a flick of my wrist, I released it and let it float in front of me, illuminating my path. I nudged it ahead and followed the narrow, dripping corridor deeper into the cavern. Flashes of blue-green light at the far end of the cave were my first indication that I was not alone.

In case the flashes were not something produced by my sire, I extinguished the glowing orb and transformed into my animal form, something I hadn't done since before I'd set foot in Lydbury. Each of my kin could take a different animal form. Mine was a mountain lion. I hadn't picked it—the form had picked me. But I loved the enhanced senses I gained: stealth, night vision, and a more refined sense of smell than my human form afforded me. I flexed my muscles and relished the increased strength, power, and grace compared to my human body.

I padded around a bend in the cave wall. Another flash illuminated a hunched figure near the back of the cave. I approached on silent paws along a path that led to a ledge overlooking the cavern floor. I kept my senses trained on the figure as I paced to the overlook. When I reached the edge, a ring of sparking light rose from the figure's outstretched hand, growing larger as it sped toward my face. I let out an instinctive, low snarl and shrank back, away from the light.

"Come down from there, son." The figure let its hood fall back to expose a mane of white hair surrounding a deeply lined face.

I pounced from my ledge to a lower perch, then landed on the cavern floor.

"You're out of practice," Cahal said. He'd gone back to fiddling with the object in his hands and didn't look up at me, even after I'd transformed back into my human form.

"I haven't been using my magic," I admitted. His scolding stung more than Arabella's constant reminders.

"Yes, I heard," he said, still without looking up from his work. "You've been masquerading as a human. Living among them. What nonsense."

I sighed. "Sire, I didn't come for a lecture."

"What did you come here for, then?" He glanced up from the object he held to glare at me.

"Mother's fading." Tears stung the corners of my eyes, but

I wouldn't let them escape here.

"I am aware." He frowned and returned to his tinkering.

"Is there nothing you can do?" I took a step forward and swept my arms out toward the cave walls. Anger replaced the sadness I'd felt moments before.

He stopped and his head snapped up, his blue eyes blazing in the dim light. "Don't you think I would have done something if I could?"

I took a step back and dropped my hands to my sides. "I don't know. You've been away so long..." I shook my head.

"I have my responsibilities and your mother has hers. She knew that when we bonded."

"But, she's fading. Aren't you...don't you want to...say goodbye?" My sire hadn't lived with us, but I knew my parents loved each other deeply. I couldn't understand why he would behave this way.

"How do you know I haven't already?" he asked, his voice low.

"Have you seen her?" My heart ached at the way my mother had looked, so frail in her bed, just hours ago.

"I've done what I can, as she asked me to." He frowned.

"She came to you?" Hope returned in a rush. She hadn't given up.

"You think you're the only one who knows how to find me?"

"I know she's lived a long life, even for the Fae. But we need her to hold on just a bit longer. Just until we can end the Hunt." We were so close. He had to understand that.

"The Hunt." He shook his head and returned to tinkering with the box in his hands. "And what makes you think you'll be successful this time?"

"We think the artifact anchoring Edric's spirit to the living world is still at Lydbury. If we can find it and destroy it, we can banish him to the Underworld for good." It sounded so simple when I put it like that.

"I suppose this is why you're wasting your talents and hiding out as a human?"

"I was better suited to this than any of the others."

"Your plan will fail, and then what? I can't hold her here forever. She deserves rest, peace."

"Our plan won't fail. I'll tear that manor to pieces before I let our plan fail. We will destroy Edric and his Hunters."

"You can't even sneak up on an old man in a cave."

"You're hardly an old man."

"If you'd been training, if you harnessed the power you possess, you could bring the fight to them. You don't need an artifact, son. What you need is to accept your heritage."

His criticism stung. Maybe if there were more of us, he might have a point. "Then what's your excuse? Why aren't you helping us bring the fight to them?"

He locked his blue eyes onto mine and scowled at me. "I am not Sworn. I'm an Elemental. My responsibilities are here. You know where yours lie. Not with those humans—those destructive animals who think nothing of polluting their world and make my work nearly impossible. The thought of you living among them disgusts me. You trained with me as a boy. You know what they do, what they're capable of, and yet you've abandoned your post and your magic to pretend to be one of them."

No surprise that he wouldn't approve of my interest in Evelyn, then. Not that it mattered. "I'm on a mission for the Court."

He snorted. "Whatever you need to tell yourself." He aimed another flash of light at the box in his hand. The flash ricocheted off the box and slammed into the cavern wall. The box shook, and he poked at it again with the tool he held in his hand.

"Being one of the Fae used to mean something. Being a member of the Queen's Sworn used to be an honor." I shook my head and began pacing. "Now it just means constant war over an ages-old grudge led by a madman hell-bent on slaughtering our kind."

"Then change it." He grumbled and fussed with the tool.

"I can't." I might be able to help stop the war, but our numbers were so diminished, even without the Hunt, I feared we wouldn't survive.

He shrugged. "Well, I can't help you."

I narrowed my eyes and glared at him. "You stand there telling me I should be using my powers. You're a healer. You should be with Mother now. Are you not at the service of our queen?"

"Clever boy. You think you have me there, don't you? Well, you know nothing. When you're as old as me, you can tell me a thing or two. Until then, allow me to remind you, your mother is nearly as ancient as I am. She doesn't need a healer. She needs to be allowed to fade. It is her right. Let her spirit return to strengthen the force that feeds our magic."

I groaned and ran a hand through my hair. "Sod it. I've had enough. If you won't help, I'm leaving." I turned my back on him and started to walk away.

"Liam," he said. I stopped walking but didn't turn around. "If you really want to help your mother and find that artifact, use your magic. Stop acting like a human."

His words were like a punch to my gut. I stalked through the darkness down the corridor until I reached the cave entrance. Arabella had been telling me since I'd first volunteered for this assignment that I should just use my magic. Maybe my sire was right. And if he wouldn't help me, then I couldn't wait any longer. I needed to destroy Edric now, before he had a chance to hurt any more of my kin. I owed it to my mother to avenge her sisters, to my cousins to avenge their mothers. But I would need to act fast. We were less than two days from the solstice, and once I used that type of magic in the manor, it would be like setting off a beacon. I would draw the Hunt directly to Lydbury's doorstep. I wouldn't have much time to find the artifact and destroy it, let alone protect Oscar and his family. And if I were wrong, if the house did not hold Edric's secrets, I'd be putting Evelyn in the middle of a war I couldn't stop.

7

AUNT Vivian served the tea in the library. I hadn't returned to this room since I'd left Liam standing by the fire staring after me. Everything in this room reminded me of the look in his eyes just before he kissed me, the feel of his lips against mine, his hands on my hips. I wondered what would have happened if my aunt and uncle hadn't come home. At least this way I had less to regret. Just a few kisses. It meant nothing.

"Ah, there you are!" Uncle Oscar walked into the library carrying a stack of books and a small wrapped package. "I've made almost no progress this morning. I had to fetch all my books and papers myself. It appears I've become accustomed to my secretary." He set the pile of books on a table and lifted the velvet-wrapped bundle off the top. "But all this messing about in my files did uncover one particular treasure." He held up the bundle. "Evelyn, I have something for you."

He held out the package to me, and I lifted it from his hands.

The dark-green velvet looked almost black and reminded me of the color of the forest at night. A cornflower-blue braided silk cord held the package together. I pulled at the knots, admiring the smooth feel of the tassels at each end. With the cord untied, I folded back the velvet to expose a wide, carved golden bracelet. I hesitated to touch it.

"It's beautiful."

"Go ahead, lift it up to the light," he said. "You'll be able to see the carvings better that way."

"Where did you find this, dear?" Aunt Vivian asked.

"Oh, I guess I forgot to tell Liam about that storage room in the cellar. It will take him weeks to catalog all that. I don't expect he'll be pleased to know there's more. But there are some treasures down there. Like this one."

I held the bracelet up to the light and admired the intricate marks carved into the surface. I'd expected the metal to feel cool against my skin. Instead my fingertips tingled where they pressed against the smooth surface. What property of the gold could produce such an effect? One part of my mind churned, examining the possibilities, while the other marveled at the magnificent piece of history I held in my hands.

"It's writing," he said. "Well, not all of it. But those marks there." He pointed out a section and slipped on his reading glasses. I rotated the band to see it better. "That's ancient Celtic. I've forgotten the translation. It's in there, somewhere." He waved his hand at the stack of books and papers he'd set on the table. "But, if I'm not mistaken, this little bangle was a gift from William the Conqueror to the wife of my ancestor, Edric Sauvage. It's said that his wife had hair the color of spun gold and was the most beautiful woman in the kingdom. I think old Willie must have been a bit soft on her, don't you agree?"

"The Faerie Queen from the tapestry that hangs in the

stairwell, right?" I asked. The pads of my fingers explored the rough edges surrounding the carvings.

"Yes, that's the one." He removed his reading glasses and folded them into his pocket, then gestured to me. "Go on, Eve, try it on. Let's see how it looks."

"Oh, I couldn't." I placed the bracelet down on the folded scrap of velvet in my hand and offered it back to Uncle Oscar, even though I longed to hold it again, to wear it.

"Nonsense. It's a family heirloom, and I'd like you to have it." He closed my fingers around the bundle and gently pushed my hand away.

I opened my fingers and gazed down at the bright-yellow gold. "It belongs in a museum, not on my wrist." But, at the same time, I wanted to sit and study it for hours, translate the writing, examine every detail.

"Never fear, there will be plenty for the museums when I'm gone. They don't need this little bauble as well." He waved a hand at me. "Go on, then. Put it on."

I lifted the bracelet and placed the velvet and cord on the table. When I slid the bracelet over my wrist, a sensation of warmth traveled up my arm, like I was dipping my arm into a bath. I stared down at my wrist, but the sensation disappeared, leaving only the expected feel of cool metal against my skin.

"Yes, just so." Uncle Oscar smiled and puffed out his chest as he slipped his hands into his pockets.

"I agree, dear. It looks lovely on her," Aunt Vivian said.

I held my arm out and admired the beautiful craftsmanship wrapped around my thin wrist. "But it's so special. I'd be afraid to wear it. What if something happened to it? I'd feel terrible."

Uncle Oscar shook his head. "It's survived this long. I don't think there's anything you can do to harm it."

Aunt Vivian smiled and clasped her hands at her chest. "And you can wear it when you go out this evening."

"Do we have plans for this evening?" Uncle Oscar asked.

"No, dear. We don't, but Eve does." She gave Uncle Oscar a quick kiss on the cheek and then walked over to the low table where she'd left the teapot and scones. "She met a charming young man in town this morning, and he's taking her to dinner."

"Well, then. I'm glad you're making friends." Uncle Oscar followed Aunt Vivian toward the sitting area.

Aunt Vivian looked up from pouring the tea to wink at me. I lingered for a moment longer, admiring the bracelet. Liam hadn't seen this yet. I wondered what he'd think of my uncle giving me a centuries-old bracelet to wear about town. He'd probably hate it.

"Are you coming, Eve? The tea's getting cold." Aunt Vivian and Uncle Oscar were already seated in the armchairs Liam and I had been sitting in last night.

"Yes, Auntie." I pushed the memories of last night out of my head and focused on my uncle. This was my first chance to talk with him about history, and I wasn't going to waste it.

"Uncle Oscar, I've been reading a lot about the woman in the tapestry." I sunk into one of the armchairs and helped myself to tea and scones. "Which of the stories do you think is true?"

He leaned back in his chair and took a sip of tea. "According to my family, Edric had been out hunting and came across a cabin in the woods. Through the window, he spotted the most beautiful woman he'd ever seen. She was dancing with her sisters. He rushed in, captured her, and took her back to his manor." He paused and scratched his beard. "This was back in the middle of the eleventh century. Things were a bit less civilized then, you understand."

I smirked. "I suppose that's how he got the name Sauvage?"

"Quite." He chuckled. "Though, come to think of it, I think he might have earned that name before he kidnapped his wife... He's known to have been a superb hunter."

"So you think it's true that he kidnapped Godda and convinced her to marry him?"

"Well, not immediately. The stories handed down say she observed him for several days and wouldn't speak or eat. Finally, just as he was growing desperate, she spoke. She told him she was a Faerie Queen and he'd stolen her away from her people, but she'd decided he was worthy of her love. She promised to stay with him so long as he never said an unkind word about her sisters or her kin. If he ever did, she would leave him. He agreed, of course, and they were married.

"They lived happily for many years, had a son, and were frequent guests of the king, who thought Godda to be the most beautiful woman he'd ever seen. But one day Edric forgot his promise. In a jealous rage, he said she spent too much time away, with her family. And that was it. Godda just disappeared. He searched for her as long as he lived but never found her. They say he died from a broken heart."

"That sounds like a fairy tale, Uncle."

He nodded. "Quite."

"I still don't believe it. I think she was just a beautiful human woman, and she's buried out there in some unmarked grave like so many other women of her time." My fingers strayed to the gold band around my wrist, caressing it as I spoke.

Uncle Oscar nodded. "I understand. I found it a bit hard to believe at first, myself. But I've reason to believe there's some truth to the stories."

"Based on your research?" Something about that tapestry haunted me. My uncle giving me this bracelet made me even more determined to discover the truth of her life, and her disappearance.

He placed his teacup on the table and stood. "Yes. But I have to admit, the details in the stories handed down in my family have done the most to convince me." He scanned his shelves and selected a small, dusty leather-bound volume with no markings on the binding. "This is an account book kept by the steward of Edric's estate." Then he selected a thin hardbound book. "And this text is from a series of lectures I did, years ago. You might find something interesting here."

I reached for the books he offered me and ran my hand over the covers, thrilled to learn more about this house and its original owner and the mystery surrounding his beautiful wife. "Uncle Oscar." I hesitated, staring down at the book covers as I formed the question I dared to ask. "Is there anything I could do to help you? You know, while Liam's gone?" If I didn't ask, then he couldn't turn me down. But now it was out there, and he had the power to squash my dreams.

He studied me for a moment before responding. "Is that something you would enjoy?"

I nodded. "Yes. Very much."

"All right, then. If you're sure, and if Liam's not back tomorrow, come see me in the morning, and we'll find something for you." He beamed at me, and I soaked it in. Things were finally starting to improve for me.

———

The return trip to the cottage was easier than the trip to the Falls. Already I felt more control over my magic and longed to stretch the feline muscles of my animal form one more time before returning to Lydbury. I transformed, prowling across the short distance across the clearing to where Arabella stood sentry outside the cottage, not far from where I'd left her.

"I almost didn't recognize you in that form," she said. "Are you trying to draw attention to yourself? Mountain lions aren't exactly common around here."

I returned to my Fae form and shook my head. "Can't win, can I? Use my magic, get a lecture. Don't use my magic, still get a lecture."

"Sheesh. Someone is a little testy. Had a nice chat with old Cahal, then, I take it?" Arabella smirked.

I ran a hand through my hair and tucked the long strands behind the points of my ears. "That man is impossible. I don't know why I bother."

"Sometimes I say the same thing about you, cuz." Arabella leaned back against the cottage wall.

I glared at her. I was nothing like my sire. "He won't help."

She shrugged. "Didn't think he would. But it was worth asking."

"How is she?" I lifted my chin toward Mother's room at the back of the cottage.

"Same. Hanging on." She frowned. I could tell she was worried. Protecting Fiona was her primary responsibility, but I knew she cared just as deeply for my mother.

"Good. I need to get back." I stretched. It had been nice to use magic freely and let down my glamour. With any luck, I'd be returning soon with an artifact for my mother to destroy.

"I thought you'd say something like that. But even if you return tonight, tomorrow is the last day before the solstice." She flexed her hands before curling them into fists.

"I know. I have a new plan." I held back my grin, knowing how much she'd approve of this new plan.

She raised her eyebrows and pushed off the wall. "Dare I ask?"

"I'm going to use my magic."

She cocked her head to one side. "Something Cahal said changed your mind?"

"Of course not." I crossed my arms. "I don't need him—or you, for that matter—to tell me that we're running out of time. I made a promise to you and Fiona. I plan to keep it."

"If you reveal yourself to them—"

I cut her off before she could finish that thought. "I know. I'll find a way to do it without them knowing."

Fiona appeared in the doorway. She'd probably heard us talking. "Liam, you're back. Your mother is asking for you."

I took a step toward the door, and Arabella grabbed my arm.

"Be careful," she said. "You don't know who else is watching that place."

"You were the one who wanted me to use my magic in the first place, Ari."

Her grip tightened around my arm. "Well, I agreed to your plan because I thought you had a point."

My eyes went wide, and I turned my face to Fiona. "You heard that, didn't you? I think Ari just said I was right."

Fiona laughed.

"Oh, please." Arabella released my arm in a huff.

"Mark this day in history, Fi," I said.

"Noted. There will be plaques in the Great Hall and bards will sing of this day." She let loose another deep-throated laugh.

Her laugh was infectious, and I joined her, only to turn

and find Arabella glaring at us from a few meters away. I ran at her and tackled her in a hug. We tumbled and transformed. Twisting in a playful scramble of fur and fangs. Her wolf growling and my lion snarling, both of us snapping and swatting until I managed to get my jaws locked around her neck and push her to the ground with a paw.

I released my hold on her and licked the fur on her head. Score one for me. It had been so long since we'd sparred like this, and longer still since I'd won. She growled and yipped.

Fiona's laughter brought us back. We returned to our human forms and I threw an arm around Arabella's shoulders as we paced back to the cottage.

"Thanks for that," Fiona said as we approached. "Watching that almost felt like old times. And I can't tell you how good it feels to laugh."

"I should go see my mother and then be on my way," I said.

"I wish you didn't have to leave so soon," Fiona said.

"I'll return soon. And we'll destroy Edric together." I shot a glance at Arabella, who appeared to still be sore over my victory. "Or maybe we'll just sit back and watch Ari do it."

"Just give me a chance and he's dust." Arabella pounded her fist into her open hand.

A thin voice echoed down the hallway, and I frowned. "Coming, Mother," I called down the hall.

Sadness filled Fiona's eyes and Arabella just nodded. I turned and walked down the hall toward my mother's candlelit room.

"Liam, my love," she said, holding out her hand to me.

"Yes, Mother." I sat by her side.

"I'm stronger than I look," she said. "But you need to hurry. There isn't much time. I'll hold on as long as I'm able."

"You deserve your rest, Mother. You've served us well." I

bowed my head and kissed her hand.

"You sound so much like your sire." She ran her fingers through my hair, and I realized that my mane of wavy brown hair wasn't that dissimilar to the messy white mop surrounding my sire's head.

"I'll be back soon," I promised. Silently, I begged the Ancients for more time. This wouldn't be goodbye. Not yet.

"Be safe," she said. "And hurry."

I nodded and stepped back from the bed. There wasn't any time to waste. Confident enough to exercise my magic, I skipped the train and conjured myself directly to the dark corner of town where I'd left my motorcycle, hoping no one would be watching when I appeared out of thin air.

8

I HAD been staring into the wardrobe so long that my mind had started to wander off, and all I could think was that everything I'd packed was terrible. A knock at my door snapped me back to reality. I left the wardrobe open and crossed my room to open the door.

"Hello, dear," Aunt Vivian said when I peeked my head out into the hallway. "I just wanted to check on you and see if you needed anything."

"I don't know what I was thinking when I packed." I sighed. "I have nothing to wear."

"Now, now. I'm sure you have something suitable."

I opened the door wider and waved her inside. She crossed the floor and stood where I'd been standing, facing the open wardrobe. She ran her hand over the hangers, then began sifting through my clothes. "Where did you say he's taking you, dear?" she asked over her shoulder. She'd paused on the only fancy dress I'd brought with me.

"I suggested we just go to the pub. He says there's one near here that's very good."

"Oh, yes! The Frog and Pêche! It's not far, walkable on a nice evening, if you don't mind a bit of a hike." She frowned at the dress. "But this is a bit too much for a date at the pub. Let's see."

Watching her pour over my wardrobe, I realized I'd reached a new low in my dating game. Who lets their elderly aunt pick out their outfit before going on a first date?

She paused on a tight black sweater. "Hmm..." She slipped the soft cashmere off the hanger and held it up. "Yes, this will do. With jeans, and those boots of yours. The ones you were wearing when you arrived. And I have a lovely scarf that will pull it all together." She handed me the sweater. "Get dressed. I'll be right back."

I was sitting on the bed, zipping up my boots, when she returned. The scarf she held out to me was black and gray with flecks of gold thread running throughout. She draped it expertly around my neck and spun me to face my reflection in the mirror.

"Lovely," she said.

"But what will I do with my hair?"

"Allow me, dear. I'm a bit of an expert at making something of our hair." I sat on a low bench near the end of the bed and let her deft and nimble fingers braid and twist my thick, glossy dark locks. When I turned back to the mirror, I sucked in a breath. She'd created the effect of a crown with a French braid that skimmed my hairline and swept back into an elegant twist at the nape of my neck.

"Auntie, you're amazing," I said, patting at my hair and not quite believing what I was seeing in the mirror.

"Well, all those faculty dinners gave me plenty of practice." She patted her own short pixie cut. "Until I couldn't take it anymore and chopped it all off into something more sensible for a woman my age."

"Oh, Auntie." I kissed her cheek. "Daddy may have got the height in the family, but you got all the beauty."

She chuckled. "Good thing, too," she said. "The last thing we needed was for your father to be tall, brilliant, *and* beautiful."

"You're brilliant, too, Auntie. You just chose a different path."

"Yes." The smile fell from her face. "As you must choose yours, dear."

The doorbell rang, and she smiled at me. "Ready?"

I nodded. Aunt Vivian gave my hands a squeeze and slipped out of my room. I grabbed my coat but left my hat and mittens behind. I'd suffer a bit from the cold, but I didn't want to be reminded of Liam tonight. Then I shut off the light and followed Aunt Vivian down the hall to the top of the stairs. I could already hear Uncle Oscar's voice in the foyer below, welcoming Nigel. I peeked over the railing and caught a glimpse of Nigel's dark hair and breathed a sigh of relief when I noticed he'd traded his wool trousers for black jeans.

I crept down the stairs. Nigel looked up at me as I stepped onto the landing. He grinned, and I returned his smile.

"Ah, there you are, Evelyn," my uncle said.

"Hello," I said.

Nigel scrambled up the first few steps and offered me his hand to lead me down to the foyer. "You look lovely," he said.

"Thank you," I said. "So do you." I lifted my jacket off the hook near the door and slid my arms into the sleeves.

"Well," my uncle said, draping an arm around Aunt Vivian's shoulders. "Your aunt and I have quite a bit of work to do. You two enjoy your evening."

"Yes," my aunt said. "Enjoy your evening." She slipped her hand around my uncle's waist and led him down the hall.

"Your aunt and uncle are rather nice."

"Yes, I like them."

"And their house is magnificent." He looked around.

"I used to be so frightened of this house when I was a child. Everything seemed so big and scary."

"Well, it is rather intimidating. It's hard to believe they can live here, among all this history."

"Oh, my uncle lives for the history."

"Yes, he mentioned that. He's a professor, then?"

I nodded.

"Well," he said, "shall we?" He offered me his arm, and I hooked my hand around it.

We'd just shut the door behind us and stepped out into the entrance when the roar of an engine and a single headlight coming down the drive caught my attention. My heart raced. Liam. I bit my lip. Nigel hadn't registered this as anything to be alarmed about, and he continued to escort me to his sleek black sports car.

Liam pulled up and stopped next to the car just as we'd reached the passenger door. He lifted his visor and looked from me to Nigel and back again.

"Eve?"

"Hello, Liam!" I forced a casual smile and hoped he didn't plan on making a scene. "Uncle Oscar will be so glad you're back." Nigel had already reached his car. He opened the door for me and stood waiting.

Liam parked his motorcycle and dismounted. He unfastened his helmet as he walked toward us, shaking out his hair. This was going to be awkward.

"I don't believe we've met," he said, narrowing his eyes at

Nigel.

Nigel extended his hand. "Nigel," he said. "Nigel Strum. And you are?"

The air around Liam seemed to crackle with tension. Or maybe that was just how it felt to me, caught in the middle. Liam didn't offer his hand, he just left Nigel standing with his hand suspended in midair, waiting.

"Eve, did you invite him here?"

"Of course." I glared at Liam. "And you're being rude."

Liam stepped between me and Nigel and shut the door to the car.

"Liam. What are you doing?"

"You should go," he said to Nigel.

"Don't be ridiculous." I tried to push Liam out of the way, but he wouldn't budge. It felt like pushing against a tree trunk, like he was rooted to the earth.

"Perhaps you should let the lady decide?" Nigel said, his voice dripping with menace. Something about it made me stop pushing against Liam and glance up at Nigel.

"Do you think you really stand a chance?" Liam asked. I couldn't believe he was threatening Nigel. This was crazy. He had no claim on me.

"Liam, stop. What are you doing? We can talk about this later. What's gotten into you?"

"I will crush you," Nigel said. They were both ignoring me at this point, glaring at each other, waiting for the other one to back down.

"I wouldn't count on it," Liam said, taking a half step closer to Nigel.

"There's nothing you can do to stop me," Nigel said.

I reached between them and tried to get their attention. My hand stretched out of my sleeve, and I felt the cold air bite at my fingers and wrist. Nigel took a step back and Liam half turned to face me. Finally, their eyes were on me and not staring each other down.

"Where did you get that?" Liam asked.

I looked up at him, confused. "Get what?"

Nigel continued to walk backward until his back was against his car.

"That." Liam pointed at my wrist and the bracelet Uncle Oscar had given me.

I shrugged and let my sleeve fall back over the gold band. Nigel took a half step away from his car but otherwise kept his distance.

"My uncle gave it to me," I said.

"Evelyn," Nigel said. "It appears that things aren't going to work out for tonight. Perhaps we could do this some other time?"

I turned to Nigel. "I'm so sorry," I said. "We can still go to dinner." I took a step closer to him, but he backed away.

"No, I think it's better that I go. I'm sure I'll see you again soon." He glanced over my shoulder at Liam. "I won't forget our date, or your invitation."

"Leave." Liam said. "Now." His voice rumbled and made the hairs on my neck stand on end.

"I'll leave, for now. But I'll be back," he said.

"You won't get past me."

Nigel walked around the front of his car and opened the driver's side door. "We shall see," he said before sliding inside and shutting the door behind him. The engine roared to life and he shifted the car into gear. I watched his taillights disappear down the drive, then I spun on Liam.

"What. The. Hell. Was. That?" I stalked toward him. "One kiss and you think you get to act all possessive? You don't own me. What do you think you're doing, acting all macho and chasing him off like that?"

He stepped backward. "It has nothing to do with you."

"The hell it doesn't. We had a date." What had happened to that kind, sensitive guy who'd offered to share his job with me? Where did he get off acting like he had any right to butt in?

He snorted. "Oh, you had a date. Do you have any idea who he is?"

I shrugged. "I know him at least as well as I know you."

"But your aunt and uncle know me. Do they know who he is? And you invited him here! What were you thinking?"

"How bad could it be? It's not like he's a thief, or a land developer, or something. What's wrong with inviting him here?" I put my hands on my hips and stared at him.

Liam just shook his head and walked toward his motorcycle. "You have no idea."

"Then tell me. If you know him, tell me who he is and why it should matter that I was going to dinner with him."

Liam kicked his kickstand up and began rolling his motorcycle toward the carriage house. He shook his head. "I don't know him."

"Then what was that scene all about?" I stalked after him.

"Just go inside, Eve," he said over his shoulder.

I jogged ahead of him and turned to face him when he stopped in front of the carriage house door. "I'm not going inside until you tell me what in the hell is going on."

"Open the door, then," he said, nodding toward the carriage house.

I lifted the handle and held the door open for him.

"And I want to know why you think you get to act like that after one kiss," I added as he slipped past me.

I followed him to the back of the carriage house. He parked his motorcycle against the back wall and hung his helmet from the handlebars. Then he spun to face me. "First"—he took a step closer to me—"it was more than one kiss." He was standing close enough that I could feel the heat of him. "Second, I told you, what happened out there had nothing to do with you."

"So you just met this person and instantly have some grudge against him that has nothing to do with me, even though I'm about to go on a date with him and you say you don't know him." I pushed my hand against his chest. "And what difference does it make how many kisses there were when you were the one who left without saying goodbye."

Liam shook his head. "I may not know him, but I know his kind, and his kind are not welcome here."

"His kind? You mean well-dressed, educated gentlemen who have manners and are about to take me to dinner?"

"You want to go to dinner? I'll take you to dinner. For the last time, this has nothing to do with you."

"I find that hard to believe." I placed my hands on my hips.

He took a step closer to me and lowered his voice. "I'm gone for one day, and you manage to walk directly into the arms of the most dangerous bloke around. I must say, that's quite a talent." He ran his fingers down my cheek.

I narrowed my eyes and scowled at him.

"It's too bad I ruined your date. You look lovely."

I pressed my hands against his chest to shove him away, but he placed his hands over mine and stepped closer. "I'm sorry I left without saying goodbye. My mother's dying."

I closed my eyes and my chin dropped to my chest. His words drained the anger from me. Uncle Oscar had said Liam's mother was sick. I had no idea it was that bad.

Liam's fingers lifted my chin until I met his eyes.

"I'm sorry," I said.

"You didn't know." He leaned down and pressed his lips against mine.

———

The wall I'd built up to resist her broke when her lips parted under mine. I knew I should push her away, but my body wouldn't obey, and my arms tugged her closer. She had no idea that she'd just exposed herself and her family to danger by letting the worst kind of predator in the front door. I didn't want to spook her, and she probably wouldn't believe me anyway. But her invitation put a gaping hole in my protection spells and now he could come back at any time.

I pulled back from the kiss to catch my breath and listened with my enhanced hearing for any sound that might let me know that git had returned. Hearing nothing, I focused my attention back on Evelyn and slid my hand down her arm to her wrist. The gold band warmed under my touch.

"Oscar gave you this?" I asked.

"This afternoon," she said. "He said it belonged to—"

"Godda," I said.

"Yes. How'd you know? Uncle Oscar said that she was the wife of one of his ancestors, and William the Conqueror gave it to her as a wedding present."

I nodded. "Godda and Edric. Their story is infamous around here." I left off how they were the reason for my presence at Lydbury.

"He also said he'd found a room in the cellar that he'd forgotten to tell you about."

"And did you tell any of this to that—" I wanted to say "creature," but I stopped myself. She was in my arms, and calm. I didn't want to see that anger return to her face. So I forced myself to remember his name. "Nigel?" I grimaced.

She shook her head. "No."

"Good," I said. So, other than the bracelet, he didn't know what artifacts Oscar had here. But he could return now as he pleased because he'd been invited, and my protection spells would no longer keep him out. To be safe, I needed to take a large bag of salt and distribute it around the perimeter of the property, and the sooner the better. Then, if he returned, at least he wouldn't be able to bring the army of spirits under Edric's command with him. But first, I wanted a closer look at that bracelet.

"Can I look at it?"

She nodded. The carriage house was dark, but I held her wrist up until the bracelet caught some of the moonlight filtering through the windows. Carvings. I couldn't read the inscription in the dim light. I let a little of my magic surface to my fingertips and placed them on the thick band. An echo of magic coursed back through me. I would need to read the carvings to better understand, but it didn't feel like Edric. This wasn't the artifact I needed. I'd never be that lucky, especially with a bracelet that had belonged to Godda. Edric wouldn't have anchored himself to something of hers, and certainly not a gift from someone he saw as a rival.

"It's beautiful," I said, certain she had no idea what she wore on her wrist. "It suits you." I cupped my hand around her cheek so my thumb was caressing her cheekbone.

"I'm so sorry about your mother, Liam," she said. "Is there any chance she might get better? Is that why you returned?"

"She's all right for now. But I'll need to go back soon." My promise to my family and the search for the artifact had to be my priority. Everything, including Evelyn's safety, relied on my success. Still, I couldn't very well continue my search tonight, and she was already in my arms. Against my better judgment, I slid one arm inside her open jacket and around her waist so I could pull her closer to me.

She placed both hands on my chest to hold us apart. "Tell me you didn't chase him off just because you were jealous," she said.

"I'm not going to tell you that I was happy to see you were going to dinner with some other bloke, but that wasn't why I chased him off." The pressure of her hands on my chest turned to something softer, more like a caress.

She tilted her head to one side. "Will you tell me why you chased him off, if that wasn't the reason?"

I cringed. "I will, but first I'd rather do this..." I bent my head down until my lips were pressed lightly against her neck. I began kissing just below her earlobe. As my lips traveled across her skin, I slid my hand from her cheek until it was cupping her long neck. Her scarf was in my way, and I pulled at it until it came free and fluttered to the ground. My lips continued down, moving along her collarbone, then up the other side to the opposite earlobe.

She moaned and clutched folds of my leather jacket to pull me closer. Sliding my hands around her waist and up, under her sweater, I stretched my fingers across her lower back, savoring the soft skin that warmed to my touch. My lips found her mouth and our tongues entwined as I guided her backward until she was leaning against the Land Rover.

Pressed between me and the car, she reached up and unzipped my jacket, running her hands across my chest, then down around my waist. Her fingers pulled at my shirt until it came untucked, and she slid her hands up underneath, pressing her palms against my skin. I nibbled at her lip and slid my hands down until they were cupping her firm ass. Then I hiked her up until her legs lifted off the ground and she wrapped them around me. My hips ground into her, pressing her body against the metal of the Rover, as my lips traveled down her neck again.

This. This was what I'd been wanting to do since I first saw her.

"Liam." She sighed.

I moaned against her neck and gripped her more firmly, my fingers digging into her jeans.

"Liam," she said again, this time slightly less breathy.

I turned my head, letting my cheek fall against her collarbone, and waited for my breathing to slow. "Yes?"

She lifted her arm to run her hand through my hair. "We can't do this here."

"Why not?" I tipped my head back, grasped her lower lip between mine, and sucked on it. She tangled her fingers in my hair and parted my lips with her tongue, deepening the kiss. Before long we were both breathing hard again.

She pulled back, letting her forehead rest against mine while she caught her breath. The puffs of air condensed in small clouds that merged with mine.

She started giggling. "It's freezing out here."

"Am I not keeping you warm enough?" My hands skimmed up her hips and under her sweater.

"Yes," she breathed.

"Yes, I'm keeping you warm enough?" I held her close and teased her mouth with mine.

"Yes," she said again.

I tugged at the hem of her sweater, inching it up.

"No," she said. "Not here."

"All right, then." I lifted her, placing her on her feet for a moment before scooping her into my arms.

"Where are you taking me?" she asked, looking up at me.

"Inside," I said.

She squirmed in my arms, trying to get down. "You can't just carry me in the front door."

"I wasn't planning on it."

I carried her around the back of the house to the mudroom entrance. Then I lowered her to the ground, keeping one arm wrapped around her waist. The door was locked, but I fixed that problem with a little bit of magic. So, when I reached for the knob, it turned freely, and we slipped inside.

"This is your master plan? Sneaking in through the mudroom?" she whispered. I shrugged out of my jacket and lifted hers from her shoulders.

"Shh." I grabbed her hand and led her through the kitchen, pausing to listen at the door leading to the back stairs. Then I lifted her onto my back, pushed through the door, and started climbing.

"You're crazy," she whispered into my ear.

"You make me crazy." It was the truth. I was bargaining with fate. One night. Tomorrow I'd use my magic to find and destroy the artifact. Then I'd go after Edric or die trying. But tonight, this was all I wanted.

"They're going to notice when I don't come home," she whispered.

"They'll never notice." They wouldn't, even if I had to use my magic to make sure they didn't. I passed the landing leading to the family wing and kept going, all the way up to my room in the attic.

I set her down inside the door and turned to close it behind us.

"It's... different than I remember," she said, wandering into the middle of the room and turning in a slow circle.

"Yeah. I moved things around a little." I leaned against the door and watched her explore my space. She walked over to a statue I'd set on top of a low bookshelf near my bed. It had been in a dark, forgotten corner of the attic, near where I'd found the gargoyles.

She ran her hand over the statue's wings and tilted her head to the side. I crept across the room until I was standing behind her.

"Is it supposed to be a faerie?" she asked.

I wrapped my hands around her waist and pulled her against me. "Supposed to be."

"Why did you put it here and not downstairs with the others?"

I kissed her neck. "It makes me smile." I moved my lips to the tender spot behind her earlobe, and she leaned against me.

"Where's the other gargoyle?" she asked. Clearly, I needed to work on my seduction skills.

"By the window."

She pulled free of my arms but held on to my hand and pulled me over to the alcove cut into the sloping roofline. I'd positioned the gargoyle on the window seat so it was looking out across the fields. She smiled when she saw it.

"Next best thing to putting it back out on the roof," I said.

She dropped my hand and sat down next to the gargoyle on the window seat. "I loved sitting here, reading, and staring out at the rain," she said. "You can see for miles from up here. I used to pretend I was a princess in a tower."

I walked over and sat next to her. "I don't know. I quite like the view from here." I traced the curve of her long neck with my finger.

She turned toward me and smiled. "You're sweet," she whispered.

"You're beautiful." I leaned forward and captured her lips with mine. We kissed softly at first, her hands gripping the fabric of my shirt to pull me closer, mine slipping under the hem of her sweater to press against her warm, soft skin. Her lips parted in response, and she leaned into me, twisting to align her body against mine, but it wasn't enough. I wrapped my hand around the back of her leg and hoisted her up until she was facing me with her knees wrapped around my hips.

"Hi," she said, pausing from our kissing to take a breath. Our foreheads and noses were touching, and I could feel her breath on my lips when she exhaled.

"Hey," I said. I smiled. I couldn't help it.

She placed her palms on my cheeks and slid her fingers through my hair, pushing it back from my face. "What are we doing?" She looked lost, confused, concerned.

"Do you want to stop?" I froze, my breath caught in my chest, waiting for her response.

"No." She shook her head, then frowned. "Do you?"

"Definitely not." I could feel my heart hammering.

"What about..." Her voice trailed off, but I didn't have a clue what she was trying to ask. She sighed. "Do you have any, you know, condoms?" she asked.

Of course. I'd forgotten about that very human concern. With a thought, I conjured a condom to the drawer of my bedside table. Then, reconsidering, I added a few more. Faeries didn't catch human diseases, and as for reproduction, male Fae could only sire one child in their lifetime. So, we were very particular about when and how that occurred. Still, Evelyn thought I was human, and I'd need to behave like one.

"I believe I have a few around here somewhere," I said.

She grinned, and I pulled her closer, then stood, lifting her along with me, careful not to hit her head on the low ceiling. Her legs wrapped around my waist, and her fingers worked to undo the buttons on my shirt as I carried her back into the main part of the room. Once I'd set her down on the bed, I shrugged out of my oxford and tugged my thin cotton undershirt over my head. Then I reached for her, but she'd beat me to it. Her hands grabbed my waistband and pulled me forward. I bent over her and inched the hem of her sweater up, running my hands along her sides as I guided it over her head, caressing her bare arms as I freed them from the confines of the cashmere.

My hand brushed against Godda's bracelet, and when I pushed it back onto her wrist, I felt that gentle echo of magic call my power to the surface. I damped my magic back down, but not before the buzzing warmth that had rushed to my hands crackled against Evelyn's skin. Her eyes fluttered and she wrapped her arms around my neck, but she otherwise didn't seem to notice.

I breathed a sigh of relief and covered her mouth with mine. The spells I planned to use tomorrow were significantly more powerful than the simple ones I'd used tonight. They would light this house up with magic so that I might have a chance to end this war. But if I failed, and those spells brought the Hunt to Oscar's manor, I'd have to join my kin to protect these humans as well as our own kind, and I might never get a chance to return. If I only had one more night masquerading as a human, I planned on enjoying every minute of it with this woman.

9

SUNLIGHT streamed in through the windows, waking me from a sound sleep. I opened my eyes and stretched, only to find myself in an unfamiliar bed, alone.

"Liam?" I called out to the empty room as I sat up, clutching the blankets to my chest.

No one responded to my call. He'd left again. I felt my stomach twist. My mind instantly started making excuses. Maybe something had happened with his mother. Maybe he'd just gone to the bathroom. His clothes were gone from the floor, and mine were folded in a neat pile on a chair nearby. The bracelet my uncle had given me had been placed carefully on top of my clothes and, under it, a piece of paper. Gritting my teeth and bracing for the cold air, I dropped the blankets and set my feet on the rug.

I dressed quickly before reading the note.

E—

Didn't want to wake you. Needed to get to work. Let me take you to dinner tonight.

—L

PS Your uncle's paper on the temple ruins is next to the faerie if you want to borrow it.

The note was sweet, and he did owe me dinner. But I couldn't shake my disappointment at waking up alone. I'd given in to my attraction to him. I'd convinced myself that he felt something for me. I wasn't expecting a commitment. I wasn't even expecting breakfast in bed. I'd just thought he'd at least be there when I woke up.

I padded down the stairs, carrying my boots and my uncle's paper. Crossing my fingers that I wouldn't run into my aunt or uncle on my way to my room, I crept down the hall. I had no idea how I would explain this to them. I hadn't come home last night because I'd never left. And I'd spent the night with Uncle Oscar's secretary. I shook my head. This was not part of my plan. My uncle had just agreed to let me help him, but now Liam was back, and I wasn't sure where that left me. Not to mention, I wasn't sure how I could possibly manage living in the same house as him for the rest of my visit without my aunt and uncle figuring out what was going on.

I reached my room and slipped inside, breathing a sigh of relief. Safe. Maybe we could find a way to work together. He'd said there was enough work for both of us. I set the research paper on my dresser and placed Godda's bracelet next to it. Then I headed for the shower and turned on the water to warm.

As I undressed, my mind wandered to Liam's hands removing my sweater, tugging off my boots, my jeans, stripping off my bra, toying with my underwear. I flushed, remembering my embarrassment that I'd not chosen a pair slightly more worthy of the occasion. Not that I'd brought any fancy lingerie. I'd assumed I wouldn't need it.

Still, my boring cotton undies hadn't appeared to phase Liam in the least. Just the thought of him running his finger under the waistband had my heart racing. My brain flooded with images and sensations from the numerous ways he'd showered my body with attention. By the time I'd had a steady stream of hot water running, I was warm enough to consider turning the dial back down to cold.

I needed to get him out of my head. We could be friends, maybe friends with benefits, but this could not be a thing. I stepped into the tub, tipped my head back, and closed my eyes, letting the water rain down on me. It was just one night. It meant nothing.

I forced myself to catalog his shortcomings. He needed a haircut. His clothes were out of style and too baggy. He hadn't even gone to university. He worked for my uncle. And he'd gone all psycho alpha male with Nigel. What had that been about anyway? He'd found a very convenient way of making me forget all about that—at least temporarily.

I toweled off and wandered back into the bedroom. One thing hadn't changed. I still wanted to find out more about Edric and Godda, and I still wanted to work with my uncle. I tugged on running tights and a sports bra, then pulled a cowl neck wool tunic over my head. The perfect outfit for snuggling in to do some reading. I grabbed the books Uncle Oscar had given me and the paper Liam had left for me. Then, hoping it would provide some luck and inspiration, I slipped Godda's bracelet onto my wrist.

On the way down the front staircase, I stopped to admire the tapestry. Liam had mentioned something about a local Goddess of the Hunt. Uncle Oscar seemed convinced that the legends were true. Perhaps reading his paper and the books he'd given me would help me understand why. As much as I wanted to go straight to my uncle's study and offer my help, I wasn't ready to be working side by side with Liam right now. The books seemed like a much safer place to start.

———

My lips felt bruised, and I could still taste her on my tongue, but right now I needed to focus. I had to find the artifact, and I'd decided to start by searching the cellar. Oscar had finally told me about it when I'd returned from salting the perimeter of the property in the early hours of the dawn. I'd lied and told him I'd been out chopping firewood. There hadn't been any sign that Nigel had returned, or brought any friends, and I wanted to keep it that way, at least until I could figure out what that half-demon wanker was after—besides Evelyn.

If Edric had recruited the demons to his cause, then this battle could be as bad as the last one. Once I found the artifact and destroyed it, Edric's spirit would be banished from walking the Earth. Maybe then, like his Hunters, any demons they'd convinced to join their cause would leave us alone. As far as I knew, the demons held no grudge against us, no reason to fight us except at Edric's bidding.

I checked in on the professor, brought him another pot of tea, and let him know I'd be working on cataloging the items in the cellar. I needed to keep him and his wife out of the cellar long enough for me to use my magic and find the artifact. Satisfied that he'd be tucked in his study for a while, I hurried through the mudroom to the cellar door and descended the rotting wooden stairs into the dank subterranean room.

I tested each step with my foot before putting my weight on it fully. Each board bent and creaked under my weight, and I wondered if the professor had even noticed the danger when he'd been poking around down here yesterday. It would be like him to only remember the room full of artifacts and neglect to mention that I might want to mind the stairs because they looked like they could collapse at any moment. When I reached the bottom, I glanced over my shoulder to check that I'd shut the door behind me. Then I conjured a ball of light in my hand and released it toward the ceiling to bathe the room in a warm glow. Barrels and bottles lined the stone walls, and sawdust covered the stone floor. A lone wooden door, partially hidden by a stack of crates, beckoned at the far side of the cellar. The crates appeared to have been recently moved aside. I'd already explored every inch of this house, from top to bottom. The last time I'd been down here, those crates had been stacked against the wall. They were empty, and I hadn't thought to move them. Had the professor really just remembered this room in the cellar? Or had he been using these empty crates to hide that door from me on purpose?

I turned in a slow circle, scrutinizing every wall and crevice. Then I released a focused blast of power, rippling out from me in all directions, meant to reveal any other hidden chambers I may have missed. I turned again, feeling out along the ripples, examining the edges of the room. I paused and stared down a corridor lined with wooden racks of wine bottles covered in thick layers of dust. I couldn't see anything, but a disturbance in the ripples alerted me that there might be another hidden room in that direction.

I cast my light down the corridor and followed behind, mentally reaching out along the ripples, feeling for the break. There. I stopped and turned to face one of the racks of wine. My fingers traced along the vertical supports until I found a hidden hinge. I pushed lightly against the rack and was rewarded with the scrape of stone against stone. When I met some resistance, I pushed harder, leaning my weight against the rack until my force overcame the resistance and a gap appeared in the stone wall behind the rack. I cast my light up to the edge of the crack and shoved against the rack again. The gap widened as the wall and the rack swung in to reveal an opening into what appeared to be a room or tunnel. Dirt and dust swirled in the musty air escaping from the gap.

I imagined the layout of the house above me and tried to determine where this passage might lead. As far as I could tell, this was the far wall of the house. Beyond this would be fields. I flashed back to standing at the attic window with Evelyn last night and tried to envision what lay in this direction. I remembered seeing the lights of town in the distance. The carriage house was on the opposite side of the house, and I couldn't remember there being any buildings on this side of the property. The only way to find out where this passage led would be to explore.

I sent a blast of magic toward the cellar door, spelling it stuck in a way that would alert me if anyone tried to open it. I hoped that would give me enough time to return and seal this passage behind me if anyone came looking for me. I'd already used enough magic that the scent of it would alert the Hunt that one of the Fae had infiltrated the ancestral home of Lord Edric, and I hadn't even started my search of the cellar room. I decided that a little more magic at this point was worth the cost. I trusted that the salt I'd scattered at the base of the iron fence surrounding the property would deter the spirits, even if the only thing keeping the demons out was an invitation. Only Nigel had the permission needed to slip past my defenses, and I could handle him. Just the thought of his hands on Evelyn had my blood boiling. I wouldn't hesitate to rip his head off if he set foot on this property again.

I slid through the gap in the wall and stepped into the dusty, stale air of the stone passageway. I cast my light ahead and found only a long, low-ceilinged tunnel with a packed earth floor. I called up my magic and shifted to my animal form. I could cover more ground, faster, on four legs than on two, and I'd see better in this darkness using my night vision. I took off at a loping run and chased after the glowing light I'd sent ahead of me.

With the exception of a few slight curves, the passage appeared to run in a straight line, directly toward the town with no end in sight. I passed no doors or intersections or signs that this tunnel had been used recently. It appeared to be a lost passage. I'd just slowed my pace to save my energy when I spotted a wall straight ahead of me. Dead end. I shifted back into my human form so I could reach out with my magic and find an opening, if one existed. I couldn't imagine anyone would put this much work into a passage that went nowhere.

The stone on either side of me was solid, as it had been throughout the length of the tunnel. But, when I laid my hands on the wooden wall blocking my path, I could sense there was something on the other side. The wide, wood planks were thick and solid, extending horizontally across the opening with no breaks or hinges that might give a hint of any opening or a way to pass through to the other side. I pressed against the wooden wall and sent a blast of magic into the wood. I stepped back and watched as the revealing spell worked. The wood planks became transparent and revealed vertical iron bars spanning the gap on the far side of the planks, and, beyond that, a passage that continued almost identical to the one I'd traveled. As the spell faded, I caught a glimpse of markings, wards from the looks of them, burned into the wood, invisible to a human eye, but obviously Fae.

One of my kind had closed this passage and warded it. The only faerie I knew who'd ever set foot in Lydbury, besides me and Arabella, was Godda herself. I wondered if she had been the one to seal this off. Perhaps she knew this passage left them vulnerable to attack, though it wasn't clear if she was keeping something out or keeping something in. Either way, I didn't have time to explore any further right now. Finding the artifact was my priority. I would return after, when I had more time, and investigate aboveground as well. Perhaps that would give me a better idea as to where this tunnel ended.

I transformed back into my animal form and returned to the cellar. Along the way I checked again for any openings I might have missed and paid close attention to the distance and direction I'd traveled. When I reached the entrance to the cellar, I transformed back into my human form and slid through the gap in the wall. Then I pulled the entrance shut behind me and added a few wards of my own to alert me if anyone else passed this way.

I walked back to the storage room hidden behind the empty crates. I ran my hand over the door, checking for any wards or markings that might have been left there to protect the contents, but found none. Then I pulled on the door handle and hauled the heavy wooden door open. Inside, I found a jumble of half-open crates, hastily wrapped packages, and loose gear cluttering every flat surface. There was barely enough room to move around. I squeezed between crates and maneuvered to the middle of the room. I jostled a stack of hunting gear and the lot nearly came down on top of me. I shielded myself and, annoyed, shot a burst of magic out to all corners of the room, searching for anything with hidden properties.

To my surprise, a shield, wedged at the bottom of the stack of hunting gear, glowed in response to my spell. I pulled it from the stack and ran my hands over the notched wood. The Sauvage crest had been painted on the front, but years of wear and gouge marks had damaged the rearing lions and intricate scrollwork almost beyond recognition. The thick wood was battered and splintered on the face, and the handle was worn smooth from use. It didn't have the sheen and polish of Godda's bracelet, but an unmistakable signature of magic thrummed inside the ancient artifact. Unfortunately, it was only a Fae protection spell, likely put there by Godda to protect Edric from harm on his hunts, back when he'd been hunting game, not Fae.

I glanced around the room. There had to be something here that tied Edric to this realm. Another glowing object caught my eye, partly obscured by packing material in a crate in the far corner of the room. I set the shield down and shimmied around boxes to get to the opposite corner. I'd need to break the spell on the shield later; magic like that couldn't be left lying around to fall into human hands. But none of that would matter if I didn't figure out how to banish Edric's spirit.

I dug the glowing artifact out of the crate and cradled it in my hands. A dagger. Again, nothing elaborate, just a simple blade with a vine-like decorative carving in the wooden handle. I wrapped my hand around the hilt, and my fingers slipped perfectly into the faint grooves worn down by years of active use. Again, the signature of magic coursed through the blade. This time the spell was more complicated, but still created by Fae.

Still, no sign of Edric's anchor object. The shield and the dagger, both objects likely to have belonged to him, both enhanced with Fae magic, were of no help to me in my quest. Perhaps Lydbury Manor had been ignored by the Hunt because there was nothing here.

Not willing to concede that I'd spent months exploring a dead end, I reeled in some of my spells and began shifting through the contents of each box, testing each item while making inventory lists so I'd have something to show Oscar, even if I turned up nothing to help my kin. Unless I found something here, I'd have to leave tonight, after dinner with Evelyn, to help Arabella prepare for battle.

10

BY lunchtime I'd finished most of my reading, and my stomach was telling me it was time to take a break. I still didn't understand why Uncle Oscar believed the legends about Godda. Rather than continue to delay the inevitable, I decided to go looking for my uncle, even if that would mean braving the awkwardness of seeing Liam without getting to talk to him alone first.

When I reached Uncle Oscar's study, his door was slightly ajar. I knocked before pushing it open. "Uncle Oscar?"

"Come in," he called.

I stepped into the room and glanced around. No sight of Liam, only Uncle Oscar, sitting behind his desk with his glasses propped on the end of his nose, sorting through a stack of papers.

He looked up when I entered, gazing at me over the tops of his reading glasses. "Eve, come in. Vivian made me some sandwiches. There's more than enough to share. I was hoping she'd send you in here when she uncovered where you'd gone off to."

I slid into the seat across the desk from him. "I've been reading those books you lent me."

"Oh, good! How are you finding them?" He selected a sandwich and motioned for me to join him.

"Fascinating." I lifted one of the sandwiches off the tray. "Only, I don't yet understand what's convinced you to believe the legends about Godda. I've been thinking that, given what you wrote about the temple ruins and Edric's reputation as an excellent hunter, maybe that's how the legends started. Like, maybe he met Godda in the temple or something, and given how beautiful she was and that it was a temple to a Fae Huntress, the legends got it all mixed up." I paused, then took a bite of my sandwich before I could continue rambling on and possibly making myself look like an idiot.

"Spoken like a budding historian. Quite good." He chuckled. "So you've been reading my paper, then?"

I nodded. "Liam left a copy for me. I told him I'd like to read it after he'd mentioned it when we went to town together the other day."

"Ah, yes. Liam. It appears he returned earlier than I'd expected. But I had a chat with him this morning, and he's off cataloging the artifacts in the cellar. Since he'll be busy with that for a while, I asked him if he'd mind if you helped a bit."

"Oh?"

"Yes." Uncle Oscar paused to chew a bite of his sandwich. "He's all for it. Left a note over there with some things you could get started on, if you like." He pointed to a filing cabinet near the door.

"Of course! I really want to help."

"All right. So long as you find it enjoyable. I hate to put you to work on your holiday."

"I love it. All of it." I leaned back in the chair and sighed, glancing around at his messy desk and bookshelves.

"Good, good." He poured me a cup of tea. "Have some tea and help me finish these sandwiches, and then we'll put you to work."

The afternoon passed quickly as I worked quietly side by side with my uncle. Liam had left me a few organizing and scanning tasks that kept me busy, especially when nearly every file contained fascinating bits of information that I kept stopping to read.

"Eve," Uncle Oscar said, interrupting an interesting story I'd been reading about the history behind those gargoyles Liam had found in the attic.

"Yes?" I pulled the remaining sheets of paper and photos off the scanner and returned them to the file folder.

"Would you mind checking in with Vivian about tea?"

I checked the clock. "Oh! How did it get so late already?" After retrieving the empty sandwich tray, teapot, and mugs from the top of the cabinet behind my uncle's desk, I headed for the kitchen.

On the way down the hall, I decided that, since I still hadn't figured out how or what I wanted to tell her about me and Liam, it would be safer to not say anything, at least for now. I peeked into the library as I walked past but saw no sign of my aunt. So I continued on to the kitchen, pausing outside the doorway to rebalance the tray. Then I heard the muffled sound of singing and chopping filter through the door into the hallway. When I pushed open the door, I found my aunt with an apron tied around her waist, surrounded by vegetables and measuring cups, with pots bubbling on the stove and caramelized aromas wafting from the oven.

"What are you doing?" I asked.

"Making dinner, dear. What does it look like I'm doing?" She snatched an onion off the table and resumed singing and chopping.

"But what happened to your cook?" If Aunt Vivian was making dinner, there was no way I could justify going out with Liam tonight—at least not without telling her about our hookup.

She paused with the knife poised over the onion. "I gave Marge the night off. It's the solstice festival tonight. Starts at sundown." She glanced out the window and then back at me. "Looks like it's probably just about to begin."

"Solstice festival?"

"Oh, it's a tradition around here. Celebrating the return of the sun and other local superstitions." She shrugged and resumed chopping.

"Uncle Oscar sent me in to ask about tea. He must have forgotten about the festival. Maybe I should bring him something and come back to lend you a hand."

"Oh, that would be lovely. How are you with potatoes?" She pointed her knife at a bag on the counter. "Those all need to be peeled for the mash. Peeler's in the drawer there."

I put the kettle on to boil water, then found the potato peeler and set to work while I waited.

"How was your date with Nigel, dear?" she asked.

The date that had never happened. "He had to go home early. It never really got started."

"That's too bad. Are you planning on going out again soon?"

"I don't know. We didn't have much in common." Or at least we never had a chance to find out if we had anything in common. I knew Liam was keeping something from me. He knew more about Nigel than he was willing to share. I'd take his word for it, for now, and assume it had nothing to do with me.

"Sometimes those pretty boys aren't all they're cracked up to be," she said. She rinsed her knife off in the sink and checked her recipe in the book lying open on the counter. Then she wandered over to the canisters on the far side of the counter, humming to herself.

"What are you making?" I asked.

"Oh, just a nice home-cooked meal. Roast, mashed potatoes, gravy, veg. Might try my hand at a pie for dessert. Or maybe a crumble." She lifted the largest of the canisters off the counter. "Oh, no. That's not a good sign," she said.

"What is it?"

She shook the container and then popped the lid open. "Just what I feared." She showed me the inside. "Looks like I forgot to buy more flour. And I need it for the gravy. And the dessert."

"Maybe I could run to the store for you?"

"That's sweet of you, dear. But the stores will all be closed tonight on account of the festival." She tapped her finger against her chin. "We might be able to borrow some from our neighbor. I was going to bring her some eggs from the chickens, anyway."

"I'll go," I said. "Just tell me how to get there."

"That would be so helpful. It's getting dark, so take the flashlight in the mudroom. If you cut through the yard, you'll intersect the road after a bit. Then just follow it to the end of the lane and you'll find a little cottage tucked behind a stone wall covered in ivy. That'll be our MaryAnn. Sweet lady, but she'll talk your ear off, so make sure you tell her you're needed home right away. We'll bring her some biscuits and replenish her flour stock tomorrow afternoon. I'll get Oscar his tea and finish up the potatoes while you're gone."

I washed my hands and dried them on a towel. Then I gave her a kiss on the cheek. "Don't worry. I'll be back before you know it." I opened the door to the mudroom and stepped onto the chilly plank floor. The cold seeped through my socks as I padded over to the boots. I slipped on a pair that fit, found my coat on the peg, tugged on my hat, and pulled on my mittens.

Just before stepping outside, I remembered my aunt's advice and grabbed the big flashlight off the shelf next to the door. The sun set early this far north. Already a few stars glimmered in the sky, and the full moon hovered above the tree tops. I hoped the skies would remain clear so that I'd be able to keep the flashlight off for most of my journey.

As I made my way across the yard in the moonlight, the steady thwack of an axe against a log cut through the crisp night air, and I smiled. That had to be Liam. I hoped he'd seen that Aunt Vivian was cooking and would be okay with postponing our date. I grinned as I thought up excuses so I could sneak away after dinner and spend more time with his arms around me and his lips pressed against mine.

I was almost to the road when howling and barking off in the distance made me pause to listen. I gripped the flashlight and placed my finger on the switch, but I didn't turn it on. I couldn't tell if the barking was getting closer or moving away. The sound echoed around me and seemed to be coming from many directions at the same time. I crept closer to the edge of the road and squinted into the darkness. There was no sign of any travelers, but the howling continued, now accompanied by hoofbeats and shouting.

The long, low bugle of a hunting horn cut through the clear night air, followed by an eerie stillness. As the echo of the horn disappeared, I realized that everything had fallen silent. I could no longer hear the hounds or even the steady rhythmic thump of the axe falling. The hairs on the back of my neck began to prickle and goose bumps rose on my arms. My body tensed to run, but I stood, frozen. Then I saw them. A group of men on horseback, tearing through the woods on the opposite side of the road, dogs bounding along and leading the way. They were weaving through the trees and appeared to be coming closer. I watched, transfixed.

"Eve!" The shout came from somewhere behind me. "Come back! Run!" I recognized the voice as Liam's and turned to look for him. Before I could spot him, I felt a thick arm, definitely not Liam's, grab me around my waist. My feet lifted off the ground and the air rushed out of me as my chest slammed into something hard. I closed my eyes and concentrated on catching my breath. When I opened them again, the ground was speeding by beneath me as I lay, belly down, across the back of a horse.

The man who'd grabbed me let out a bellowing whoop to the others, then yelled, "I got one, lads!" His call was answered with cheers and shouts.

I squirmed, struggling to free my hands that had been pinned between my body and the warm hair of the horse's back. My wrist wedged against leather when I tried to turn and get a closer look at who sat on the saddle. I lost my grip on the flashlight, and it fell, hitting me in the head before tumbling to the ground. That was the last thing I saw before my vision faded to black.

———

I'd just raised the axe over my head, ready to swing and slice another log, when a low, sustained note from a hunting horn sliced through the crisp night air. I dropped the axe and turned to face the sound. The Hunt had returned. They'd sensed the magic I'd used today. A chill ran down my spine. That horn signaled they were in pursuit, and close, by the sound of it. I hoped my defenses would hold against them. I took off running in the direction of the horn, planning to hide near the edge of the property and wait until I was sure they couldn't cross onto Lydbury proper.

The tree line at the edge of the property loomed in the distance. The road beyond the property line was barely visible between the trees. But I could see there was someone standing there, in the middle of the road. I focused on the lone figure, intuition or Fae senses, I didn't know which, telling me this was a human. My gut wrenched with recognition. Evelyn. She'd already crossed over the property line and was outside the protection spells I'd set.

"Eve," I shouted, spelling my voice toward her so she would hear me across the distance. "Come back! Run!"

I could see them now, the Hunters, crossing the field on the far side of the road, emerging from the woods. I ran harder. Evelyn turned toward me, and I caught a glimpse of her face before a Hunter snatched her up and slung her across his saddle.

"No!" I screamed. The Hunter swung around to follow the road, avoiding the property line, and the others followed. I was still too far away. I pushed harder and skidded to a stop in the middle of the road where I'd last seen her standing.

The Hunt was gone. I'd lost her. I hadn't been fast enough. I stood in the middle of the lane, staring down at her new hat, now lying in the dirt. It must have fallen off when the Hunter snatched her up. I didn't pause to see if anyone was watching before I called up my magic and transformed. Once in my animal form, I sniffed at the hat, breathing in her scent, and took off after the Hunters. With every breath, I cursed myself for letting my guard down. I'd thought I had the upper hand. I should have been more cautious.

I ran fast, keeping to the shadows, closing the distance. I had no idea where they were taking her. I just knew I had to get her back. They'd only ever captured faerie folk before. Evelyn should have been safe. She'd wandered off the property, and outside my protection. But still, she should have been safe. Part of me worried that the half-demon pretty boy had tipped off the Hunt and was just using Evelyn to get to me. If that were the case, I was leaving the house open, undefended. But there was nothing there for me now. I'd have to trust my protection spells would keep Oscar and Vivian safe. Right now only Evelyn mattered. And defeating Edric.

I slowed when I realized that I'd lost the path. I circled back until I'd picked up her scent again. Then I found the spot where they'd turned and I started running again. In the distance, moonlight glinted off stone. They'd veered off in the direction of the old temple. I growled and pushed myself harder. We'd never been able to find Edric's hideout. Now I finally had a chance to trace him back to his lair. If that band of marauders had decided to infiltrate an ancient temple dedicated to a Fae goddess, there would be hell to pay. I almost hoped that they were hiding there, just to see the look on Arabella's face when she came to destroy them.

I needed a plan. Alone, I was no match for Edric and his Hunters. I wouldn't be able to defeat them without help. But, if I called Arabella, Evelyn would surely be killed in the ensuing battle. Perhaps I could find a way to sneak in, unseen. I could rescue Evelyn and then call Arabella and the Queen's Guard to help me destroy Edric and banish the Hunters. But first, I needed to get Evelyn out of there before Edric got his hands on her, and before she learned enough to earn her a death sentence from the Fae. I pushed harder, driving my paws against the earth, following their trail and closing the distance on the standing stones.

As I'd anticipated, the trail ended near the outside ring of stone that used to be a foundation for the temple. I began to pace the perimeter, trying to pick up the scent and searching for a hidden entrance.

"Well, well, well." A familiar figure stepped out from behind one of the towering, vertical stones. "What do we have here?" Nigel stood facing me, blocking my path. "A mountain lion? In merry old England? Why, I never."

I growled and flashed my fangs at him in the moonlight. The fur on the back of my neck stood on end and I crouched, ready to pounce.

"Ah, ah, ah," he said. "I wouldn't do that, if I were you." Two spirits flickered in my peripheral vision.

My suspicions were confirmed. I'd been lured into a trap. I took a step backward and the spirits closed in on me, pinning me between them with no escape except to turn tail and run. I couldn't conjure myself away in this form. I'd need to transform first, leaving me defenseless and vulnerable to their attack. I searched for an escape route as they closed in on me.

"Chain him," Nigel said.

I lunged out of reach of the spirits and flew at Nigel, leaping off the edge of a collapsed stone and aiming to pin him under my front paws. The glint of a knife in his hand caught my attention, and I knocked it from him as we tumbled to the ground. He rolled away from me as we landed, chasing after the knife, and I skidded on my paws, turning quickly to catch him before he had a chance to run away.

But he wasn't running away. He was running at me, knife

in hand. I dodged his blow and he tumbled. I pounced and missed him but managed to knock the blade away again. By now the spirits were nearly on me, closing in fast. I ducked behind a stone for some protection as I transformed, then I grabbed for Nigel's discarded knife. The spirits surrounded me, holding steel manacles and chains. I lunged at them and stabbed each of them, using my magic to amplify the iron content in the blade, iron being deadly to spirits, where only man-made metals were deadly to Fae.

The spirits disappeared, and the chains clattered to the stones at my feet. Only, I knew the spirits were connected to Edric and would return so long as he remained. I would only have a few precious minutes before they reappeared. I reached for my magic and tried to conjure myself away. Nothing happened. That's when I felt it. The place had been cloaked in protection spells, not unlike what I'd done around Lydbury. Spirits and demons didn't have this kind of magic. One of my kind was helping the enemy. I needed to get Evelyn and get out of here to warn Arabella.

I turned and found Nigel facing me. "Where is she?" I asked.

He flashed a sly smile. "Now, why would I tell you that when I could just take you to her?"

"You'll need better goons than those if you think you're going to take me anywhere." I shifted the knife in my hand. "I'll ask you again. Where is she?"

I crouched and took a step toward Nigel. He backed out of my reach and we began to circle each other on the flat rock. The two spirits began to flicker into being again, just beyond the edge of the stones and out of my reach.

"Thought you could take us on all by yourself, Fae?" Nigel taunted.

"Since when did demon folk start doing dirty work for the spirit world, halfling?" I swiped at him, but he slid out of reach.

"What makes you so sure that we're not the ones in charge here?"

"Joined the Wild Hunt, have you, then? Losing your touch with the ladies? Decided clubbing them over the head is a bit easier than turning on the charm these days?"

Nigel flashed a signal at the spirits and they flew at me. I took my eyes off Nigel for a moment and moved to defend myself against the spirits. As soon as I took my eyes off him, Nigel attacked. He grabbed the knife from my hand and slammed the butt of the blade into my skull. My vision swam, and my knees buckled.

"Not a half-bad idea, that," Nigel said, dusting off his black trench coat. "Cuff the bastard."

The spirits slapped the cuffs around my ankles and wrists and chained them together. I was beginning to regret my decision not to send for Arabella and the Queen's Guard before rushing into this fight.

Nigel stood facing me. He spat on the ground. "Cocky faerie bastard. Your kind will never learn, will they?" He took a step closer to me and turned to the spirits who were holding on to my arms. "Hold him up!"

The spirits yanked at my arms and forced me to my feet.

"Wanted to do this last night," he said. "Better late than never, I guess."

His fist connected with my jaw and my head twisted. Pain sparked through my face and my vision went blank. Nigel's laughter haunted my last conscious thoughts like the beginning of a bad dream.

11

MY body felt sore all over and my head throbbed. I closed my eyes and rubbed the lump forming on my head, trying to remember how I'd ended up here. I'd been on an errand for my aunt. The last thing I remembered was standing in the road and seeing men on horseback with dogs riding toward me. There had been a hunting horn and Liam's voice calling to me, then nothing.

I sat up slowly and realized I'd been lying on a dirty, cold stone floor. I scooted backward until I could lean my back against the wall. When the wave of dizziness passed, I studied my surroundings. This wasn't a room. It was a cell with three thick stone walls and bars closing off the fourth side. There were no windows, and the candles that gave me just enough light to see by were both located outside the thick bars.

I pushed myself up, using the wall for support. Then I took a few tentative steps toward the bars of my cell. The room shifted as I tried to focus and keep my balance. The blow to my head was making me see double. But I managed to stay upright, setting one foot in front of the other until I clasped my hands around the cold steel bars. I pressed my forehead into the gap between the bars and let my temples rest against the cool metal. I closed my eyes and leaned against the bars until I felt steady. Then I opened my eyes and waited for them to focus. Without moving my head, I glanced to my right and to my left, hoping I'd recognize something, anything, that would give me a clue as to where I was being held prisoner.

Shuffling footsteps made me suck in a breath and hold it. I listened, my heart beating madly. I turned my eyes in the direction of the sound but didn't dare move my head. If I moved, I knew my vision would blur and the dizzy, nauseous feeling would return.

A robed figure appeared at the end of the corridor outside my cell. The hood of the robe cast a shadow over the figure's face, and the thick fabric folds obscured the rest of the body. With each step toward me, metal scraped against stone. I glanced down at the figure's bare feet, which were poking out from under the robe with each step. Shackles circled each ankle, just visible beneath the hem of the robe, and chains dragged against the rough stone floor.

I shivered. I was being held prisoner and no one knew where to find me. I released one of the bars and reached for my phone, but my pocket was empty. That's when I remembered I'd left my phone in my room at Aunt Vivian's house. I groaned.

The robed figure stopped in front of my cell and extended a bowl toward me, slipping it between the bars. They kept their head down and their face hidden in shadow.

"What is this?" I asked.

"Food."

I reached for the bowl, trapping their hands under mine and holding tight. The figure's head snapped up, and their hood fell back just enough for me to catch a glimpse of the face underneath. Piercing blue eyes peered out at me from above a delicate, thin nose and lush, full lips framed by long golden hair. A woman.

"Where are we?" I asked. "Who are you?" If this person was also a prisoner, maybe I could get them to help me. After all, they were at least moving around while I had been locked in this cell.

The woman shook her head slightly in answer to my questions.

"Eat," she said. Her eyes traveled to the gold band around my wrist, then flicked up to meet mine. I released her hands and backed away from the bars, hugging my wrist against my chest and out of her reach. She said something in a language I didn't understand. Then, without waiting for a response, she turned and shuffled back down the hall.

I lifted the spoon from the bowl she'd handed me and stirred the contents. The foul odor made me wrinkle my nose, but the food was hot and my stomach was empty. I lifted the spoon to my lips and tilted it onto my tongue. The sour broth made me wince, but I forced myself to swallow and keep it down. I stirred again and scooped another spoonful, bracing myself for the taste. I slurped the liquid off the spoon and swallowed.

By the time I'd finished the bowl, my head had stopped throbbing and my vision had cleared. I set the bowl down just inside the bars and paced to the wall, where I could sit and stare down the corridor, watching and hoping for the woman to return.

The longer I waited, the harder it became to keep my eyes

open. Just as I'd let myself begin to drift off, two men appeared, supporting a third between them. They tossed the third man into the cell across from me and slammed the door. They didn't even spare me a glance as they returned the way they'd come.

"Wait!" I called. "Wait!"

They didn't respond, and their backs disappeared around the corner.

"Damn!" I picked up the empty bowl and threw it against the wall, shattering the clay and sending the metal spoon clattering to the ground.

The prisoner across from me moaned. I turned to face him, two sets of bars between us. I squinted in the dim light, but they'd thrown him to the back of the cell and his face and body were hidden in shadow.

"Hello?" I whispered. "Hello? Are you okay?"

He moaned again and rolled onto his side. "Eve," he whispered.

"That's me," I said, shocked that this person would know my name. "Do I know you?" I squinted harder into the shadows.

"Must. Find. Eve," he panted, stopping to breathe between each word. He shifted again, and I saw his matted brown hair.

"Liam?" I grabbed the bars and shook them. "Liam? Is that you?"

He moaned and pushed himself to a sitting position. He raised his head and his hair fell back from his face. I cried out when I saw the blood. "What did they do to you? Are you okay?"

The robed woman shuffled into view between us.

"Shh," she said.

I turned to her. "Help him!" I said. "Can't you see that he's hurt?"

"Eve?" Liam said, blinking at me across the corridor.

"It's me, Liam. I'm right here. What happened? Are you okay?"

"Hush," the woman said. She stepped closer to me, blocking my view of Liam. "You shouldn't talk to him," she said. "It will only make it worse for you both."

"Make what worse? How could it be worse?" I shook the bars to illustrate my point.

She placed her hands over mine on the bars, her eyes going once again to the bracelet on my wrist, then shifting up to meet mine. "Hush."

I grabbed her wrists and pulled her against the bars. "Tell me where we are."

"I can't."

"Why not?"

She just shook her head.

"Why am I here?"

"The Master will make it clear when he sees you. But first I must ready you."

Behind her, Liam lunged for the bars of his cell. "Let her go!" he said. "Take me instead."

The woman turned her head to look at Liam, but I didn't let go of her wrists. She pulled against my hands, trying to get a better look. She said something to Liam in a language I didn't understand.

Liam pushed himself to his knees and blinked at her. Then he said something to her in response. They spoke the same language. She made a wailing moan in response to whatever he'd said to her, and then she dropped her head to her chest. I could feel the sobs shaking her body as I held on to her wrists.

"What did she say?" I said.

"Eve," Liam said. "Tell me what she looks like."

The woman looked up. Her wet eyes met mine.

"Golden-blond hair," I said. "Blue eyes. Do you know her?"

Liam moaned. Then he spoke again in that language.

The woman bit her lip and sobbed again. "Let me go to him," she said.

I let go of her wrists and she flung herself across the corridor, sliding on her knees to face Liam. She reached for his face and my heart sank. They were speaking rapidly now. I took a few steps back from the bars and started to turn away.

"Eve," Liam called. "Wait."

"It's all right," I said. I turned and paced to the back of my cell.

"No, you don't understand," he called to me.

The woman stood and approached the bars of my cell. "He is my kin," she said.

My head snapped up. "Kin?"

"Eve," he said. "She's going to help you."

"But I'm not leaving without you. And you're hurt," I said. "She should help you."

"I'll be fine. Just promise me you'll listen to her."

The woman looked nervously over her shoulder down the corridor. "I must go," she said. "They must not find me here. Stay quiet. I'll return soon."

She disappeared down the corridor, and I paced back to get a better look at Liam. His face was swollen on one side, and a bruise darkened his jawline. The blood dripping from his nose had mostly dried, but the front of his shirt was spotted with it.

"How did we get here?" I asked, keeping my voice barely above a whisper. "Do you know where we are?"

"You were captured," he said. "Don't you remember?"

"No. I remember shouting and dogs barking, and a horn. I remember hearing your voice calling to me, but I couldn't see you. I don't remember anything after that."

He sighed. "Some men, wild men that come out on the night of the solstice and get a little crazy, grabbed you. I chased them, trying to rescue you." He grinned. "I guess I made a mess of that." He ran his fingers over his bruised jaw and brushed away some of the dried blood.

"But what is this place? What do they want?" I sank to the floor and sat facing him.

He shook his head. "They've mistaken you for someone else. I hope when they realize their mistake, they'll let you go. It's me they want."

"What do they want with you?" I knew he'd been hiding something.

"It's a long story," he said.

"Well, we're not going anywhere." I waved a hand at the bars separating us.

He sighed. "True." He leaned his head against the bars and met my eyes. "I'm sorry," he said.

"You didn't kidnap me and drag me here."

"No, but it may be my fault. They want something from my family, but we don't have it to give."

"Money?" I really should have known better than to hook up with my uncle's secretary, especially after I'd already suspected he was up to no good.

He shook his head. "No. If it were that easy, this would have been settled long ago."

"Well, what do they want, then? Does it have to do with that woman? The one who said she's related to you?"

"In a way. She was also taken by them. We thought she

was dead." He shook his head. "They think we have something of theirs. But we don't."

"Are they like the Mafia? Or terrorists or something? I don't understand."

He shrugged. "Not quite. More like a family row. Sometimes they get a little mad and rough us up a bit, trying to get us to admit we have what they're looking for."

"But they took me." There was no way someone would mistake me for being part of Liam's family.

"I think they took you to get to me."

"They took her because they think she's one of us," the robed woman said. She had returned and was carrying another, larger bowl and a clean cloth. She also had a key.

"One of you? You mean part of your family?"

Liam said something to her in that language of theirs, and she responded. It definitely didn't sound like any language I'd heard before. Maybe Liam's family came from one of those Northern European countries. Maybe it was Danish or Icelandic, or whatever they spoke up there in those frozen Nordic countries. I wanted to ask, but I didn't want to be rude. If they wanted me to understand what they were saying, they'd speak English.

The robed woman took a step toward the door to my cell.

"What are you doing?" I asked. "I don't need that. He's the one who's been bleeding. Help him."

The woman shook her head and inserted the key into the door to my cell. "I need to get you ready to see the Master. He'll be calling for you soon."

"But Liam—"

"It's okay. I'll be fine. Whatever happens, listen to her. Do what she says."

I had no reason to trust this woman, but I had to admit he

had a point. If I could manage to get out of here, I could get help.

"Fine," I said.

The robed woman stepped inside my cell and shut the door behind her. I glanced at the key in her hand and considered making a break for it now while I still could.

"There's nowhere to run," she said. "They'll catch you before you even make it down the hall."

"I doubt that." Even if she hadn't been shackled, I was confident I could outrun her and anyone else down here. Four years on my university track team and a pile of medals from national competitions meant outrunning a bunch of thugs should be no problem for me.

"Your overconfidence will get you killed," she said. "When you see the Master, you must be silent. Invisible." Whoever this Master was, he was clearly someone of whom this woman was utterly terrified.

"Listen to her, Eve, please," Liam said. He sounded like he was in pain. I resisted my urge to run. If she could get me out of here and Liam trusted her, I'd listen. For now.

She walked toward me with the bowl of water. "We need to get you clean."

"Why?" This part made no sense to me.

"The Master is very particular." She handed me the bowl. An herbal fragrance wafted up on the steam rising from the liquid swirling inside. "And we need to do something about that." She pointed at my wrist.

I set the bowl down on the stone floor and clasped my hand over the bracelet. "You can't have this," I said, hugging my arm to my chest.

"She's right, Eve," Liam said. "If anyone here sees you wearing that bracelet, they'll never let you go."

"How am I going to explain to Uncle Oscar that I lost his family's precious heirloom?"

The robed woman's face creased in anger, and she said something low and menacing in that other language. Liam responded in a soothing tone. Her mouth softened, but her eyes remained narrowed and suspicious.

"Give her the bracelet," Liam said.

"Why can't I just give it to you?"

"It will be worse if they find it on me," he said. "Please, Eve. She'll return it once we're free. You need to listen to her."

The woman held out her hand and took another step toward me. I slipped the bracelet off my wrist and stepped to the side so I could see Liam. He nodded at me. I took one last look at the bracelet and placed it in the woman's hands. I really did not like this plan.

"Quickly, now," she said, closing her fingers around the gold. "We don't have much time."

———

I watched my long-lost aunt, the youngest of Godda's sisters, prepare Evelyn for presentation to Edric. She washed Evelyn's face and hands and made her change into a simple white gown. Then she brushed out Evelyn's hair until it flowed in dark waves down her back. Evelyn was beautiful. I feared for her life.

Sorcha had promised me that she'd protect Evelyn. She'd told me that Edric would inspect the Fae who'd been captured in that night's Hunt. She said he usually picked the most promising of them to interrogate first. I'd begged her to help make sure that Evelyn would not be selected. She'd promised to use whatever magic she had available to her to escape with Evelyn and any of the Fae who had not been chosen. I would need to find my own way out and free any remaining captives in the process.

When she finished, Sorcha left Evelyn's cell and disappeared down the corridor. Evelyn paced to the bars and gazed down at me.

"She'll keep you safe," I said.

"What about you?"

"I'll be fine. Don't worry about me. Just follow her instructions. Promise me."

"Liam..."

"Please? Promise me."

"I'll listen to her, but you better promise I'm getting that bracelet back once we're out of here."

A commotion at the end of the corridor made us both turn our heads. Two spirits came toward us, laughing and joking in loud, drunken voices. Spirits couldn't get drunk. So these two specimens must have died pissed. They stopped in front of my cell.

"This one?" said the tall, burly spirit.

"Looks like the one," his shorter, wiry friend responded.

The first spirit unlocked my cell and they crowded inside. Each took one of my arms and hauled me to my feet.

"Stop!" Evelyn cried. "Where are you taking him? Let him go!"

The two spirits just cackled and dragged me toward the cell door.

"Promise me," I said to Evelyn.

One of the spirits mimicked me in a whiney sing-song voice. They both started cackling again.

"Let him go!" she shouted. "Stop!"

They pulled me down the corridor, dragging my chained feet along the stone floor.

"Liam!" Evelyn yelled after me. "I promise! I won't leave you here!"

I sighed and went limp, letting the two spirits lead me where they would. Evelyn was under Sorcha's protection now. I needed to focus on staying alive and learning as much as I could about this place. After Sorcha escaped, she'd send Arabella and the Queen's Guard here. Together we could defeat Edric, even if we were only able to banish him until the next solstice. At least it would give us more time to destroy him for good.

The spirits hauled me down corridor after corridor. Each section identical to the last. Finally, they stopped in front of an arched doorway blocked by a barred metal door. The shorter one unlocked the door and they tossed me inside. Then they slammed the door closed behind me. The clang of metal against metal rang in my ears as they walked away, still laughing and joking with each other.

The chamber they'd tossed me into was dark. So dark I couldn't make out the walls, or what else might be in there with me. I felt my way along the floor. My hands and feet were still chained together, making my progress slow. I decided to see if my magic would work here. I lifted my hands up in front of me and conjured a ball of flame. I held the chain over the flame and stoked the heat until the metal began to turn red, then golden, then melt. One link broke, separating the chain tying my hands to my feet. Then I moved on to the link that would separate the chain keeping my hands tied together.

That link melted, and I was just about to move onto the chain keeping my feet linked together when a low, menacing growl made the hair on the back of my neck stand on end. Every instinct screamed run, but I knew there was nowhere to go. I conjured a ball of light and sent it out in the direction of the noise.

The hunched and hairy form of a hell beast crouched in the darkness, close enough to pounce on me. It was as large as a bear but had pointy ears and fangs like a dog and smelled like compost and ash. Saliva dripped from the end of one fang, landing on a paw nearly as big as my head and drawing my attention to four deadly claws, each as long as my forearm. I'd seen enough. It was time to find a way out of here.

I sent a conjured flame flying after the ball of light, hoping to get the beast to back off. He just growled again and shifted forward. Those thick, sharp claws clicked against the stone floor, and his long canine teeth flashed in the light. I routed my glowing ball of light around the perimeter of the room, only to find more hell beasts crouched in the darkness, waiting to make a move.

I didn't have time to free my feet. I needed to defend myself now. I called up my magic and hoped there weren't any spells in this place that would keep me in my Fae form. I transformed, then leapt for the nearest beast with my rear paws still chained together. I latched on to the beast's neck with my jaws and held tight while it bucked and tried to shake me off. I ripped and tore with my teeth, digging in and holding fast with my claws. The beast bellowed and swiped at me, trying to free itself from my grip. The other beasts circled the dark perimeter of the chamber, waiting for this battle to play out before they made a move.

The beast I fought reared when I dropped to the ground, providing me an opening to slice my claws across the its belly. I jumped free and faced the others while it convulsed and collapsed behind me. As other beasts circled, I watched, deciding which one would be my next target. I knew my survival depended on me destroying these creatures, and I still needed to find a way to free my legs. I couldn't use magic in this form. So I needed to let them come to me, or I needed to give myself enough time to transform and burn through the final chain before returning to the fight.

A movement from one of the beasts caught my eye, and I pivoted to face the animal. The moment I turned away, another of the creatures jumped at me from behind. The claws raked my back and I rolled toward the dead beast. I landed next to its enormous paw. Jumping to my feet, I turned to face the others, who were closing in on me. I backed up toward the dead beast and scraped the chain restricting my hind legs against its razor-like claws. While I worked, another of the beasts lunged for me. I swiped out at it, just missing, but I succeeded in getting it to back off.

I moved my hind leg back and forth, rubbing the chain against the dead beast's claw and getting a few good slices in before the next attack. I lunged, and my front paw swatted the hell beast's claws away. I snapped at its neck and my fangs grazed its tough hide but couldn't find purchase. It retreated and focused on the chain again, pulling and scraping frantically against the jagged edge of the claw. One half of the link snapped. I began scraping the claw against the other half.

Another attack, this time two beasts closing in on me and the third lunging for my neck. Pointed canine teeth sliced at my throat as I sprung up on the back of the dead beast. From my higher perch, I pounced down onto the closest beast and landed on its back. I buried my teeth in its neck and ripped at its hide. My claws sliced against its shoulders as it twisted, trying to toss me. I jumped free as it collapsed, blood pooling around it and spreading out across the stone floor.

I was thankful Evelyn couldn't see me right now. No matter how attracted she might be to me in my human glamour, this would be enough to send her running, possibly straight to Nigel. Oh, he'd love that. I snarled and sliced at my next attacker, imagining Nigel's face in its place.

The chain between my hind legs finally snapped, and I ran at the next attacker, leaping and tackling it, pinning the hell beast beneath my paws so I could tear at its throat. Three down, three to go. Blood dripped from the wounds on my back, trickling to the ground beneath me while the remaining beasts circled, cautious, watching for their opening. These were the cunning ones. The ones who had waited while their mates had struck and died. Hell beasts weren't intelligent, but they were ruthless and cunning.

I noted the scars marking the hides of these three. They'd seen other battles like this and had survived. They circled me, and I watched them, panting, gathering my strength for the first attack.

The smallest jumped at me, and I lunged to meet it. One of the others snagged a claw in the metal cuff on my leg and pulled. The metal scraped against my skin as I was pulled backward. I twisted, trying to land a blow on the creature who held my leg. One of the others attacked my shoulder and snapped its teeth, just missing my neck. I hurled myself at my captor and tumbled with it across the floor. I sliced and stabbed and snapped and bit. I was so close to victory. These three were not going to stop me.

I went for their wounds first, opening old scars, slicing new ones. I harnessed my rage and lashed out at them. One after another, they went down. The last one standing held its ground as it bled out from a wound I'd carved into its side. When it finally collapsed, I let myself feel the pain.

I stood in the middle of the empty room, panting. My body stung wherever I'd been scratched, and blood matted my fur. I knew I'd heal faster in my Fae form, but I needed to rest before I could find the energy to transform. I watched the lumpy forms scattered around me, checking for any signs of movement. Then I scanned the perimeter of the room, searching for any other openings, aside from the one where they'd tossed me in. I stalked through the darkness obscuring the perimeter of the room, investigating every corner, searching for another way out.

I found another barred door on the opposite side of the room. A quick look between the bars revealed a corridor similar to the one I'd been dragged down. Against the back wall, I spotted a tunnel. No bars blocked the entrance, but the curved wall prevented me from seeing very far inside. I sniffed and listened, half expecting more creatures to emerge. But none came.

I gathered my strength and transformed. My blood-matted fur became blood-soaked clothes, and I limped closer to the door, trying to keep the metal cuff on my ankle from rubbing against the raw skin. I considered using magic to break the lock on the door. Perhaps this tunnel led to a way out.

"I wouldn't go in there, if I were you," boomed a voice from somewhere above me. I froze midstep. Laughter echoed against the stone walls of the room. I backed away from the door and squinted up at the ceiling, which I couldn't see.

Lights flooded the room, and I blinked as my eyes adjusted.

"Well done, Fae," the voice called. I could now make out figures standing on a balcony above me. In the light, the room I stood in resembled an arena—an arena smeared in blood and littered with the stinking carcasses of dead hell beasts.

"Though I don't think the demon woman will be pleased

that you destroyed all her pets," another one said. The others erupted in whoops and hollers.

I counted the men assembled around the balcony. There were ten, maybe fifteen, of them. Mostly spirits, with a few demons in the mix. The spirits had all the strength of the solstice behind them, plus whatever power Edric tapped into. This allowed them to appear more solid and gave them an almost human grip on the world. That was why they'd been able to chain me and toss me into this prison. But even in this state, they still preferred to glide across the earth, rather than walk like the humans they used to be. And if you looked closely, they still shimmered a bit around the edges. The demons were easier to identify, at least if you were Fae. The horns that they could easily glamour to disguise themselves as human were always visible to the Fae because the Fae controlled all magic, even the simple glamour spells. Even though there weren't many demons in this crowd, I would be no match for them in my current state. I needed time to heal, and a way out.

As I considered my options, the one who'd spoken first started banging on the balcony railing and calling for the crowd to quiet.

"All right, gentlemen," he said once the others had stopped shouting. The last few whispers died down and a hush fell over the assembled men. "You've had your show. Settle your bets and let's bring our new champion before the Master."

The men crowded around one demon with thick horns that curled around his feathered cap, and they resumed shouting. The two thugs who'd thrown me into the pit approached a spirit who seemed to be the leader. They spoke briefly. Then the leader pulled a lever and one of the walls shifted to reveal a staircase leading up to the balcony. The thugs descended the stairs and glided across the bloody stone floor toward me.

"Captain says we can leave the chains off, s'longs you be-have yourself," the shorter, wiry spirit said.

"Gonna behave?" the taller, burly one asked.

I glared at them. "Where are you taking me?"

"You heard the captain," the wiry one said. "We're taking you to see the Master."

The Master. Sorcha had warned me that he was Lord Ed-ric. I'd wanted to stay as far from him as possible. Once he saw me, he'd know who I was, with or without my human glamour.

"Shouldn't I get cleaned up first? Maybe change into something more suitable for an audience with your master?" I asked. I didn't know if charm worked on a spirit; I'd never tried before. I flashed them my most roguish grin and chan-neled a hearty dose of magic behind it.

The burly spirit chuckled and elbowed his companion. "That's not a bad idea, Bub."

The wiry one narrowed his eyes at me. "Captain didn't say nothin' about new clothes," he said.

I stepped closer to the nearest hell beast. I'd survived this trial only to face certain death once Edric laid eyes on me and realized I was his nephew. If I was going to meet the Master, I needed a weapon. Iron. But these Hunters carried only steel.

"Guess you're going like that, then." The burly spirit cack-led, and his friend joined in. Together, they dragged me up the steps. I could only hope Sorcha had escaped with Evelyn to warn the others.

12

AFTER they came for Liam, I paced in my cell. I didn't dare sit and risk ruining the white dress I'd been given to wear. The woman in the robe had instructed me to keep my eyes down and not say a word unless someone spoke to me directly. All I could do now was wait for them to come for me and worry about Liam.

Soon enough, she returned. I rushed to the bars.

"Where did they take him?" I asked. "Is he okay?"

"Hush," she said. She unlocked my cell and beckoned to me. "It's time. Follow me."

She led me down the corridor and I followed as we turned down another that looked the same. We stopped outside another cell and were joined by two other women, also wearing white dresses like the one I'd been given. One had long brown hair that fell in waves to her waist. The other had strawberry-blond hair that reminded me of California. Neither met my eyes, nor did they speak to the woman in the robe. I let them walk ahead of me and fell into place at the end of the line.

The woman led us up a curved staircase and into a large chamber. Pillars lined a path down the center of the room. She walked toward the pillars and we followed. When she reached the pillars, she turned and shuffled down the path between them toward the figures waiting near the opposite wall. I tried to keep my eyes on the floor in front of me, but I snuck glances at the smooth stone walls. There were no windows and no artwork, no markings of any kind that might give me an idea where we were.

I remembered what I'd been told, and when we stopped, I didn't dare look up. The robed woman arranged us in a line, facing the small group who waited there. With my eyes on the marble floor, I guessed from their boots that this was a group of men.

"Master," the robed woman said in a hushed tone, "these three were captured by your Hunters this evening."

One pair of boots stepped forward and paced in front of us. I tried to keep my heart from hammering and attempted to breathe normally. My palms began to sweat and I pressed them against the sides of my dress. The boots stopped in front of one of the other two women.

"Her hair," he said. His voice was gravelly and deep. "Reminds me of summer." He took a step closer to the woman. "Let me see your face," he said.

He made a noise of disapproval and turned to the next woman in line. "Look at me," he said. "Not highborn, but might be useful."

He stepped in front of me and stopped. "Look up," he said. I obeyed but tried to keep my eyes trained on a spot in front of me and didn't meet his gaze. "Well, look what we have here. Something new," he said, excitement creeping into his voice.

For a moment, I was back in my boss's office, frozen, unsure how to react.

"Look at me, girl," he said.

I turned my face toward him but kept my eyes downcast as I promised I would.

He paced around me, studying me from every angle. "I think I'll start with this one," he said. My heart sank. I'd followed every instruction and still he'd chosen me. "Take the others back. I'll deal with them later."

"Yes, Master," the robed woman said. I followed her with my eyes, but she didn't look at me once before turning and leading the others away. She'd left me alone, when Liam had said she'd promised to help me. I wanted to shout after her, but I held my tongue and looked down at the ground.

"Tell me what you know, girl."

"I don't understand," I said, not taking my eyes off my bare feet. "Know about what?"

"Don't play the fool. Tell me where she is."

"Where who is?"

He took a step closer to me and grabbed hold of my shoulders. "None of that, now. Tell me where they're keeping her. Where is she?" He shook me once, hard.

"I don't know. I don't know who you mean."

"My wife, you fool. Where is my wife?" He shook me again.

"I don't think I know your wife. I don't know where she is. Please. Let me go."

"You're not going anywhere until you tell me what you know." He released my shoulders and paced away from me.

"I don't know anything. Please." I took the opportunity while his back was turned to get a look at him. He was dressed like he was going to a Renaissance fair. He wore a leather armor vest over a tunic and pants. Knives hung from his belt alongside a white horn attached to a leather strap.

He pivoted to face me, and my eyes dropped to stare at my feet.

"Impossible," he said. "Tell me where they're keeping Godda."

My head snapped up, and I met his gaze before I could control my reaction. "What did you say?"

"You heard me, girl. Tell me where they're keeping my wife."

"Godda." I blinked. "Your wife?"

"Are you really this daft? Yes. My wife. Godda. Where is she?" He sank into a throne-like chair and drummed his fingers on the arm.

"But that would make you..."

"Lord Edric Sauvage, master of these lands, entrusted by the king of England to keep the peace. Yes, I am." He signaled to one of his men. "Now you, girl, will answer me. Tell me where they're keeping my wife."

"But Lord Edric is dead. You can't be..."

"Of course I'm dead, you ridiculous girl." He set his goblet on the arm of his chair and waved his fingers back and forth through the solid metal. Then he flicked his wrist and his hand became solid again as he lifted the goblet in the air.

"Impossible." Maybe he was a magician. There was no way I was standing here talking to a ghost.

"And yet, here I am. And here you are. Now, we can do this the easy way, where you tell me what I want to know. Or we can do this the hard way." He motioned to his men, who took a step toward me. "Which will it be?"

"I told you, I don't know where your wife is." I wanted to believe this man was delusional, but he did resemble the paintings I'd seen of my uncle's dead ancestor. Perhaps this man was an actor playing a part in a reenactment for the festival. If so, he was doing a spectacular job staying in character.

"Either you are the most skillful liar I've ever met, or you are completely naive." He stood and walked toward me, circling me once before continuing. "I don't think you're that talented of a liar, but you've clearly been marked by a Fae, so I suspect you're not as naive as you're acting. Shall we do this the hard way, then?"

Marked by a Fae? What did that mean? I wanted to ask, but I feared what reaction that would bring. Perhaps if I played along, he'd let me go.

He waved an arm, and the two men, who I assumed were guards of some sort, walked toward me.

One pinned my arms behind my back and the other wrapped his hand around my hair and pulled, exposing my throat. He held a knife against my skin and pressed the point under my chin. I pulled away from the knife, only to find myself pressed against the man behind me. Lurching away, I nicked my skin on the knifepoint. A trickle of warm blood dripped down my neck, ending the idea that I'd been plunged into a festival drama.

"Now, let's try again," said the man who thought he was my uncle's ancestor. He stood over me and stared down at me.

Fear coursed through my veins. "I don't know anything," I said. "I swear it." My body began to shake. Tears filled my eyes. I'd never see my family again. I tried to breathe and recall everything I'd learned about Edric and Godda.

Edric nodded at the man holding the knife to my throat. The knife point moved from my chin to slice at the shoulder of my gown. The fabric split and fell away to expose my shoulder. I grabbed for the fabric, only to find the knife returned to my throat. I froze, and a whimper escaped my lips.

"Sharp, isn't it?" Edric asked. He ran his hand over my exposed shoulder and down my bare arm. "The one who marked you has good taste. But my Godda was more beautiful. And I want her back. I know the Fae have her. Tell me where she is."

"Godda's dead," I said.

"Is she, now?" He frowned. "We both know that can't be true. If she were, then she would be here, with me. I've searched the Underworld. She's not there." He gripped my earlobe and squeezed it. "I'll ask again. Where is she?" He tugged my head closer to the blade, and I pulled against him, trying to inch away.

"I don't know." Tears escaped from the corners of my eyes and slid down my cheeks.

"Your tears won't sway me, girl. I won't stop until she has been returned to me, if I have to find and kill every single one of her kin." He nodded at the man holding the knife.

"Master," said a voice from the back of the room. The guard holding the knife hesitated.

"You're interrupting me," Edric said. "This better be worth it."

"One of the prisoners has successfully defeated the beasts. We have a new champion," the voice said.

"Bring him here," Edric said. He waved his hand at the guard with the knife, and the man released my hair and stepped back. I let my head drop forward and kept my eyes down as I listened to the footsteps approach.

"Master," a voice behind me said. "The new champion."

I watched Edric from beneath my brow. He sat forward on his throne and placed his elbows on his knees.

"Well, isn't this interesting." He stalked toward the man

they'd brought forth who stood to my right and a little behind me. I couldn't see him without turning my head. So,
I kept my head down and tried to catch a glimpse from the
corner of my eye.

Edric's feet disappeared from view as he slowly circled the
man.

"Yes," he said. "This is very interesting." He returned to his
throne, paused for a moment, then pivoted to face us.

Extending his arms out to his sides, he addressed his men.
"Hunters, it appears we have a distinguished guest for our
festivities this evening." Directing his attention to the man
they'd brought in, he continued, "How kind of you to join us,
and how convenient that you've earned the honor of becom-
ing our Solstice Champion." He dropped his arms and took a
few steps forward before continuing. "You will be our honored guest for our solstice celebration this evening."

He nodded to the guard holding my arms behind me. "Take
them back and get them cleaned up and dressed. The festivities will begin in an hour."

"Yes, Master." The guard released my arms and grabbed the
back of my neck with one hand.

Edric's attention returned to the champion. "The girl will
join you this evening at our celebration." Then he spoke again
to the guard holding me. "Leave them in the same cell and
bring her the clothing and supplies they'll need. Let her tend
to the champion."

"Yes, Master," he said. He gripped my upper arm and led
me away. When I turned, I finally got a chance to look at the
man they were calling the champion. I forced myself not to
react at the sight of Liam standing in front of me. Deep gashes covered his body. Some still oozed blood. Dirt and blood
matted his clothes and hair. But underneath the filth, it was

Liam, and my heart lurched. I wanted to run to him, but I held myself still. He didn't look at me before he turned to follow one of the other guards. Clutching my shoulder strap to keep my dress from sliding to the floor, I fell into step behind him.

The long walk down the center aisle and down to the cells below gave me more than enough time to catalog the injuries covering his back. He looked like he'd been left in a cage with wild animals. No matter what he said, I wasn't letting him out of my sight again. We'd get out of here together, or not at all.

———

They tossed Evelyn into the cell after me and slammed the door behind us. A guard passed a stack of clothing through the bars and set it on the floor. I waited until we were alone before I lunged for her.

"Are you okay?" I tilted her face up until I could look in her eyes.

"Am I okay? Look at you," she said. She pulled back so she could look me over. "You're a mess. What did they do to you? Are you hurt?" She leaned toward me and placed a hand on my cheek. I winced.

"I'm fine. Or, I will be," I said. I touched the spot of blood under her chin. "He kept you and sent the others back to the cells?"

"That man is insane, Liam. He thinks he's Lord Edric! Can you believe it? I told him Edric is dead, and he tried to tell me he was a ghost. He did this magic trick where he made it look like his fingers could pass through a solid object." She shook her head.

I frowned. "He's not a ghost, Eve." I'd been hoping to avoid this conversation. But, since we were both still here, I was going to have to do some explaining.

"I know! But what is going on? And where are we?" She paced to the bars of the cell, glancing back and forth down the empty hall.

I shook my head and dove in. "What I mean is, he's not *just* a ghost. Ghosts can't take physical form. He's a spirit. And not just any spirit. He really is the spirit of Lord Edric."

She spun around and stared at me. "Are you teasing me?" When I didn't respond, she continued. "You're joking, right? You don't believe him, do you?"

I walked over to her, taking her hands in mine. "I know this sounds crazy to you. You don't have to believe me. But you must know that he's dangerous. We need to find a way out of here."

She narrowed her eyes. "It does sound crazy. But I agree with you about the fact that we need to get out of here." She leaned back and looked down the corridor again. Then she turned to face me. "Do you have a plan?"

"Not yet. I'll tell you what I know and maybe we can come up with one together." I knew I had to tell her something to prepare her for whatever Edric had in store for us, but I couldn't tell her everything without putting her life in more danger even than it already was. I'd have to choose my words carefully.

She nodded. "Okay."

"Edric's spirit returns around each solstice. He leads a band of other spirits who are seeking revenge, or just interested in causing trouble. The locals call it the Wild Hunt. They captured you, and they're holding us prisoner. I'm fairly certain that Edric is up to something, inviting us to his party."

"Are you trying to tell me that all those men out there are spirits? All of them?" She looked at me like I was trying to convince her the sky was orange. I couldn't blame her.

"They're solid. One of them held a knife to my throat. They dragged you down that corridor."

These were spirits at the peak of their strength. To the untrained eye, they would easily pass for human. It would be easier to just let her continue to believe whatever she'd decided to believe.

I sighed. "Yes, but that's not what's important. What's important is getting out of here."

"What about the woman? The one I gave my bracelet to? The one you said was your relative. Wasn't she supposed to help get us out of here?"

"She's my aunt, and she's a captive. Like us." Even though I could really use her help right now, I hoped Sorcha had managed to escape with the other prisoners.

"So, she's real. The rest of them are just ghosts."

"They're real. They're spirits, not ghosts. Spirits of real people." And Sorcha was Fae, but if I could keep her from learning about us, then maybe the Fae would have no reason to kill her, assuming we managed to escape whatever Edric had planned.

Evelyn covered her face with her hands. I wrapped my arms around her and held her against my chest. "Please, believe me, Eve." She leaned against me, and I tilted her face up so I could look her in the eyes. "We're both in a lot of danger right now and we don't have much time. I promise you, I'm telling you the truth."

She frowned. "Let's get you cleaned up." She pulled away and reached for the bowl of water and the cloth they'd left for her to use. I watched her, trying to think of what I could do to get her to believe me.

"What did he say to you?" I asked as I peeled off my shirt. Most of the gashes had started to heal already, but I was still covered in dried blood. The fabric ripped away from partially healed wounds, causing them to start bleeding again.

"He wanted me to tell him where we're keeping his wife, Godda." She pulled a stool over and motioned for me to sit on it.

"What did you tell him?"

"What was I supposed to say? She's dead." She dipped the cloth into the bowl, submerging it to absorb the liquid.

"You said that? You said she's dead?"

Evelyn glanced up at me. "She is, isn't she?"

"No one knows."

She scowled as she wrung out the rag. "What do you mean? She lived centuries ago. She must be dead by now."

"What did he say when you said that?"

"He said he'd searched the Underworld and she wasn't there, so she couldn't be dead. He kept insisting I knew where she was and was lying to him. That's when he said that thing about me being marked by a Fae. What do you think he meant by that? Fae? Like a faerie? He thinks I've been marked by a faerie?" She snorted. "I think I'd know if I'd ever seen a faerie, let alone been marked by one, whatever that means."

My mind replayed what Edric had said when they'd brought me to him. He'd looked between me and Evelyn and said, *Interesting.* My stomach sank. What had I done? Was it possible that I'd marked her in some way? I searched her body as she moved around me.

"Liam?" she asked. "Are you okay? Did I hurt you?"

"No, no." I wrapped my arms around her waist and pulled her down onto my lap. "You didn't hurt me." I pushed her hair back from her face and leaned in to kiss her lips.

"I'm glad you're okay," she said, resting her forehead against mine. "Now, let's figure out how to get out of here."

She dipped the cloth into the water and squeezed some of the moisture from it before bringing it to my face. Very gently, she wiped away the blood, dabbing around the cuts and bruises.

"What happened to you?" she asked as she worked. "Did they beat you? What did they mean when they said you'd defeated all the beasts?"

I sighed. "They threw me in a dungeon and left me to defend myself against the current residents."

"Animals?" She stared at me with her mouth open.

"A few," I said.

"They left you to fight off animals? With what? Your bare hands?"

I shrugged.

"No wonder you look like that. I need soap. And some antibacterial ointment. You could be infected." She started to get up, but I pulled her back down.

"It's okay. They're not infected."

"You don't know that."

"Let's just work on getting out of here. Then you can clean them with as much soap as you'd like." I raised an eyebrow and grinned at her.

She swatted at me with the damp rag. I dodged it, kicking the bowl in the process. Water sloshed up the sides but didn't spill. "Enough messing around," she said, dipping the rag drop back into the water and wringing it out. "We may not have much time."

"All right." I took the bowl and the rag from her. "Let me finish this. You go see what they left us for clothes. Maybe it will give us an idea about what's in store for us tonight."

She kissed my forehead and stood. I knew how much danger we were in. If Edric knew Evelyn and I were somehow connected, he could use that against us. And I wasn't entirely sure that being Edric's "honored guest" was a good thing. I hoped Sorcha had escaped with the others, as promised. We needed to figure out a way to stay alive and stall him, in the hope that help was already on the way.

I watched her walk to the bars of the cell and bend to retrieve the clothes. She was beautiful. If Edric forced me to reveal myself in front of her, I'd lose her forever. Our laws were clear about what happened to humans who discovered us. Fiona would kill her to protect our kind, and I would be powerless to stop her.

"Looks like they left a gown for me and some pants and a shirt for you."

I splashed the water onto my face to clear my head, then rinsed the blood from my hair. She held the folded bundle of clothes out to me. I took them from her and handed her the bowl.

"Party clothes," I said.

"Why is he doing this?" She turned her back to me and faced the wall as she pulled the white gown over her head and stepped into the emerald-green one they'd left for her to wear. She pulled the straps up over her shoulders but left the back open.

"Remember I told you that he thinks my family has something that he wants?" She held her hair up, and I reached for the zipper on her dress. I let my knuckles run over her spine as I pulled the zipper closed. I leaned down and kissed her bare neck.

"He thinks you have Godda?" she asked.

"Yes."

"But Godda disappeared. That's what the legends say."

I nodded and stripped out of my jeans. "Precisely. She

went missing. She never returned. But he's convinced she's not dead. Probably because, as he told you, he can't find her spirit."

"But how could she still be alive? She'd be close to a thousand years old by now." She wasn't wrong, but that was well within the possible life span for Fae, even for those who chose to reproduce. Not that I could explain that to her.

"She's not." Or at least, we were all fairly certain that she wasn't. She really had just disappeared. Of course, all this happened long before I was born. I pulled on the clean wool trousers and slipped the black shirt over my shoulders.

"Why would your family know anything about Godda, anyway?"

"We're related."

"You're related to Godda?"

I nodded.

"So I was right. She was just a woman and not a Faerie Queen. Did you tell my uncle this?"

That wasn't the conclusion I'd expected her to come to, but it was better than the reality. "No. We didn't really discuss it." At least it was easy to tell the truth to answer her question.

"Is that why you're working for him?"

"Partly. I became interested in history because of my family. And it's my interest in history, especially my family's history, that earned me the job with your uncle." No lies, but definitely not the entire truth.

"So, this spirit of Edric thinks you're going to be able to tell him where Godda is because you're related?" She reached for the front of my shirt and began buttoning it.

"Yes." I watched her hands work and wished we were safe, back at the professor's house.

She paused, clamping one hand over her bare wrist. "That's

why you said I shouldn't wear the bracelet, isn't it? Do you think that's why they captured me? Because of the bracelet?"

"Maybe. Or maybe it was just to get to me. Maybe they knew I'd come after you." I reached out and wrapped my arm around her to pull her close. She leaned her head against my chest, and I buried my face in her hair.

"Hate to break up the reunion," said a voice at the cell door. I looked up and locked eyes with Nigel.

"You," I said, tensing.

"Nigel!" Evelyn said, stepping away from me. "Wait. What are you doing here? Can you get them to let us out?" I hated the sound of relief in her voice, but there was no time to warn her now.

"I'm here to escort Evelyn to the party," he said.

"No," I said. I reached for Evelyn's hand.

"What are you doing here with these people?" She squeezed my hand and didn't let go.

"She's not going anywhere without me," I said.

"Oh, don't worry. You're coming, too. Your escort will be along to retrieve you shortly. She's a bit delayed. She just found out that she lost a few of her favorite pets today," he said, looking at me.

Great. The demon woman was coming for me. I didn't know who she was, but from the talk in the arena, I anticipated the worst. I turned toward Evelyn.

"Eve." I tilted her chin up so I could meet her eyes. I didn't like the idea of sending her with Nigel, but she'd likely be better off with him than with me right now. "Be careful." I kissed her once and let her go. I had a sinking feeling that we were about to be the honored guests in a very dangerous game.

13

NIGEL opened the cell door and offered me his arm. He led me down the corridor, away from the cell, away from Liam. I'd almost been convinced that Liam was telling me the truth about the spirits until Nigel showed up, looking sharp in his dark jeans, button-down shirt, and sweater. But now I only had more questions.

"You didn't answer me. What are you doing here?" I asked him.

"Maybe I came to rescue you," he said. His short dark hair was swept back off his forehead in a perfect wave, and his imperfect nose and sharp cheekbones created odd shadows on his thin face as we moved through the torch-lit corridor.

"I'd like to believe that, but how did you even know I was here?" The last time I'd seen him he'd been backing away from me. Come to think of it, he'd been backing away right after he'd seen my bracelet. Liam had warned me about Nigel. If Nigel was associated with this place, perhaps Liam had been right. I tried to pull away from him, but he held my hand in place.

"Ah, ah. Better not run. You're new around here, and it looks like no one warned you. It's best to stay home on the nights around the solstice. You never know what or who you might run into out there."

"Who, or what, are you?" I asked. "And are you really here to help? Can you get us out of here?"

"What? And miss the festivities?" He let go of my hand to adjust his tie.

"I'll take that as a no, then." I twisted away from him. "If you won't help, then take me back to Liam."

He reached out to grip my forearm, tugging me back to his side. "Liam can't help you, either. Even he knows that you're safer with me than with him. Why else do you think he let you leave with me?"

"Then tell me what's going on." This was insane. "Are those really spirits of dead people? Are you one of them?"

He laughed. "There is more to the world than you ever imagined, Evelyn. Yes, spirits are real, so are faeries and demons. You've met some already, and you'll meet more tonight."

"But you're not, right? Are we the only humans here?" I asked.

"Who? You and me?" He seemed surprised at my question.

I nodded. "And Liam." Liam had to be human. I'd seen him naked. There's no way he was a ghost, and I think I would have noticed horns or wings or whatever.

Nigel laughed. "Evelyn, my girl, I do believe that you'll be the only human guest at the party this evening."

I blinked as my brain tried to process what he was telling me. "So, you're...you're one of them?"

He waved his hand in the air above his head, and two tiny

black horns materialized. "No. I'm something else. Technically, I am half human. But the other half—the better half, I'd say—is demon. They call my lot cambions."

I took a step backward and gaped at him. He had horns. And he was half demon. And spirits were real. This was too much to process. I was about to turn and bolt away from him and back to Liam when he grabbed my arm.

"Ah, ah, ah," he said. "I wouldn't do that if I were you." He grinned at me, and I shivered.

"Where are you taking me?" I asked, trying to twist out of his grip.

"To the party, of course. You heard Lord Edric. You're to be an honored guest at this evening's festivities." He wrapped my hand around his arm and started up the stairs, dragging me along behind him. "And, just because I like you, I'll give you a hint. If you know what's good for you, you'll stop acting so human. He'll keep you around longer if he keeps thinking you're somehow connected to the Fae."

"He thinks I'm connected to the Fae?" The last word squeaked out and echoed off the walls of the stone stairwell.

Nigel smirked. "Ridiculous, isn't it. And a bit insulting, if you ask me. But he appears to have caught a whiff of something between you and Liam. And what he wants is to find his wife. Help him do that and he'll never trouble you again."

We reached the top of the stairs and stepped out into the large room with the pillars. In the short time I'd been in the cells below, the room had been transformed. Delicate lights were suspended from the ceiling, though I couldn't tell how. There didn't appear to be any wires holding them up. Garlands of holly and pine had been wrapped around the pillars and draped along the walls. Crystal stars sparkled near the ceiling, and music filled the air, even though I couldn't see any speakers or musicians. Only a few people, or spirits, roamed about the room. If this was supposed to be a party, it appeared we'd arrived early.

"You're quite lucky, you know," Nigel said. "Lord Edric's solstice party is really the best party in town. Much better than the bonfires and dancing in the town square."

I searched the room for any sign of Liam, but he hadn't arrived yet.

"Don't worry, he'll be along shortly," Nigel said, as though he'd read my mind. "Though I have a feeling his escort will be keeping him occupied this evening. Don't be upset if he doesn't ask you to dance. Or even remember you exist." He laughed.

Fear gnawed at my belly, and I tried to pull away from him again.

"I'm afraid you're stuck with me for the evening. I do think that should be preferable to returning to the cells, which is your other option."

I stopped pulling and stood rooted in place. More guests had arrived. The chamber started to buzz with chatter and the music played louder.

"Better," he said. "But I don't intend to just stand here all night and miss out on the fun." He extended his hand toward the center of the room. "Shall we dance?"

He didn't wait for a response, he just started walking toward the middle of the room, pulling me along as he steered us between clumps of people. I stared at everyone we passed. They all looked solid and human, except a few who I noticed had horns like Nigel.

"It's not polite to stare," he whispered in my ear. He'd caught me swiveling my neck to study a man with a shiny bald head, bare except for a pair of curved golden horns.

"Lesson number one if you want to survive: try not to stare at the horns. Dead giveaway that you're human."

We slipped around a group of men and out into an open space where the music was impossible to ignore, and couples danced surrounded by a ring of onlookers. Nigel took my hand in one of his and wrapped his other around my waist. I followed his lead, only tripping and stumbling a few times before I grasped the basic steps. He moved us gracefully around the floor while I continued to stare, wide-eyed, at the other guests.

I kept searching for Liam in the crowd. I'd almost given up when I spotted a stunning woman with thick dark hair, swept up in a mass of curls on top of her head. She'd dressed in a low-cut, strapless ruby-red dress that left her bronze shoulders and arms bare, save for a golden band that snaked around her left bicep. When she turned, I spotted the blood-red horns nestled in her dark curls. I was so enchanted by her that I almost didn't notice Liam at her side.

Nigel followed my gaze and chuckled. "See, I told you he'd be along."

Liam's eyes never left the demon woman. She greeted others and chatted with people, but he barely noticed anyone but her. My heart twisted, even as my brain insisted that she must have cast some sort of spell over him. I turned back to Nigel to ask him if demons could cast spells and found him smirking at me.

"Seems like lover boy has found himself a new lady," he said.

I scowled. What right did I have to be jealous when I'd been so angry with Liam for chasing off Nigel in a display of what I'd thought was some territorial nonsense. Only, Liam had said he wasn't jealous. He'd told me it had nothing to do with me, that I'd managed to find the most dangerous guy in town. I froze and tripped over Nigel's feet. He righted me, and I fell back into step, but my mind was elsewhere. Liam had known. Liam had known that Nigel was half demon, and that's why he'd chased him off. But how had Liam known what Nigel was if Liam was just a human, like me? How did he know so much about demons and spirits?

Then I remembered what Nigel had said in the corridor. I looked up at him. "You said I would be the only human at the party. What about Liam?" I had a feeling I wasn't going to like the answer.

"I wondered how long it would take you to ask," he said.

"Is he one of you? A what did you call it? Half-demon thing?"

Nigel raised his eyebrows. "Cambion, love. And no. No horns on that one. He's all Fae. And Fae royalty, at that." The corner of his mouth quirked. "Surprised he never told you. But I suppose if he told you, he'd have to kill you. Those Fae are more strict about their secrets than MI6."

I stopped dancing and walked toward the ring of onlookers. Nigel followed me, grabbing hold of my wrist when he caught up with me.

"I thought we had an agreement. No running off."

"I don't feel like dancing anymore." I needed to find a way to get rid of him so I could talk to Liam. "I'd like something to drink."

"I suppose that can be arranged. Spirits don't drink, but demons do, so there must be some refreshments around here somewhere." While he looked around the room, I checked that Liam was still where I'd last seen him. The demon lady was chatting with a group of men as he stood by, hanging on her every word and smiling like a dope.

"I think I saw something over here," I said. I grabbed Nigel's hand and pointed toward a wall that would bring us close to where Liam stood.

"All right," Nigel said. He started off in that direction, taking a firm hold of my hand and trailing me along behind him.

I watched the crowd and waited for my chance. I looked for a large group standing near Liam but behind the demon lady. I'd only have a moment to break Nigel's grip, grab Liam, and pull him out of sight so we could disappear among the other guests. Perhaps if I could talk to Liam, I might be able to break the spell that woman had over him. I'd have to if we were going to have any chance to come up with an escape plan.

Nigel wove us through the crowded room, taking us past, but out of sight, of Liam. I waited until we'd passed them, then spotted my opportunity. I slipped my hand out of Nigel's to push away a man—more likely a spirit—who'd reached out to grab at me as we passed. Nigel turned to confront him. While he was distracted, I lunged for Liam. Latching on to Liam's arm, I hauled him with me into a clump of guests.

"Hey!" he said.

"Shh," I said, pulling him with me and ducking behind one of the columns. I flattened myself against the stone and positioned him in front of me, wrapping my arms around his neck and forcing him to look down at me and meet my eyes.

He blinked as his pupils slowly began to focus on my face. "Eve," he said.

Relief flowed through me, and I let out a sigh. "Liam. We don't have much time."

"She enchanted me," I said. My brain was foggy. I shook my

head to clear it. The demon woman had not been pleased that I'd killed her hell beasts. Upon arriving to retrieve me from the cell, she'd announced that I'd be her pet for the evening. A Fae enchanted by a demon. I'd never hear the end of this from Arabella if I ever got out of here alive.

"She's a demon, Liam." Evelyn's shocked face stared back at me as my vision cleared.

"I know." I'd just finished trying to convince Evelyn that spirits existed, and now she was telling me that I'd been enchanted by a demon. Since when did Evelyn know anything about demons?

"So is Nigel," she said. Things began to make sense again. He must have shown her his horns, the bastard.

I raised my eyebrows. "He told you?"

"You were trying to keep me away from him because you knew what he was, weren't you?"

I nodded.

"You could have told me."

"You wouldn't have believed me."

"You're probably right." She frowned. "He also said that you're...not human."

I cringed. Of course he'd told her that.

"We shouldn't talk about this here." The last thing I needed was for anyone to find out that Evelyn didn't know the first thing about the Fae. Edric would discard her immediately if he knew she couldn't help him. But, if I could keep them from realizing their mistake long enough, I might be able to get her out of here. I looked around, trying to see if anyone was close enough to overhear our conversation.

Evelyn pulled me back behind the pillar. "Don't," she said. "He'll see you."

"Who?" It wasn't exactly the most private location for

a chat. I conjured a shield to hide us from the other guests and keep those nearby from listening to our conversation. It would screen us from view, making it appear like there was nothing here, and deter wandering guests from stumbling through and discovering us. Anyone who was searching for us and knew to look for magic would find the shield. But it might give us some time and privacy to talk.

"Nigel told me that I had to stay with him, but I needed to talk to you. I couldn't leave you under that demon's spell. We need to get out of here."

I placed my palm on her cheek and let it run down along the side of her neck until it rested on her shoulder. She'd been captured, imprisoned, threatened, held at knifepoint, and shackled to a half-demon escort, and all because I'd let my guard down.

"I'm sorry," I said.

"When were you going to tell me?" she asked.

I shook my head. "I just wanted to keep you safe."

"Look at where we are, Liam! We're surrounded by creatures I didn't even know existed before tonight. And you... you let me think... Why did you sleep with me when you know it's impossible for us to be together? Were you ever planning to tell me?" She glared at me with her arms crossed.

"No." I couldn't lie, even if I wanted to.

"So you were going to just disappear again?" She'd started to shake, but I didn't sense her fear this time. She was angry, and she had every right to be.

"I told you I wouldn't, and I meant that. I've never lied to you. I can't lie."

"You just left out the part about being Fae." She squinted at me. "Wait. What do you mean 'can't'? Like Pinocchio?"

"Who's Pinocchio?"

Evelyn groaned. "Little wooden boy. Couldn't tell a lie or his nose would grow."

"You believe in little wooden boys who can talk, but Fae, spirits, and demons are too far-fetched for you?"

She rolled her eyes. "It's a story for kids, and you're not answering my question."

"No. I can't tell a lie. Not even one that would make my nose grow." I grinned.

"Not funny." She frowned at me. "What *can* you do? Fae are supposed to be immortal, but these spirits and demons could still kill you, right? What about magic? Do you have any sort of powers?"

I hesitated. Whatever I told her might make things worse. I might be able to convince Fiona to let Evelyn live if the only thing she knew was that we existed, and that I was Fae. If I told her anything about my powers, Fiona might not be so easily convinced. Even if I failed, I wanted to know that Evelyn would live.

"Liam?"

"Yes, I have magic. But if I tell you more, they might kill you."

"They who?" She shook her head. "Never mind. It doesn't matter. Whatever magic you have, we need it. I'm just a human who's supposed to be going to grad school in a few months. I certainly don't have any special powers that might help us escape from this band of vengeful spirits and creepily attractive demons."

"It would be a lot safer for you if you could pretend you never heard about this Fae thing and go back to just worrying about my being your uncle's secretary," I said.

She glared at me. "If we don't find a way out of here, we're both going to die. So, start talking."

"Right. Well, yes, I have some magic, but I can't just conjure us out of here, if that's what you mean."

"What can you do?"

I cupped my hand between us and conjured a ball of light, then let it float toward the ceiling.

Evelyn gasped. Her eyes followed the light up until it disappeared, blending in with the decorations. "You really are one of them," she whispered.

"I'm not one of them. I'm Fae. My mother is the Queen of the Faeries."

"I thought Godda was Queen of the Faeries." Her jaw dropped open. "Wait. Is Godda your mother? Is that why Edric wants you? But that would make you hundreds of years old or something..." She glanced away, clearly doing the math in her head.

"It's not like that. Godda was my aunt. My mother was her second-in-command and took over as queen when Godda disappeared."

"So that's what Nigel meant. He said you were Fae royalty." Her eyes widened. "And you said your mother is sick. If she dies, do you become king or something?"

"No. The title is handed down to the eldest female in the line, my cousin Fiona. I'm just one of the Sworn in her Court. Or, I will be once I take the Oath."

She pressed the heels of her hands against her temples. "This is insane."

"Eve, I shouldn't be telling you any of this. Humans can't know about our existence. It's our way. Ever since what happened with Edric and Godda. It's the only way we'll be safe."

She looked thoughtful again. "Edric said you marked me. What does that even mean?"

"I don't know. I didn't do anything to you. I wouldn't hurt

you." Until Evelyn had told me what Edric had said, I hadn't even known that was possible. I certainly wouldn't know how to do it on purpose. Perhaps I had somehow managed to mark her on accident. I wished there was someone I could ask about this, but we were on our own, for now.

"Nigel said Edric and his Hunters would kill me if they found out I'm of no use to them, and now you've told me that the Fae will kill me just for knowing they exist. Is there any way for me to get out of this alive?"

"I won't let them hurt you. Edric or Fiona. We'll find a way to get you out of here. Alive."

"And what about you?"

"I can take care of myself."

"With a ball of light? I don't think that's going to help. What else can you do? Do you have wings?" She ran her hands over the back of my shirt.

I grinned. "Most Fae don't have wings. But we do have animal forms."

"You can turn into an animal?"

I nodded.

"Can you do it now?"

I frowned. The shield I'd created around us was too small to hide me if I transformed. If I made it any bigger, we'd begin to attract attention. Certainly, they were already searching for us.

"Now's not the best time. It will draw too much attention. Besides, I can't use my magic in that form."

"So our only defense is the ball of light?" She raised her eyebrows, clearly unimpressed with my magic.

"I can do more than that."

"Such as?"

"Well, for starters..." I dropped my human glamour. I'd

only been using it for her, anyway. It didn't work on spirits and demons. Muscles filled out my baggy clothes and the tips of my ears went from round to pointed as I stretched to my full height. Evelyn took a step backward, and I grabbed for her so she wouldn't slip outside the shield.

"Oh." She blinked at me. "So that's what you really look like?"

I nodded. "And I can conjure myself places, but only if I know where I am in relation to where I'm going. I could probably carry you with me, but I've never tried, and I don't know where we are, so that isn't going to help."

"All right. What else?" I could tell she was trying not to stare at my ears.

"I can also conjure things away, or to me. But again, only if I know where I am in relation to where the thing is going. So, I can't get us any weapons, not that they'd do us much good against these spirits and demons."

"How do you fight a spirit or a demon?"

"Spirits are easier. They can be harmed with iron or salt. But they can only be banished if you destroy the thing that's holding them in this realm."

"You mean, like a Horcrux?"

"What's a Horcrux?"

"You're really not human, are you? It's from a book. The bad guy used objects to hide bits of his soul. There were seven."

"Seven seems a bit...much. I certainly hope Edric hasn't read this book. I've been looking everywhere, and I haven't been able to find the one that's holding him here."

"That's why you've been interested in the artifacts at Lydbury."

"Yes. I found a dagger and a shield that both showed signs

of magic, but neither anchored a life force."

She nodded, her brow wrinkled in thought. "So, even if we find some iron or salt, we can't get rid of Edric. What about the demons?"

"You need a special weapon. We don't have it. Unless they have one lying around here somewhere, which probably wouldn't be very popular, given the guest list. I think we'll have to settle for avoiding them."

"Is that really the best you've got?"

"Demons don't have magic, at least not the same way we do. The Fae, I mean." I paused to gauge her reaction.

She rolled her eyes at me. "Yes, I knew what you meant. Continue."

"Right. Well, they can do a bit of glamour."

"Is that the thing they do to hide those horns of theirs?"

"Yes, exactly."

"But they couldn't do that ball of light thing that you did. Is that what you mean?"

"Precisely." I nodded. "Of course, they can do other things..."

"Mind control?" she asked. She was likely thinking of the enchantment that demon woman cast on me. I felt my face grow warm.

"Yes. It's more like a strong persuasion to do as they wish. An enchantment that creates a bit of an obsession in the victim."

"Interesting. How do you know if you're being enchanted?"

I shrugged. "You don't, really. At least not until it's over and you snap out of it. If you snap out of it." I studied her face closely. "Did Nigel...?"

"No," she said, cutting me off before I could finish my question. She scrunched her face a bit. "At least, I don't think he did. I'd know it if he did, right?"

"You would have just blindly obeyed him, thinking it was your idea. Later you might have wondered what you were thinking, or realized you didn't want to do or say any of those things." If he'd tried anything, I would make his death a slow and painful one.

"Okay. I don't think he did that. That's interesting, isn't it?"

"Perhaps. Let's save that for later. I think we have more pressing matters to attend to."

"Yes, like keeping you away from that red-horned she-devil so she can't get her claws into you again."

I smiled. "You almost sound as though you care." I pulled her close to me.

"Well, you looked like an idiot."

I scowled at her. "You're ruining the moment."

She smiled. "A cute idiot," she added.

I leaned down and kissed her smiling lips. She wrapped her hands around me, and for a moment, I dared to hope that we'd find a way out. And maybe even a way to be together. But I sensed a shift in the air and began to worry we wouldn't be able to stay hidden much longer.

"You're handling all this quite well," I said.

She shrugged. "Right now, all I care about is getting us out of here. I'll probably freak out later. If there is a later." She frowned.

"I promise I'll get us out of here. But first, we need a plan," I whispered, my nose still pressed to hers. "Quickly."

14

I LEANED into Liam, my brain sorting through everything he'd told me, everything I'd learned, searching for a solution. Now that I knew the truth about Edric and Godda, I attempted to piece together a plan, but I still had so many questions about this supernatural stuff. Nothing seemed to fit together in any useful order. We needed to escape, but we didn't even know where the exits were or how well they would be guarded. I took a step back, away from Liam, and shivered.

"Not very polite, you know," a voice said. I turned and found myself staring at Nigel. I felt Liam grab for me, but Nigel beat him to it, wrapping his hand around mine and pulling me next to him. He slung an arm over my shoulder and turned to Liam. "Tsk-tsk," he said. "The two honored guests, off hiding themselves in a corner, sneaking a snog." He shook his head. "Best come rejoin the party before Edric notices you've gone missing."

"Take your hands off her," Liam said.

Nigel clucked his tongue. "Ah, but you forget, she's my date for the evening. Don't worry, I'll let your escort know I found you. She was quite upset that you'd run off. I calmed her down a bit." He looked out over the crowd, then turned back to face Liam. "Here she comes now."

My muscles tensed, and I searched among the figures in the direction Nigel had been looking. There she was with her dark hair curling around blood-red horns above her beautiful—even while scowling—face. The she-devil looked like she might tear someone's head off at any moment. I turned to Liam, my eyes wide in fear.

"Run," I said.

"I'm not leaving without you."

"Neither of you are going anywhere," Nigel said. He tightened his arm around me. I squirmed and pushed him away.

Liam looked from me to the demon woman and back again.

"Go," I said. "You're no use to us if she gets her claws into you again."

His eyes went wide. "Claws," he repeated in an almost inaudible whisper. Then he disappeared.

Nigel gave up trying to keep his arm around me and clasped a firm grip around my wrist instead. He held tight as he spun around, searching the room for Liam. I didn't bother looking. Instead, I kept my eyes locked on the demon woman as she pushed through the last few groups separating her from where we stood.

"Where'd he go?" she asked.

"He was here a moment ago. Then he disappeared."

"Don't let her out of your sight," she said. She ran her eyes over my body, and I shivered. "He won't leave without her."

"Maybe she doesn't mean as much—" Nigel started to say, but the demon woman cut him off.

"Silence!" she hissed. "We've tried this your way and look how well that's turned out. Enough. I'll find him. You make sure this one stays with you. You let her go again, and we'll see how *you* fare against my pets."

"Yes, Mother," Nigel said.

The demon woman was Nigel's mother? I stared at him as she nodded once and spun on her heel. She stalked away from us, and I turned toward him with raised eyebrows.

"Mother?"

"Upset that I didn't introduce you properly?"

"That woman is your mother?" I pointed at the swaying figure that was slicing through party guests as she cut a path away from us.

Nigel straightened his tie with his free hand. "I said I was half demon. What did you expect?"

"I guess I just assumed it was your father who was—"

"The demon half?" Nigel raised his eyebrows. "No. My father was a lying, cheating, no-good bastard, but he was only a mortal."

"She doesn't look old enough," I said, staring after the flash of red dress disappearing into the crowd.

"Yes, yes." Nigel waved his hand. "Your humanity is showing again. Best zip that up before we return to the party."

"How kind of you to be concerned." I glared at him.

"Don't take your frustrations out on me. I'm just trying to show you a good time. And keep you from getting killed by a raging-lunatic spirit. You should be thanking me."

I tried to yank my wrist out of his grip, but he held fast. "You're hurting me."

"Would you prefer I use less conventional methods to keep you at my side for the remainder of the party?" He raised an eyebrow at me, and I remembered what Liam had told me about demon powers.

"No."

"All right, then. Let's get back to the party." He relaxed his grip around my wrist and slid his hand down until it clasped my hand tightly.

"What's she going to do to Liam?" I asked.

He shrugged. "Make him her slave."

———

I watched the party from my perch in one of the balcony boxes above the main floor. I saw Nigel's exchange with the demon woman, and then I saw her stalk away. I waited until I was certain that Nigel hadn't tried to enchant Evelyn. I didn't like the grip he had on her, but I supposed it was better than the alternative. The balcony was mostly deserted, and I'd cloaked myself to remain unseen as I searched for Edric in the crowd below.

I wanted to stay so I could keep my eye on Evelyn and wait for Edric to appear. But I didn't have much time, and I needed to find a weapon and a way out. Evelyn's warning reminded me of the tunnel in the hell beast arena. So I decided to take a chance and transport myself back into the dungeons to see if I could find a weapon. If my aunt hadn't found a way to escape already, maybe she could help. If anyone knew how to get out of here, it would be her. And if I could find her, and get Evelyn to her, they could all escape to safety while I faced Edric.

I pictured the dark corner of the corridor outside the cells and hoped no one would be standing there when I appeared. When I opened my eyes, the chatter and music of the party had disappeared. I pressed myself against the cold stone walls outside the cells where they'd held me and Evelyn and listened to the silence, waiting to make sure I was alone. Then I crept down the hall, feeling with my magic for any others, friendly or unfriendly, who may have remained below. I followed my senses and turned down another corridor, retracing the route I'd taken earlier when I'd been dragged to the arena. The sense of my kin grew stronger as I approached the arena, and I hurried.

"Sorcha," I whispered into the darkness of the arena. A flash of light at the far side of the arena caught my eye, but I paused first to examine the door. A blast of magic revealed the carvings in the stone archway. Wards. This was the magic that had prevented me from conjuring myself directly out of the arena and would also prevent me from conjuring myself inside from the party. I couldn't undo another Fae's magic, so I'd have to take that into account in our escape.

I pushed open the barred door and slipped inside. Then I crept across the room toward the flash of light I'd seen. No beasts remained. Someone must have removed their bodies after the fight. In the dim light, I could just make out a cluster of figures huddled together at the far end of the arena. I ran to them.

"Nephew," Sorcha said in greeting when I reached her. She took a step toward me and reached out her hand. I saw the flash of gold on her wrist and realized she was wearing Godda's bracelet. I grasped her hand in both of mine and glanced past her at the two Fae females huddled against the wall in identical tattered white garments. They shivered and stared at me with wide eyes.

"Where are you taking them?" I asked.

"Through there," she said. She nodded toward the tunnel entrance I had seen earlier.

"Do you know where it leads?" I asked.

"No," she said. "They kept the beasts back there, and they didn't bring them through the dungeons. So they must have let them in that way. If they're conjuring them in through here, then there must be a place where the wards are relaxed."

"Who created these wards, those keeping us here and the ones cloaking the temple ruins?" In those first moments of joy, when I saw that Sorcha lived, it didn't occur to me that she might have been the one helping Edric and his Hunters. Even now, I dreaded her response would reveal that my long-lost aunt had acted against her kin, even if it had been against her will.

Her eyes flicked to the prisoners she'd set out to free. Then, in a hushed voice, she said, "Eventually they break. He tortures them for information. Then, when they can take no more, but before he's exhausted them beyond their ability to conjure, he bargains with them."

"For protection?"

"For magic that will hide this place, magic that will keep Fae from escaping, anything he thinks will help him. Once they've completed their end of the bargain, he kills them. He knows we can't undo what another has done. He knows the bargains will remain so long as he does. He makes sure of it."

"He hasn't used you this way?"

She shook her head.

"Why didn't you warn them?"

Her blue eyes glared at me. "Don't you think I've tried? You don't know what he does to them. What he'll do to you when he finds you. Come with us." Her hood had fallen back, revealing her golden hair, now loose and cascading around her face. Nearly as ancient as my mother, she still appeared young enough to be my older sister.

I shook my head. "I can't leave without Eve. I have to go

back for her."

"Our responsibility is to our people." She looked over her shoulder at the Fae who were waiting for her near the tunnel entrance. "You'd put their lives at risk for the sake of one human?" Of the seven sisters, Sorcha looked the most like Godda. They'd each had different sires, since male Fae could only sire one child, but Godda and Sorcha, the oldest and youngest, had ended up looking nearly identical despite that fact. Sorcha hadn't said so, but her appearance may have been what had ultimately prevented Edric from killing her.

I wanted to join her, but Evelyn was defenseless and innocent. She deserved a chance to live. "It's my fault she's here."

Sorcha narrowed her eyes at me. "Your feelings for her are getting in the way of your responsibilities. Did you come here to save her? Or to put an end to the Hunt?"

"I can do both." I'd find a way to destroy Edric before he could harm anyone else, even if it meant my own death.

She shook her head. "You know what you have to do. Most of the guards are at the party, but our absence will be noted soon. We need to go," she said.

"Go," I said. "Get them to safety. Find Ari, if you can. Tell her where we are." I knew she'd tell Ari and the others more than that. She'd tell them about my distraction, and Evelyn would be at Fiona's mercy if we got out of here alive. But I couldn't help that now. I needed backup.

Sorcha nodded. Then she turned and guided the others into the passage. She paused in the tunnel entrance and glanced at me over her shoulder.

"Good hunting," she whispered. Then she disappeared.

I turned and made my way back across the arena. We had a way out. Now I needed to get Evelyn and find whatever was holding Edric here so that I could destroy him. But first, I needed a weapon. I scoured the arena with my magic, searching for anything sharp and made from iron. Something near the wall caught my attention, and I switched directions to investigate.

My ball of light illuminated a hell beast claw lying partly covered in dirt on the arena floor. The claw was coated in a thick layer of dried blood. I'd never had much talent for Elemental magic, despite having such a powerful Elemental for a sire. Still, like any good apprentice, I knew the basics.

Cradling the claw in one hand, I focused on the iron in the dried blood. With my other hand, I reached for one of the metal rings imbedded in the stone wall. Similar rings, likely used to chain up the beasts occupying the arena when they weren't fighting, dotted the walls at regular intervals. I couldn't manufacture a weapon from nothing, but I could alter the makeup of the claw, so long as I had a source of additional material to pull from. Recalling an old lesson, I swapped out the organic material from the claw with iron from the metal ring until I was left with an iron claw and an organic ring.

I needed to find the object holding Edric here if I hoped to banish him completely. But even if I could only eliminate him temporarily, it might be enough to get Evelyn to safety and buy time until Arabella arrived. I tucked the claw into my pants and exited the arena the way I'd come in. Then I conjured myself back to my hiding place on the balcony overlooking the party.

15

NIGEL spun me around the dance floor. It gave my body something to do while my mind churned through everything I'd learned about Edric and Godda and my eyes searched the room for any sign of Liam.

"Why are you helping them?" I asked, looking toward the Hunters gathered at the edges of the dance floor.

"Why shouldn't I help them?" Nigel spun us closer to the center of the floor, away from the leering spirits.

"Edric's illogical and he's going to destroy the Fae just because he can't find his dead wife." I caught a glimpse of a red dress in the crowd and checked to make sure there wasn't a pointy-eared guy with wavy brown hair hanging on her every word. There wasn't. I sighed with relief, but then my heartbeat sped up again as I resumed worrying about where he could be and what could be keeping him.

Nigel intercepted my gaze and smiled at me. "You have to admit, it's a bit romantic."

"It's not romantic. It's insane." I scowled and turned my

head so I could glance past his shoulder.

Nigel shrugged. "If you went missing, wouldn't you want your true love to search for you to the ends of the earth and beyond?"

I started to reply, but he cut me off.

"Oh, that's right." He cocked his head. "Your Fae prince did try to come to your rescue. Though, I suppose that isn't turning out quite as well as planned, is it?"

"Liam isn't mine. And he may be trying to help me, but he isn't killing innocent people." I shifted my body, trying to increase the space between us.

Nigel kept his embrace firm, allowing only a tiny sliver of air between our bodies. "Are you quite sure about that?"

"Who did he kill?" I asked.

"I was referring to the true love bit, but if you'd prefer to discuss the body count, I'd say it's not so much 'who' as 'what' he's killed in his pathetic attempts to save you."

"So what if he killed a few of these spirits. They're already dead, anyway."

Nigel shook his head. "He didn't tell you about the hell beasts?"

I snorted. "You can't be serious."

"You don't know the first thing about hell beasts." He looked down his nose at me. I didn't think people actually did that.

"You're right. I don't. I don't know about any of this, and I was perfectly happy that way." Well, maybe not *perfectly* happy, but at least not in mortal danger.

"Then perhaps you need to be more selective about the blokes you snog." He grinned.

I narrowed my eyes and scowled at him. "Oh, and I suppose you think you would be a better choice?"

"Of course I would. If that obnoxious Fae hadn't gotten in the way, we could have had our nice, civilized date, and you'd never be in this mess."

"No. Instead I'd be dating a demon. Remind me again why that's better? Are there any men left in England who don't have supernatural powers? Or is it just my dumb luck to have run into all of you within days of setting foot in this cold and drizzly country?"

Nigel laughed. "Just say the word, and I'll take us somewhere more comfortable."

"I'm not leaving without Liam." I turned my head and scanned the crowd.

"I thought you said he wasn't yours. If that's true, then he's not your problem, love. You should be worried about saving your own skin. Aren't you at all concerned that he left you here to rot?"

There was a possibility that Liam had managed to escape and left me behind. But he'd said he'd help me escape, and now I knew he couldn't lie to me. Still, Nigel's words inserted a sliver of doubt, and I didn't want to give him the satisfaction of knowing it. "He won't leave without me."

Nigel started to reply, but cheers erupted at the far end of the room. The music stopped and everyone turned their attention to the source of the commotion. My stomach flipped and fear coursed through me, making my skin prickle. I strained to catch a glimpse past the other guests, hoping I wouldn't see Liam captured.

Nigel leaned toward me, his lips hovering just above my ear, and whispered, "You better hope you're right and your Fae prince shows up before Edric finds out he's done a runner."

The crowd parted and Edric emerged, boisterous and regal

in his finest armor. The Hunters cheered as he passed, calling out to him and shouting his name. He acknowledged them with a wave but continued walking, directly toward me. I gulped. Nigel was right. If Edric knew that Liam had escaped, he'd take it out on me. I needed to stall him and give Liam more time.

Edric stopped in front of me, and I tensed, but tried to keep my face relaxed. Nigel stepped aside to make room, but continued to watch my every move. I ignored him as Edric reached for my hand, lifting it to his lips. Only a brush of air caressed the back of my hand. No skin contact. He lifted his head to meet my eyes, but didn't let go of my fingers.

"I don't believe we were properly introduced earlier," he said. "What is your name, girl?"

My throat felt dry and my skin prickled at his touch. It felt like a damp towel had been wrapped around my hand. There was no pressure or warmth in the touch, and I fought the urge to shiver.

"Evelyn," I finally managed say.

"Evelyn. What a lovely name," he said. The other spirits had closed in behind him. They leered at me over Edric's shoulder.

"And how are you enjoying my humble solstice party?"

"It's quite impressive," I said.

"Has your escort been keeping you entertained?" he asked.

I glanced over at Nigel, and he winked at me. I forced my lips into a smile. "Yes," I said. "He's been very...entertaining."

"Good, good." Edric released my hand and began looking around the ballroom. "Now, where is our champion?"

My heart raced. I needed to distract him. "Lord Edric," I said. "I have a question for you."

Edric turned to face me. His hands rested on his hips, just

above his belt, and his chest puffed under the armor plate covering it. I had his attention. Now I just needed to come up with a question to ask. A flash near the arched stone ceiling caught my eye. I assumed it was a trick of the lighting, but I didn't dare glance away or let it distract me. I needed to keep Edric's attention on me until Liam returned.

"What is it, girl?" he asked.

"They say that when you were alive, you were the greatest hunter in all of England. Is that true?" A plan had begun to take shape in my mind. If I could get him talking, maybe he might unknowingly give me a clue about the object holding him here.

Edric's brow wrinkled over his hooded eyes. "I'd say more than just England, girl. Alive or dead, I'm still the greatest hunter. Aren't I, men?" He opened his arms and glanced around as the spirits surrounding him roared their approval.

I rubbed my damp fingers against the smooth silk of my dress and waited for the cheers to die down. "Of course. I only just wondered if you had a secret to your success?"

He tucked a thumb into the strap on the hunting horn hanging across his chest as he considered the question. "Who needs tricks when you have skill?"

Pieces of what I'd read and what Liam had told me about the artifacts fell into place. "It's just, I thought you had an enchanted shield that protected you from harm."

Edric leaned closer, and I took a step back, colliding into Nigel. "Who told you that, girl?"

His nearness reminded me of the knife that had been held at my throat. I shivered, and Nigel slipped a hand around my waist to steady me. "I...I don't remember..." I shook my head to clear it and find my courage. Then I stepped away from Nigel. "I just thought it odd that such an expert hunter would need an enchanted shield to protect him."

"Watch it, girl. Your kind aren't usually welcome here. We've made an exception for you on this night, so long as you continue to behave." Edric glanced around. "Now where are Lilium and the champion hiding?"

Stubby red horns surrounded by black curls bobbed through the figures gathered behind Edric. I panicked.

"Looking for me?" a familiar voice called out, and the spirits surrounding Liam dispersed.

Liam stepped into view, and I reached for him, but Nigel's strong hand on my waist held me in place. The demon woman emerged from behind Edric at the same time, and she paused to stand just behind his shoulder.

"Lilium," Edric said without turning to look at her, "I thought you were keeping a close eye on this one?"

"I was, Your Lordship," she replied, her voice a sultry purr.

"So how is it that he is not with you?"

"The girl helped hide him," she said.

———

"Nonsense." I stepped forward, trying to position myself between Edric and Evelyn. "I just didn't enjoy being under your spell. It made me a rather dull party guest."

The demon woman grabbed my arm and pulled me toward her. She placed the fingers of her other hand near my temple. I had a moment to shield my thoughts before she began probing at my mind, reaching for my memories. I couldn't risk succumbing to the demon woman's power again. So I avoided her glaring eyes as she searched for a way to break my defenses.

"He's hiding something," she said, releasing me in frustration.

Edric stepped closer. "Where have you been, Fae?" He wasn't close enough to me yet. I needed to draw him within reach so I could stab him with the iron claw.

"In the dungeons." He knew I couldn't lie. I could only hope he wouldn't connect me to Sorcha and ask me about her, or the other prisoners.

"You'll never find a way to escape," she said. "We've made sure of that."

"Why would he try to escape?" he asked Lilium before turning his attention to me. "I heard how you fought your way in here, Fae. My men thought it would be fun to put you up against Lilium's beasts, and somehow you managed to kill them all to become our Solstice Champion. Do you know what that means, Fae?"

I shrugged. "You enchant me and toy with me for entertainment?" I longed to reach for the claw, but the crowd was too close. His lieutenants would be on me the moment I revealed my weapon. I'd only have one chance to stab him, grab Evelyn, and escape.

Edric laughed. "Oh, you'll be our entertainment. That much is true. And sooner than planned, since you decided to run off without your chaperone." He shook his head. "I thought I could appeal to your sense of honor, but you and your kind have no honor, do you? Godda broke her promise to me. Why should I expect any different from her kin?"

Rage boiled through me as I lunged toward Edric. "Godda did no such thing. You were the one who broke your promise to her." I jabbed my finger into his chest armor, but it met with no resistance. Instead, it felt like I'd plunged my hand into a swampy pit. Disgust contorted my face, and I shook my hand as if that would help get the slick feeling off faster.

"What do you know of it, Fae? Hmm?" Edric leaned toward me, pressing his face close to mine.

"I know what happened," I said. "Every Fae child has heard the story. We know you're a selfish liar."

Edric threw his head back and laughed. "I'm sure they tell little Faelings all sort of nonsense. But I was there." His eyes narrowed. "She left me." He clenched his fists and raised them between us. "And I will find her and bring her home." The spirits gathered behind him cheered.

Motion at the edge of my vision distracted me. A quick glance revealed Evelyn struggling with Nigel. He was holding her back, trying to keep her quiet. I would have told her to listen to him and stay out of it, but I didn't dare take my eyes off Edric.

When the cheers died down, Edric spoke again. "You have nerve, Fae. You insult me and disregard my hospitality. I'm afraid your time as guest is over." He flicked his wrist, and his lieutenants straightened to attention at his side. "Prepare the champion for sacrifice. Restrain him." The crowd roared in response.

Before I could move, Edric's lieutenants slapped shackles around my wrists and tugged at the chains, testing them. Evelyn made a strangled sound as they led me to the platform with the altar at the front of the room. I couldn't look at her.

I twisted and strained against the chains. Sacrifice did not sound promising. I scanned the faces staring up at me and easily spotted Evelyn fighting with Nigel, trying to pull him toward the platform while the demon woman whispered to Edric. The Hunters had lost all pretense of playing at being human. They floated, hovering above the ground, loosening their hold on the illusions that gave them corporeal forms. Some of them wisped through the air, flitting from group to group in a blur of excitement. The few demons in attendance moved toward the edge of the room and began to cluster near the exit. Only Nigel and Lilium remained in the midst of the chaos.

"Silence!" Edric's voice boomed.

The room fell quiet at Edric's command. The blur of movement stilled, but the spirits didn't regain their human forms. They hovered, waiting for the Master's next command.

"As is our tradition, one who has shown great strength will be sacrificed so his strength will flow to us and allow us to ride and hunt this solstice. The Lady Lilium has agreed to assist us in this regard."

The demon woman nodded to Edric, and the crowd cheered. She walked toward Nigel, who was keeping a firm grip on Evelyn's arm, and whispered something to him. Then she stalked toward the platform.

Evelyn turned her face toward me with wide eyes. She shoved the halfling, trying to break free, and winced in pain when he didn't break his hold. I pulled against my chains and tried conjuring fireballs in my hands. Light flashed, but the flame wouldn't burn. The demon woman, Lilium, smiled. She had me right where she wanted me, defenseless and displayed in front of an appreciative audience.

"Remember, Lilium," Edric called to her. "We need him alive."

I prepared my mental shields, readying myself for her assault. But instead of attacking my mind, she flicked her wrists, and a long, winding form flew at me. At first, it looked like a scarf, stretched out horizontally and flying through the air directly at my face. As it twisted and drew closer, the form gained roundness and girth.

Moments before it hit my torso, my brain registered the form and I recoiled instinctively. But it was too late. The serpent slammed against my chest and wrapped itself around me. Its body was thicker than my arm, and I estimated its length to be at least as long as I stood tall. It wound around me, scales glinting in the light. Then it began to squeeze.

I sucked in a breath and tried to hold my rib cage firm, breathing shallowly so I wouldn't give it the chance to crush my lung capacity. But my chest muscles were no match for the lean serpent. I began to sweat and shake as I tried to keep my muscles tense. Patiently, it chipped away at my endurance, tightening its grip as soon as I gave it an opening.

Lilium stepped up on the platform and swaggered toward me. "Fae," she said. "You'll pay for what you did to my pets." She stepped in front of me and ran a hand lovingly over the serpent's body. It stretched its long neck toward her and flicked its forked tongue. "And you'll pay for the hell your kin thrust on me and my family."

Great. Another creature of the Underworld had a grudge against my family. Her nails pierced the shirt fabric stretched across my shoulders and dug into my skin. The punctures burned, sending a red-hot searing pain up my arm. My chest collapsed as I exhaled. The serpent wound itself tighter around me, and my mental defenses collapsed. Another stab of pain, and my vision blurred.

16

I FOUGHT against Nigel, screaming at them to stop. Nigel tried to clamp a hand over my mouth, but I bit him and twisted away.

The crowd had closed in on the platform, and I couldn't see around the hovering spirits. I could see through some of them, though, enough to make out the hazy details of what Nigel's mother was doing to Liam up on that stage. Why hadn't he conjured himself away from here? Why was he putting up with this torture?

"Nigel, please," I begged. "Please. Help him!"

"I can't interfere," he said. "And if you know what's good for you, you'll let me get you out of here while they're otherwise occupied."

"I can't leave him here. They'll kill him. You heard Edric."

"He said they needed him alive."

"He said 'sacrifice,' Nigel." I glared at him. "I know what that means."

Nigel shrugged. "I can't say he doesn't deserve it."

"For what?" I shoved at Nigel's chest. "For killing some hell beasts? He doesn't know where Godda is. Neither of us do. You know that."

Cheers erupted behind me. I'd shifted my attention to Nigel and turned my back on the stage. I spun around in time to see Liam's head fall to his chest. It bobbed there as he hung suspended between the chains that held his arms outstretched. The demon woman turned to face the audience, a sly smile spreading across her face. The crowd went wild.

"Don't worry, Edric," she called. "He's still alive." She flicked her wrist, and Liam's head snapped up, eyes open and staring blankly, unseeing, out into the audience. "But now he's under my control."

The Hunters began to roar and yell in appreciation. My heart lurched. Up until this moment, I had convinced myself we'd find a way to escape. Seeing Liam's blank stare, seeing him at the mercy of that merciless woman, made a chill creep over me. If I valued my life, Nigel was right. I needed to get out of here. Fast. The world suddenly seemed much scarier than it ever had back in sunny California.

"Silence!" Edric called. The Hunters obeyed. "Find out if he knows where Godda is," he commanded.

"He doesn't know," I moaned. My voice carried farther in the silence than I had intended. Edric's eyes turned to me, and all the others followed his lead, including Nigel's mother.

"We'll see about that," she said. She stepped toward Liam and placed her fingertips at his temples.

Edric leaned closer to me. "How are you so certain that he doesn't know?" he asked.

"He told me, and Fae can't lie."

"The girl is correct. The Fae doesn't know where your wife is hiding," Lilium said.

"He's using his powers to keep the location from you," Edric yelled. "It must be there."

"He's keeping nothing from me. His mind is completely open. He is at my command."

Edric glanced between me and Liam. "His feelings for the girl?" he asked Lilium.

Nigel's mother closed her eyes a moment. Nigel tensed beside me, his hand gripping me tighter.

"They are what we suspected."

"Good." He turned to Nigel. "Bring her to the platform."

"But, sir," Nigel said. "You said..."

"Bring the girl," Lilium commanded. Her voice rang out, echoing off the arched stone ceiling.

I stared at Nigel, silently begging him to help. But he pushed me forward and forced me toward the stage. Edric followed in our wake. I watched Liam's face as we approached. His eyes remained unfocused, staring out into the crowd. Nigel reached to guide me, but I shook him off and continued walking toward Liam. If Nigel wouldn't help me, I'd figure out how to save Liam on my own.

I stepped up onto the platform. Edric and Nigel followed closely behind, both of them pressing me toward the demon woman. She'd removed her hands from Liam's head and positioned herself in front of him on the platform so I could no longer see him.

"The sacrifice will be most powerful if he submits to it willingly," Edric said to Lilium as we approached. "If you indeed have control over the Fae's mind, release his chains and call off the serpent."

The sly smile reappeared on the demon woman's face. The spirits standing guard released the cuffs around Liam's wrists, and they snapped open and clattered onto the platform. The serpent uncoiled itself and slithered over to Lilium. She reached a hand down, and it climbed her arm and draped itself across her shoulders. Defenseless, Liam's body sagged like a puppet resting on its strings.

At the demon woman's command, Liam's mind took control of his body, and he snapped to attention. Fear coursed through me. With a flick of her wrist, she'd brought Liam under her command, and he had magic and training. I had nothing. She could break me with a thought.

"Good," Edric said. He turned to Nigel. "Now, make sure the girl knows nothing of Godda before we eliminate her."

My heart beat faster. My mouth went dry. I gulped and stared at Nigel, even though I knew it was pointless to hope he wouldn't follow orders.

Nigel stared back at me until Lilium snapped him out of it by saying, "You heard the Master. Are you a demon or not? Do I have to do everything?"

Nigel took a step toward me, then he was in my mind. I closed my eyes and twisted away, lifting my hands to cover my temples, but it was too late.

I'm sorry, he thought at me. *I have to.*

Get out! I screamed at him in my mind.

Memories filtered through my consciousness, rewinding back through my time at Lydbury. To Oscar and Vivian. To Angie dropping me off at the airport. Back to the events leading up to my trip. He didn't need to see this. These were my memories. My feelings. I winced and moaned.

He paced around me, replaying moments I didn't ever want to see again. Then he stumbled. He recoiled from my pain. "She doesn't know anything," he said aloud, for Lilium and Edric to hear.

"You already knew that," I snarled at him. Once again, I

was powerless. Only this time, I had nothing to lose. I lunged at him.

He stepped back, colliding with his mother. She spun on him in a rage. In the process, she lost control of Liam. She swiped at Nigel, her snake hissing and striking as she lunged for him. Nigel glanced toward me, then grabbed his mother and shoved her toward the back of the platform. She struggled against his hold, then they disappeared.

There wasn't time to consider where they'd gone. Edric was already commanding his guards to recapture Liam. I yelled a warning, and Liam's eyes blinked and focused. Then he crouched into a fighting stance as Edric's guards glided toward him.

At the same time, I rushed toward Edric, forgetting that he was a spirit and his form wasn't solid. Connecting with him was like jumping into a cold, wet marsh. Instinctively, my eyes snapped shut, and I recoiled. My hand landed on something solid, and I grabbed for it, pulling it with me as I stumbled backward. A cord snapped, and just as I thought I'd got my feet under me, I tripped as the tension released and lurched backward again.

I opened my eyes and looked down at my hand. In it was Edric's hunting horn that had been hanging across his chest. The crowd fell silent, and an eerie stillness surrounded me. I looked up and found Edric staring at me.

"Now be a good girl and give that back," Edric said.

I gripped the horn and glared at him. I had something he wanted. He had something I wanted. I glanced at Liam. The guards hovered near him but hadn't tried to restrain him yet. He was crouched between them with his back to me, and I didn't want to distract him.

I turned to face Edric. "Let him go," I said.

Edric took a cautious step toward me. "Give that to me, and I'll consider it," he said.

I wondered if I'd heard him correctly. He was willing to trade a hunting horn for Liam? That's when I realized what I must be holding. I remembered what Liam had said about Edric's soul.

"Horcrux," I said, gripping the horn tighter.

"What did you call me?" Edric's hands clenched into fists at his sides.

I looked down at the horn and wondered what animal he'd stolen it from. It was hollow inside and bone colored. There were carvings etched on the outside surface, and leather wrapped around a piece of metal at the tip, which I assumed served as the mouthpiece. The laces that had attached it to his belt dangled from a strip of leather wrapped around the midpoint of the horn. I glanced back at Edric and raised the horn, slowly, as though I were about to hand it to him. Hope flickered across his eyes.

Then I yelled, "Liam, catch!" I waited for him to turn, then tossed him the horn. He caught it, realized what he had, and set it aflame in his hands.

I watched as the horror dawned on Edric's face. He screamed, a piercing, whistling noise that sounded more like a gust of wind howling across a field than a human cry. He lunged for me, losing his grip on his human form and rushing toward me like a wall of thick smoke. Then the smoke disappeared, and a black object, hooked and pointed at one end, clattered to the ground at my feet.

Liam rushed to my side and threw his arms around me. Then the world disappeared. I gasped for air in the darkness, cold pressing in on me from all sides. I could no longer feel Liam's arms around me. I couldn't breathe, and I panicked.

"Shh…" I wrapped my arms around Evelyn and tried to muffle her screams by pressing her against my body. "It's okay," I whispered. "It's okay, we're safe now." Or at least safer than we were before. I hadn't had time to warn her I was about to conjure us out of there. And she'd had no idea what to expect. I decided I should be grateful she was at least conscious and standing on her own two feet, even if she was hysterical.

"Eve," I tried again, whispering softly to her. "Eve, shhhh. It's okay." I smoothed her hair with my hand. "Hey, I need you to listen to me, please? Please, Eve?" Her screams had turned to muffled sobs, and now they were dying down to hiccups.

"What." She inhaled a deep breath. "Was." Exhale. "That." Another deep inhale, like she was teaching herself to breathe again. I'd forgotten what it was like to travel like that for the first time.

"I conjured us out of there. Sorry, I didn't have time to warn you."

"Air," she breathed. "There was no air."

"Yeah." I frowned and cupped her face in my hands. "I'm sorry. Are you okay?"

She nodded. "I think so," she whispered.

"Nice work back there." I smiled and kissed her forehead. "Now, we better get out of here before they find us. Can you run?"

She cocked her head at me and looked at me like I'd asked if the sky was blue. Then she reached down to the hem of her dress and began to tear.

"Help me with this," she said as she pulled and the fabric began to rip a long slit up the length of her leg.

I got the general idea of what she was after, and I removed the lower two-thirds of her skirt with magic, revealing her long, lean legs. Runner's legs.

"Thanks," she said.

I tore my eyes off her legs and blinked at her. "Right," I said. "Let's go."

I opened the door to the arena and waved Evelyn inside, ahead of me.

"It's dark in here," she said. "And..." She covered her nose and mouth with her forearm. "What's that smell?"

I conjured a ball of light and let it float ahead of us. "Hell beasts," I said. They may have been removed, but she was right, the arena still stank of their blood.

Her eyes went wide. "This is where you—"

"Yes," I said, interrupting her. I took her hand, the one that wasn't covering her face, and led her across to the tunnel. Her hand hung limply in mine, and she craned her neck to study the room.

"Why would you bring us back here?" she asked.

"There's a tunnel," I said. "Up here."

Noises in the corridor behind us reminded me that we needed to hurry. Edric and his Hunters may be gone, but Lilium's demons might still be after us. I extinguished the light and started moving faster, allowing my senses to lead the way.

"Stay close to me," I whispered.

Evelyn gripped my hand tightly and sped up to match my pace. When we reached the mouth of the tunnel, I pulled her inside and held my open palm between us. I conjured a dim light and let it glow so I could see her face.

"I'm going to need to transform into my animal form," I explained. I watched her face closely for a reaction, but she just nodded. "That will make it easier to follow the trail out."

"Okay," she said. "It can't be any worse than anything else I've seen today."

I laughed. "Good point." I let the ball of light grow and released it far ahead of us in the tunnel, hoping the glow wouldn't be visible to anyone searching the arena. I would be able to use my night vision, but I didn't want Evelyn running in the dark.

"Ready?" I asked.

"Wait," she said. "Is there anything you can do about my shoes?"

I cringed. I couldn't just conjure her a pair of running shoes out of thin air. The slippers they'd given her to wear to the ball seemed sturdy. At least they didn't have high heels.

"I can prevent them from slipping off your feet, but that's about it, I think."

"Do it," she said.

I spelled them to her feet, and then, without further warning, transformed.

Evelyn took a step backward and pressed herself against the wall. She looked terrified. I had no voice to reassure her, and I decided it would only make it worse if I growled. Instead, I bowed to her, stretching my front paws out before me and lowering my head until it nearly touched the ground.

She took a cautious step away from the wall. "Can you understand me?" she asked.

I nodded.

"Okay. You win. That is probably the strangest thing I've seen today."

I rolled over onto my back and exposed my belly to her, arching my head back so I could still see her face.

"Yeah." She laughed. "Belly rubs later. Let's get out of here."

I pounced to my feet, and she jumped back. I crept closer and rubbed against her legs. Those legs. I purred.

She laughed and gave me a little shove. "Go," she said.

I took off at a loping run, and she easily pulled alongside me. I focused my senses on following the scent of Sorcha and the others. I lost myself in following the trail, and we'd been running for some time before I realized I'd picked up the pace considerably. I turned my head to see if she'd fallen behind, but she'd kept pace with me. This girl was strong and fast, and I loved it.

I was so lost in the joy of running alongside Evelyn and absorbed in the amplified senses of my animal form, that I didn't notice the wall until we were nearly upon it. I slowed and skidded to a halt. Evelyn stopped alongside me and placed her hands on her head, breathing hard. I considered the vertical iron bars posted across the opening of the tunnel. Beyond the bars, the tunnel was boarded up, with wooden planks covering the opening. I nosed around at the feet of the iron bars, searching for the scent of the others who must have passed this way.

"Did we miss a turn?" Evelyn asked.

I growled softly and shook my head. They'd been here, I could smell it. But then they'd disappeared. Something about the bars tugged at my memory. I'd seen this somewhere before. I transformed so I could use my magic and confer with Evelyn.

"They were here," I said. "But they didn't go that way." I pointed toward the bars.

"Did they..." She paused and made an explosion gesture with her hands. "Poof," she added.

I snorted. "Maybe. If Sorcha knew where they were." But how would she have known? I turned to face the bars. "Wait,"

I said. "I think I know where we are." I raised my hand, palm facing the bars, and cast a revealing spell. Markings in the planks began to glow.

"What are those marks?" Evelyn asked.

"Wards. Fae wards. It's a protection spell, meant to keep out creatures who mean to harm us." I let the spell fade and turned to face Evelyn. "But what's more important is that I know where we are."

She gestured toward the now-invisible marks. "From those?"

"No," I said. "I think I ended up on the other side of these marks when I was exploring in the cellar at your uncle's house."

"Are you saying that this tunnel leads back to Lydbury?"

I nodded. "I'm not positive, but how many other boarded-up tunnels can there be just lying about underground near here?"

She raised her eyebrows.

"Yes. Okay. Valid point." I crossed my arms. "Perhaps it's best not to conjure us across, then."

"What would happen if you're wrong?"

"We'd be stuck between."

"With no air?"

I nodded.

She shook her head. "What else have you got?"

"I think we could pass through the wards. I'd just need to create an opening."

"But those are iron bars."

"Iron is Fae friendly. It's the man-made stuff that doesn't agree with us. Watch." I ran my hands over the bars and felt the metal heat under my touch until it became like taffy. Then I stretched and bent the bars to create a space wide enough to walk through.

Evelyn tiptoed forward and reached out a hand to touch the bars.

I caught her hand in midair. "It's still hot."

"That's amazing," she said.

I shrugged. "That's just the first part. Now we have to get past the wards." I stepped through the bars and placed my hands on the planks covering the opening. Then I muttered an incantation my mother had taught me years ago. It was the same incantation that unlocked the cottage where she lived, and where Arabella, Fiona, and I had grown up.

The wards glowed, giving off a pale-green light. Then a crack appeared. One vertical seam running from floor to ceiling. I slid my hands along the rough, unfinished wood until they were alongside the seam. Then I pressed. The wood groaned and crackled when I pressed against it, but the gap widened. I pressed harder, pushing until the gap was big enough for us to shimmy through.

"I'll go first," I said.

Evelyn nodded.

I slipped through the gap and cast a light down the dark tunnel. My paw prints still marked the dirt covering the tunnel floor. I poked my head through the gap and called to Evelyn to follow.

Once we were both through, I sealed the gap. Eventually, I'd probably have to come back and repair the iron bars on the far side. But that could wait until another night. All that mattered now was we were finally headed home.

"How far?" Evelyn asked.

"It's still a bit of a walk from here." I grinned at her. "Unless you feel like running some more?"

"Are we safe now?"

I shrugged. "Safe enough, I think."

"Is Edric really gone?"

"I think so."

"And what about Nigel and his mother?"

"I don't know." The moments leading up to Evelyn telling me to destroy the horn were still pretty hazy.

"I think Nigel saved us," she said. "But I don't know what made him change his mind."

"Maybe you finally convinced him."

"He was controlling me. Do you remember?"

I shook my head. "It's all jumbled. I don't know what's real and what she made me see." I stepped toward Evelyn and wrapped my arms around her. "It's going to be okay, now."

"What if they come after us?" She shivered. "He knows where I live."

"I won't let him hurt you."

"And what about your people? They're going to kill me for knowing what I know."

"I'll deal with them. I won't let any of them hurt you. You destroyed our biggest enemy. They'll make an exception." I tilted her head up until I could see her face. "Trust me?"

She sniffled and nodded. I leaned in and brushed her lips with mine, but one taste wasn't enough. I pressed my lips to hers again, longer this time. Her lips parted in response, and she slid against me. I ran my hands over the silky fabric of her dress, and she tightened her grip around my waist.

I kissed along her jaw and whispered in her ear, "Race you home."

She laughed and took off running. I transformed and then followed, pulling alongside and then ahead.

"No fair," she said. "You have four legs and I only have two!"

I growled and tossed my head, pulling farther ahead. She answered with a burst of speed and closed the distance. We played that way, most of the way home, taking turns in the lead, until the door to the cellar appeared before us.

We were both exhausted when we stopped in front of the door. I transformed and pushed open the door that I knew would lead us into the cellar at Lydbury. Giddy with the excitement of destroying Edric and escaping the dungeons, I didn't sense Arabella stalking toward us until it was too late.

"There you are," she said. "I've been searching everywhere for you, and what do I find?"

"Arabella, wait," I said. "Let me explain."

"I warned you. You didn't listen. She knows too much." Arabella flicked her wrist at Evelyn. I threw up a shield in reaction, but I wasn't fast enough. Some of Arabella's spell got past my shield. Evelyn's legs folded, and she started to collapse. I ran to her and caught her before she hit the ground.

"What did you do?" I screamed.

"You know the rules, Liam. Why are you protecting her?"

I felt Evelyn's neck for a pulse. Her heart was still beating faintly. I didn't inherit my sire's healing magic, so I concentrated on giving her some of my strength. "Come on," I whispered to her. "What did you throw at her, Ari?" I yelled over my shoulder.

"You can't be serious."

"It's not your call to make!" Sharing my strength with Evelyn made me weak. After all the fighting and the torture and the running, I wouldn't be able to keep this up much longer.

"It's not yours, either!"

"You don't understand. We owe her our lives. Just help me," I begged. "Please?"

"I can't believe you. You've spent too long among the humans. You've lost your mind. She's just a girl. In a hundred years, you won't even remember she exists."

I growled, deep and low, in my chest. "You have no idea what she did to save us. You don't get to decide her fate."

"Fine," she said. "I'll help you get her upstairs. Then we're calling Fiona to settle this." She crossed over to Evelyn's other side and helped me lift her. I stumbled and nearly blacked out as I pushed up onto my feet.

"Thank you," I said.

"You look like hell."

"It's been a long night."

17

I WOKE up in my room at my aunt's house staring at the unfamiliar ceiling. The events of the past few days came rushing back to me. I threw the duvet off and sat up, ready to search my body for wounds and bruising to prove that I hadn't been dreaming. Dizziness made my vision blur and my head swim. I wobbled, and a strong, dark-skinned arm reached out to steady me. I looked up and met the round brown eyes of a beautiful woman with twisted hair sticking up in short spikes.

"Hello, Evelyn." She knew my name, but I was certain I'd never seen her before.

"Do I know you?" I asked.

She laughed. "Not yet, though I hope we'll have a chance to get to know each other better. But first, why don't you lie down again. Your injuries required quite a bit of healing, and I'm afraid you're not yet ready to jump out of bed."

I reclined on my elbows and she pulled the duvet up over me. Then she propped some pillows behind me so we could talk without me straining myself.

"Is Liam okay?" I asked. "And Aunt Vivian and Uncle Oscar?"

"Yes," she said. "Everyone is well and asking after you. Especially Liam." She smiled. "But you needed time to heal, and I wanted to have a chat with you before I let the others in."

I blinked at her and tried to remember what had happened after Liam and I had returned.

"My name is Fiona," she said.

"You're Liam's cousin."

"Yes," she replied. "Liam told me what happened with Lord Edric. It sounds like I have much to thank you for."

"I just—"

"You were very brave, and quick thinking, and helped to put an end to a great enemy of my people. You may have even helped to end a war, though only time will tell that, I'm afraid."

"Liam said—"

"Yes." She nodded. "Liam told you that you'd have to die when we found out you know our secrets. That is our way."

My eyes widened. Had she come to kill me? Would she have let me live just to kill me?

"I am, however, willing to make an exception for you," she said. "I can see how much you mean to my cousin. He cares for you a great deal. I know he thinks our troubles are over now that the Wild Hunt has ended. But I need him by my side to help me rebuild."

I didn't say anything. I worried that, if I spoke, I might say the wrong thing and she might change her mind about letting me live.

"But," she continued, "if I let you live, I can't have you out in the world knowing what you know. You'll need to decide.

You can either give up Liam, and I'll erase your memories of the past few days, or you can accept a place in the Court as one of my Sworn, and I will grant you immortality."

I opened my mouth to respond, but she held up her hand to stop me.

"Wait," she said. "I want to give you time to consider your options. You have family and a future, human. This will not be an easy decision for you. You will have until the coronation ceremony to decide. I can't tell you exactly when that will be. It may be soon, or it may be weeks from now. Until then, you must promise me that you will tell no one of what you've seen and what you know. If you do, I will know. My offer will be withdrawn, and your fate will be sealed, as will theirs."

I swallowed.

"Do you agree to these terms?"

"Yes, Your Majesty," I said.

She smiled, but there was sadness in her eyes. "I am not yet queen, human. That honor still belongs to another." She stood and turned to leave. "I will let the others know that you are ready to receive visitors. I know they are anxious to see you."

"Wait!" I called after her. "What about Aunt Vivian and Uncle Oscar? What will happen to them?"

"Oscar is a direct descendent of Edric and Godda. He was already aware of our existence, but you will not speak openly of this with him. Do you understand?"

I nodded. I wasn't entirely sure that I did understand, but I was too stunned by this new information about my uncle to clarify. Fiona had her hand on the doorknob, about to leave the room, when I thought of another question.

"Does Liam know about the offer you've made me?"

She turned to face me. "I told him I would consider his plea on your behalf. But he does not yet know about this offer. It must be your decision. I'll not have him influencing you."

I nodded. "Thank you," I said.

"You needn't thank me, human. I should be the one thanking you." She bowed her head to me. "You have my thanks, and my offer. I'll leave you now." She turned and slipped out of the room.

I sighed back on the pillows. Sworn and immortal. Or I could return to my normal life with no memories of this other world. I didn't owe them anything. I'd spent enough time in their world to know that it was dangerous. But then again, so was my world. I wanted to ask Aunt Vivian for advice, but I'd just promised not to do that. I frowned. Fiona had said it must be my decision.

My phone began to ring, and I jumped at the sound. When I reached over to the bedside table to grab it, Angie's face filled my screen. I swiped to take the call.

"Angie?" Seeing her reminded me of what I'd be giving up if I accepted Fiona's offer.

"Hey, girl! Where have you been? I've been texting and calling. I left you so many messages. I was beginning to get worried about you. Are you okay?"

I considered how to respond to that, given my current state and the events of the past few days. "I'm fine," I said. "I've just been busy." Which was true. I had been busy. The rest I would have to keep secret, possibly forever, or at least until the memories had been erased.

"Too busy to call your best friend?"

"Sorry."

"It's fine. I just wanted to see how things are going. Have you decided when are you coming home?"

"I..." I hadn't planned that far ahead, and now I faced an

even bigger decision. If I chose to become Sworn would I even be able to continue working with my uncle and going to graduate school? If I chose to forget would I be compelled to leave? "I don't know. I don't have a return ticket yet."

"Well, figure it out and let me know. I'm back next week."

"Okay. I will." I paused, considering what else to say, my mind still stuck on the decision that loomed before me, and the questions I hadn't thought to ask.

"Hey, Evie?"

"Yeah?"

"Whatever it is that you're not telling me? It's gonna be okay, girl."

I cringed. Keeping secrets from Angie was hard enough without her knowing I wasn't telling her everything. "Thanks, Ang. I've missed you."

"Miss you, too. And if I don't hear from you in a few days, I'm flying out there to see for myself what's up with you."

I laughed. "Bye, Ang."

"Bye, girl!"

After hanging up with Angie, I sent a quick text to my mom so that she wouldn't worry about me. The last thing I needed right now was her asking questions I couldn't answer. Then I turned the sound off and dropped my phone on the table. Fiona's offer weighed on my mind. I'd always thought my future was so clear. I had it all figured out. But now this whole new world had opened up for me and I wasn't so sure anymore.

A knock at my door pulled me from my thoughts.

"Eve?" Liam's head appeared around the edge of the door.

"Hi," I said.

"Can I come in?"

"Yes!" I smiled at him. "I'd get up, but your cousin said I can't get out of bed yet."

"Did she say anything about me getting into bed with you?" He shut the door behind him and leaned against it. Then he flashed me his adorable sheepish grin. He'd resumed his glamour, and his hair had returned to resembling a shaggy mop on the top of his head. A scruffy beard obscured his chin, and he was wearing the same stretched and misshapen wool sweater that he'd had on when I met him. But somehow, he looked different now. I could almost see through his magic to the tall frame, lean muscles, and pointy ears underneath.

I grinned. "Come here."

He sat gently on the bed next to me. "I was so worried about you." His fingers skimmed my jaw.

"I'm fine."

"But you weren't," he said. He shook his head. "You don't remember, do you?"

I searched for the last thing I remembered. Liam transforming into a mountain lion. Us running through the tunnels. Laughing. Then nothing. I shook my head.

"It's okay now. Fiona fixed you." He smiled. "I think that means I've convinced her to let you live. I mean, she wouldn't have gone to all that trouble to fix you up just to kill you, would she?"

I grimaced.

"Sorry," he said. "I'm sorry." He clasped my hands in his. "I didn't mean it like that. You should know I'd never let her hurt you. You know that, don't you?"

"Shh..." I said. "It's okay."

"Did she say anything to you?"

"She gave me some things to think about," I said. "How is your mother?"

"She's fading. But there is one last problem she must deal with before she goes." He sighed. "Actually, it involves you."

"Me?"

"Yes. It has to do with Godda's bracelet. We were waiting for you to recover before we dealt with it."

"The bracelet belongs with your people. As long as Oscar agrees, your mother can have it, or give it to whomever she chooses."

"I'm afraid it's not that simple." Liam shook his head. "You're not going to believe this, but it was there the whole time. Right under our noses."

"What was?"

"Sorcha discovered it. She first noticed it in the dungeons, but she couldn't be sure until she returned to our lands and conferred with Mother and Fiona."

"Noticed what?"

"The markings on the bracelet. When Godda disappeared, she hid her life force in that bracelet."

"She's in the bracelet? You can bring her back?"

"No. Not like that. The markings explain everything. It was part of the final spell she cast, the deal she made with Edric. He swore to honor her and never speak against her or her kin, and in turn, she agreed to give up everything, become human, and be with him. She did love him, you see."

"But I don't understand. How did she end up in the brace-let?"

"Edric broke his promise. When she disappeared, her life ended. She couldn't return to the life she'd given up. But the spell kept her life force safe, so it could be released by her kin to return to the source we draw on to supply our magic."

"So, what do you need me for?"

"You're the owner of the bracelet now. Oscar gave it to you. Mother needs you to unlock the spell."

"And how does she expect me to do that?" Fiona's offer

had been immortality, not magic.

"I guess we'll find out when you meet her."

"You're taking me to meet your mother?" I raised my eyebrows.

"Not today. Fiona says you need more rest."

I shook my head. "There's so much I don't know about your world."

"You can't be expected to know everything. You didn't even know my world existed a few days ago." He squeezed my shoulder, then trailed his fingers down my arm.

"Are you sad?" I asked. "About your mother?"

He nodded. "She's lived an impossibly long life, even for one of us." His gaze drifted away from mine, and he focused on the wall above my head. "But it's more than that. After she's gone, I'll need to decide."

"Decide?" This sounded familiar. Only, apparently he was allowed to talk with me about his decision.

His lips pressed together and he nodded. "When they crown Fiona as queen, Arabella and I will be expected to swear our Oaths."

He'd mentioned this when he'd first told me that his mother was Queen of the Fae. But with all that had happened since then, I'd forgotten. Fiona had also mentioned something about needing Liam by her side. This was probably what she'd meant.

"Your cousin needs you," I said.

"I'd be committing myself to a life of war and vengeance."

"But Edric's gone."

He shook his head. "Edric may be gone, but I'm not convinced this is over. Ari's already gone looking for the demons. They should never have joined with Edric and his Hunters. We need to find out why they're against us and what it means for our future. There are so few of us left now."

"All the more reason why you should remain at Fiona's side." I'd seen what Nigel and his mother could do. He'd been inside my head. If Fiona erased my memories, I would never have to remember that experience. But I would also be completely unprepared if he ever found me again. I shivered.

"I was just beginning to enjoy it here." He smiled.

"Working with Uncle Oscar?"

"And spending time with you."

"Would you have to leave?"

He shrugged. "Oscar still needs help with his projects. But, as far as Ari is concerned, my work here is done."

I yawned. "Sorry," I said.

"No," he said. "I'm sorry. I should let you get some rest."

He started to stand, but I pulled him back down.

"Stay for a while," I said. "At least until I fall asleep."

He pulled the duvet up over my shoulders and curled alongside me. My mind kept going over Fiona's offer and everything Liam had told me about Godda and the Oath. But Liam began tracing patterns on my arm with his fingers, and soon I relaxed enough to drift off to sleep.

———

While I waited for Evelyn to heal enough for us to travel to the cottage, I avoided contact with my family, especially Arabella. Oscar had been keeping me busy, and I'd nearly cataloged the entire cellar room before Fiona cleared Evelyn for travel.

"She's ready." Fiona said, appearing in the doorway to the cellar room.

I looked up from the crate I'd been repacking and labeling. "Should we leave now?"

Fiona nodded. Her face was grim.

"What's going to happen to her, Fi?"

"That's her decision."

"But you'll let her live?"

"She's earned that much." Fiona glanced around the room. "Oscar says you've done good work here. He'd like to see you stay on."

"Even though he knows?"

She nodded. "We had a long talk. I think he might have always suspected you weren't as wholesome as you appeared."

I laughed. "He doesn't mind that we meddled with the artifacts?"

"We agreed that the enchantments were too dangerous to leave. Now that Edric's gone, Sorcha was able to remove all trace of magic from the dagger and the shield. To a human, there's no difference."

"So there's no reason for me to continue here?"

"He understands you won't be returning," she said. "What you do next is up to you." She crossed her arms and studied me silently. "I should go and prepare Flida for your arrival," she said.

I bowed my head to her. When I raised it, she was gone. I finished taping down the lid of the crate. Then I took the stairs two at a time in my hurry to get up to Evelyn's room. I found her standing in front of her mirror fussing with her hair.

"Leave it," I said. "You look great."

She frowned. "What do you even wear to meet the Queen of the Fae?"

I slid up behind her and wrapped my hands around her waist. "Are you worried because she's queen or because she's my mum?" I asked, watching her face in the mirror for a reaction.

She glared at my reflection. "You should be the one worried. Are you really wearing that?"

I hadn't even noticed my clothes. I stepped away from her to examine my ensemble. She had a point. I snapped my fingers and dropped my glamour, exchanging the dusty, moth-eaten sweater and jeans for a dark-green belted tunic and formfitting tan pants.

Evelyn spun to face me, her lips curled in consideration. "If this is what passes for Fae casual, no wonder you were so human-fashion challenged."

I brushed my hands down the front of my tunic. "What's wrong with this?"

She sighed against me and wrapped her arms around me. "Nothing."

I kissed the top of her head, inhaling the tropical scent of her shampoo. "All right. Take a deep breath," I said. "And don't freak out."

I waited for her to inhale, then I conjured us to the lawn outside the cottage.

"Okay?" I asked, leaning back and looking down at her.

She nodded. "That wasn't as bad."

"I had a chance to warn you this time."

She laughed and pulled away from me, turning to take in the lush grass and drooping green trees that surrounded Mother's cottage.

"It's beautiful," she said. "You grew up here?"

"Hard to believe?" I asked.

She looked at me. "No," she said. "Actually, you look very much at home here." She gestured to my clothes and grinned.

I laughed and reached for her hand. "Come on," I said. "Let's go inside."

I led her through the entry and caught a glimpse of Arabella before turning toward my mother's room. If she knew what was good for her, she'd stay as far away from me as possible. We hadn't spoken since she'd helped me carry Evelyn to her room, and I was in no mood for a fight. I let Evelyn walk ahead of me down the hall and glanced back over my shoulder to make sure Arabella wasn't following.

Fiona greeted us when we stepped into the candlelit room. Sorcha sat at my mother's bedside, holding her hand and talking with her in soft tones. Mother's pale skin appeared nearly translucent and blended with the white bedding, making her dark-brown hair stand out in contrast. I wound my arm around Evelyn's waist and led her to the bedside opposite Sorcha.

"Mother," I said.

"Liam!" She turned to me, slipped her hand from Sorcha's grasp, and reached for mine. I clutched her outstretched hands and bent to place a kiss on her soft, dry cheek.

"I've brought Eve," I said.

Evelyn stepped forward and dropped into a curtsy. I bit my lip to keep from laughing.

"Hello," she said.

"Come closer, child," my mother said, letting her hands slip from mine so she could beckon to Evelyn. I traded places with Evelyn, and she let my mother grip her hands. "I hear you saved my son from that awful barbarian that I had the misfortune to call brother-in-law." Her voice was barely more than a whisper, but it still conveyed all the strength and humor of her youth.

"No, I just—" Evelyn started to respond, but Mother cut her off.

"Don't be modest, child," she said. "I'm glad you were there with Liam. It sounds like you make a good pair."

"Thank you, ma'am," Evelyn said, ducking her head at the compliment.

"It appears you not only helped get rid of our enemy and return a sister to me, but you also brought us quite a treasure." Mother turned to Sorcha and held out her hand.

Sorcha slipped Godda's bracelet off her wrist and placed it in Mother's open palm.

"We've been holding on to this for you," she said, offering the bracelet to Evelyn.

"Thank you," Evelyn said. "But I think you should have it."

"Nonsense, child," Mother said. She placed the bracelet in Evelyn's palm. "I will be gone soon and have no need for such things." She wrapped Evelyn's fingers over the gold band and rested her long, thin hand on top. "But there is something I would like to take with me."

Sorcha reached for Mother's arm, but Mother didn't let go of Evelyn's hand.

"Flee," Sorcha said, using my mother's childhood nickname. "Let me do it. Save your strength."

Mother didn't move, except to glance at Sorcha out of the corner of her eye. "And what should I save it for?" she asked. "Edric is gone. You've been returned to us. There is nothing left for me to do but free our sister from her prison and join her."

Sorcha stood and leaned over my mother, wrapping her arms around Mother's frail frame. Still, Mother didn't let go of Evelyn's hands. But she glanced up, past Evelyn, to meet my eyes. I swallowed my tears and nodded at her. Then I stepped forward and slipped my hand around Evelyn's waist.

Mother cupped her hands under Evelyn's and began to speak in the ancient tongue. Sorcha sobbed silently but held my mother as she recited the words that would free Godda's life force. The bracelet began to glow, and Evelyn's fingers arched away from the metal. But Mother didn't release her grasp. She just continued her chant.

Light shined out through the markings on the band, and the bracelet began to spin in Evelyn's open palm. Mother continued her soft and steady chanting, and Sorcha held her and gave her strength. Evelyn leaned into me, her arm rigid and straining. She tried to pull her hand away, but Mother wouldn't release her grasp.

The band was a blur of shining gold. The light pulsed in time with Mother's chanting. Then, my eyes blinked shut against a flash of bright white light. When I opened them, Mother lay limp in Sorcha's arms, and the bracelet sat still and plain in Evelyn's outstretched palm. Sorcha sobbed, and Fiona stepped forward, Arabella at her side. Evelyn cradled her hand, still holding the bracelet, and buried her face against my chest.

I watched as Sorcha and Fiona laid Mother's body flat on the bed. They crossed her hands over her chest and brushed her hair from her face. Arabella disappeared and returned with a crown of flowers and a wooden staff. She handed me the staff before placing the crown on Mother's head. Fiona coaxed Evelyn from my arms so I could tuck the staff beneath Mother's hands.

Tears dripped from my eyes as I placed a kiss on each of her cheeks and said goodbye. Then I wrapped my arm around Evelyn and led her out onto the lawn. I wanted to get her home before our kin gathered for the wake. I would need to be here to greet the mourners, and I decided that Evelyn would be more comfortable with her aunt and uncle.

Evelyn still clutched the bracelet to her chest. Her face had gone extremely pale and she trembled.

"She's gone," she whispered.

I tucked her into my arms and held her close. She leaned against me for a moment, then she pulled back and looked up at me with wide eyes.

"I should give this to Fiona," she said, holding out the bracelet in her open palm.

I shook my head. "Not now," I said. "Maybe later. Right now, I should get you back to Lydbury. I have things I'll need to do here."

"Oh," she said. "If that's what you want." She looked down at her hand and ran her thumb over the smooth metal.

"You really want to stay?" I asked Evelyn. A hand touched my arm, and I turned my head to find Arabella standing next to me.

"Not now," I growled at her.

"Please," she said. Tears glistened in her eyes. "Talk to me." Her fingers dug into my arm.

I released Evelyn and spun to face Arabella, shaking her fingers from my arm in the process. "Now is really not a good time."

"You think I don't know that? Flida was like a mother to me. Don't shut me out. You're all I have left. You're all *we* have left. We need you." She stared me down with her hands on her hips.

"Edric's gone. Mother's gone. I owe you nothing." I started to turn away, but she grabbed me again. I growled low in my throat, but she didn't release me.

"We're family. And we need you," she said.

I grabbed her hand and pried it off me. "Maybe you should have thought of that before you nearly killed her," I said, taking a step closer and stabbing my finger into her breastbone.

"You had no right."

She winced and backed up. "Be reasonable. How was I supposed to know?"

"It wasn't your call to make."

"Fine. I'm sorry I nearly killed your human. Are you happy now?" She threw her hands up.

I shook my head. "You're not sorry. You're just like my sire. You hate them. Do you really expect me to believe you care?"

"Don't be a fool." She glared at me.

I laughed. "I knew it. You'd do it again if you had half a reason." My fists clenched, and I burned to transform and resume the fight we'd had on the lawn just a few days ago.

"Stop it," Fiona's voice cut across the lawn. Arabella and I froze. "Stop it before either of you say something you'll regret."

Arabella took a step backward, toward the cottage.

"Go," I said.

She opened her mouth to respond, but Fiona cut her off.

"Arabella, inside, now."

Arabella snapped her jaw shut, and I could hear her grinding her teeth. But she obeyed, turning her back on me and pushing past Fiona and into the darkness of the cottage. Fiona held my gaze for a long moment, then disappeared inside.

I turned toward Evelyn and found her staring at me, eyes wide. "Explain," she said, biting off the word.

"It was a mistake," I said, trying to shake off the adrenaline rushing through my body.

"That's not what you just said. You said she tried to kill me." She pointed toward the cottage.

"But she didn't." I reached for her.

She twisted away from my hand and took a step back. "Tell

me what happened."

I jammed my fingers into my hair and dug the tips into my scalp. This was not going well. "Ari was there when we returned through the tunnel after escaping from the dungeons. She attacked you."

"When were you going to tell me this?"

"You didn't remember." I shrugged. "It didn't seem important."

"Liam, your cousin hates me." She folded her arms across her chest.

"She doesn't hate you. She was just doing what she thought needed to be done. It's her job to protect Fiona."

Evelyn frowned. "You just said it yourself, though. You said she hates humans. You said your father hates humans."

"That doesn't mean they hate *you*." I stepped in front of her and placed my hands lightly on her shoulders.

She shook her head. "I've caused enough trouble for you and your family. Maybe you should just take me back to Lydbury."

"I want to be with you." I cupped her cheek with my palm and tipped her head up until her eyes met mine.

"You need to be with your family." Tears welled in her eyes.

"Don't you see, I've put them first my whole life. I've done everything they've asked of me, and more. But I can't fight this war anymore."

"What are you saying?" She placed her palms against my chest.

"I won't swear the Oath."

She groaned. "Don't you see? Everything you did, you did because you love them. You can't walk away now." She paused and frowned. Then she added, in a low voice, "I won't let you give up your family for me."

"Then I won't give them up, but I'm not giving up on you, either." I skimmed my hands over her shoulders and down her sides until they reached her waist.

"Your cousin hates me." She slid her hands up my chest until they rested on my collarbones.

I smiled. "You already said that."

"It's still true." She raised her eyebrows, daring me to contradict her.

I kissed her forehead and her muscles relaxed. "Give her time," I whispered.

"Liam—"

I caught her lips with mine and cut off the rest of her sentence. *Enough talking.* We'd been through so much. I'd nearly lost her. I wouldn't lose her again. I kissed her until she relaxed in my arms and leaned into me.

"Let me get you back to Lydbury," I whispered, leaning my forehead against hers so the tips of our noses touched. "We can deal with Ari tomorrow."

Evelyn sighed. "Okay," she said.

"You ready?" I asked.

I waited for her to inhale, then, focusing on the carriage house, I conjured us back.

18

I SUCKED air into my lungs and leaned against Liam. When I opened my eyes, we were standing outside the carriage house. The Christmas lights Aunt Vivian had strung up in the bushes twinkled in the darkness.

"Will you be back tonight?" I asked.

Liam shook his head. "The wake will last until dawn, and the coronation will begin at sunrise."

"Oh," I said, remembering my agreement with Fiona. "That soon?"

"It's our way," he said. "But I'll return as soon as I can."

"Actually," I said. I bit my lip. "I think Fiona wanted me to attend the coronation."

"See," he said. "Fiona likes you."

I rolled my eyes. "We'll see." I had no idea how I would get to the coronation. Maybe I would have to decide first, before they let me attend. "Will you come back to get me?"

"I'm not sure what Fiona has planned. She may send me. If not, someone will come to get you." Liam leaned down to kiss me, then he disappeared.

"So," a voice said from the shadows, "the queen is dead. Long live the queen."

A shiver ran down my spine. I turned, slowly, to face the figure whose voice I'd already recognized.

"They're all looking for you," I said. I tried to keep from trembling.

"Oh, it sounds like they have better things to do this evening." Nigel stepped out from his hiding place and into the moonlight. His features appeared angled and hawkish in the harsh lighting.

"Why are you here?" I asked.

"I wanted to say goodbye." He cocked his head and smiled at me.

"Goodbye." I folded my arms across my chest and waited for him to leave.

"I also wanted to give you a warning." His smile faded.

"So give it."

"I won't come after you." He slipped his hands into the pockets of his black wool jacket. "But, you should know, my mother might."

"What happened back there? Did you have a falling out?"

"She certainly wasn't pleased that I let you two get away," he said. "But I tried to explain that I was saving her skin." He shrugged, hands still buried deep in his pockets. "She may not have entirely believed me."

"So you're running away?" I asked.

"Care to join me?" He arched one perfect eyebrow at me.

"You've lost your mind." I shivered.

"Quite possibly." He took a step toward me, and I resisted the urge to back away. "I didn't want to hurt you," he said.

I tensed. "Are you done?"

He watched me closely. "I'm not the enemy, Evelyn."

"You could have fooled me."

He shook his head. "You'll see," he said. "The enemy is coming. Protect yourself." He snapped his fingers and disappeared.

I exhaled and let my head fall back. Stars glimmered in the night sky above. Only a handful of hours remained for me to make a decision about my future, and now I had confirmation that a demon woman would be hunting me down. If Fiona erased my memories, I wouldn't know what danger I was in when Lilium came for me.

I shivered in the cold, crisp night air and wrapped my arms around myself to keep warm. I walked along the path to the mudroom entrance and crept through the kitchen and up the stairs. As much as I wanted my aunt's advice, I knew I couldn't consult her on my decision. So I decided I'd use the large house to my advantage and avoid them.

I loved my family. The thought of living long after my parents and brothers were gone frightened me. Fiona hadn't said that I needed to stop seeing them if I chose to become Sworn. But how would I explain to my family when I never seemed to age? Liam's mother and Sorcha had lived for nearly a millennium, and they looked no older than my grandmother.

I paced around my room. I picked up clothes and tidied my dresser. I flipped through photos on my phone. Then, frustrated, I turned off the screen and tossed my phone onto the bed. I stalked over to the window and stared out at the moonlit garden below.

As many times as I went over it in my head, one thing remained constant. I didn't want to give up the knowledge I'd gained. I didn't want to leave Liam and his world behind. I wanted to know more. I wanted more time with him. I didn't know what would happen with us, but I didn't want to give him up any more than he wanted to give me up.

I'd come here with a plan for my future. I still wanted to work with my uncle and maybe go to graduate school. But nothing I could learn in a classroom would teach me about the Fae. I wanted to learn more about this world that I'd only just discovered. I wanted to learn how to protect myself, and I wanted to find a way to help.

I lay down on top of the bed, still fully clothed, and stared up at the ceiling. I couldn't sleep, and I couldn't stop thinking. So I crept up to the attic. I knew Liam wouldn't be there, but it made me feel better to be closer to his things. I pushed his door open, pulled a blanket off his bed, and dragged it over to the window seat. Then I wrapped the blanket around my shoulders and curled up next to the gargoyle on the bench. I leaned my head against the window frame and stared out across the fields and let my mind churn. At some point, I must have closed my eyes.

When I opened them again, a faint light glowed above the horizon. I glimpsed a flash out of the corner of my eye and turned to see Sorcha standing in the alcove with me. She stared down at the gargoyle and then reached a hand out to touch the statue.

"Fascinating," she said.

"You should see the statue of the faerie," I said.

She glanced at me as though noticing me for the first time.

"Fiona sent me," she said. "It's time."

I stood and let the blanket fall onto the bench. I ran my fingers through my hair and looked down at my rumpled clothes.

"I should change," I said.

Fiona waved her hand, and when I looked again, I was

wearing a long tunic and leggings, similar to what Sorcha wore. She held out her hand to me.

"Come," she said.

I placed my hand in hers and braced myself for the empty, airless space. But traveling with Sorcha was different. This time it felt like we'd plunged into a tropical sea. When we surfaced, we were standing in a forest.

Sorcha released my hand and began walking along a dirt path. I followed her between the lush, ancient trees coated with lichen and moss. A break in the trees ahead revealed a clearing filled with Fae. Tiny winged faeries hovered and swarmed above the heads of stunningly beautiful males and females, all lean and lanky and dressed in belted tunics and tapered pants in earth tones. Clustered at their feet and atop boulders were squat creatures with long noses, large, pointy ears, and short wings folded tight to their bodies. Everywhere I looked, I found a new type of Fae to admire.

I tried not to stare and gape too much as Sorcha and I edged around the gathering crowd to join Liam and Arabella next to a glimmering pool at the foot of a rushing waterfall. They stood shoulder to shoulder staring out over the still waters toward the falls. I hoped this meant that they'd resolved their differences. It would make what I was about to do a lot easier.

I stepped beside Liam. He reached for my hand without looking over at me, and my fingers interlaced with his. Sorcha left us standing there and continued walking to a large boulder near the edge of the pool. She stopped at the foot of the boulder and turned to face the crowd. Then she held up her hands to silence those gathered behind us in the clearing.

A hush fell over the assembled Fae. The sound of the waterfall filled the air, broken only by the chirp of a bird or the wind in the treetops above. Two figures appeared near the base of the falls and walked arm in arm around the edge of the still pool. As they approached, I recognized Fiona on the arm of a much older Fae male with bushy white hair and a long white beard. He led her to the boulder, and stopped next to Sorcha.

Sorcha began speaking in a language I couldn't understand. I guessed it was the language of the Fae, the same language she'd used when she'd spoken with Liam back in Edric's dungeons. Fiona bowed her head, and the male produced a staff similar to the one Liam had tucked into Flida's arms after she'd passed.

The old Fae handed the staff to Sorcha, who held it up for all those gathered to see. She said something, and they responded in unison. Then she tapped Fiona's shoulders with the staff and presented it to her. Fiona accepted the offering and turned to face the gathering. The male reached up and placed an iron crown atop her head. The band was a simple design, made to look like a series of twisted and braided vines.

Fiona let Sorcha and the male help her step up onto the boulder. When she reached the top, she held the staff high and said something. I couldn't understand her words, but I sensed the emotion behind them. Liam gripped my hand in reaction, then released it when she finished speaking so he could clap and cheer with the crowd.

As the cheering died down, Arabella stepped forward. She knelt at the base of the boulder and bowed to her queen. Fiona descended to stand before Arabella and receive the first Oath from her Sworn.

When Arabella finished speaking, Fiona bent and kissed her forehead. Then Arabella stood and took her place at Fiona's side. The cheering resumed in response.

With the roar of the crowd in my ears, I stepped forward. Liam hissed, and his fingers brushed my arm as he reached for me, but I moved too fast for him to react. In a moment, I had taken Arabella's place, kneeling at Fiona's feet. The assembled Fae fell silent. I didn't know the proper words, so I improvised.

"I swear my life and my loyalty to the Queen of the Fae." My heart hammered as I waited for her response.

"This is your decision?"

"It is."

"Then I accept you as Sworn to the Fae Court." She bent and placed a kiss on my forehead. Then I stood and found a place next to Arabella.

The Fae in the clearing whispered and clapped but didn't cheer.

Liam stared at me across the grass. While he hesitated, Sorcha came forward to swear her Oath. I still couldn't understand a word being spoken, but it didn't matter. I'd made my decision, and now I had to wait while Liam made his. While Sorcha knelt, Liam never took his eyes off mine. I couldn't tell what he was thinking; I only wondered what he would decide.

Once Sorcha stood and stepped aside, Liam looked away, locking eyes with Fiona. He took a tentative step forward, paused, then closed the remaining distance. He glanced once more at me before kneeling at Fiona's feet.

After Liam stood, Fiona addressed the gathering again. Then she turned and retraced her path around the pool toward the base of the waterfall. Arabella fell into step behind her queen. Liam, Sorcha, and I followed. The old Fae remained behind, and the Fae who had gathered to see the coronation began to disburse.

When we reached the base of the waterfall, Liam pulled me aside.

"Why did you do that?" he asked.

"Fiona gave me a choice," I said. "She said she'd let me live, but I needed to either become Sworn and immortal, or return to the humans with no memory of the Fae."

"Why didn't you tell me?"

"I needed to make my own decision. Just like you needed to make yours."

"You gave up your humanity to be one of us?"

"Well, not exactly one of you."

"Why did you do it?"

"I can't turn my back on this world now that I know it exists. And I don't want to give you up, either."

Liam threw his arms around me and kissed my face. "You're amazing," he said. "You're perfect."

"You're Sworn," Arabella said.

Liam froze. I looked over his shoulder and found Arabella staring at me.

"So that's the deal she made with you," Arabella said. "Fiona always did have a soft spot for her cousin Liam."

"Ari, she took the Oath. Let it go," Liam said.

I slipped past Liam to face his cousin. If I was going to spend eternity with Arabella, I couldn't let Liam fight my battles for me. "I understand why you did what you did," I said. "But we're on the same side now. We both want the same thing. Can't we start over?"

"Start over?" She scowled. "We'll see. Liam's marked you and Fiona's made you one of us, but you're still human. It's going to take more than that for me to trust you."

"Fair enough," I said. It was a start.

Arabella nodded and walked away. I turned to face Liam.

"About that marked thing," I said.

He looked down at his feet and stuffed his hands in his pockets. "About that," he said.

"How does she know? Does she know what it means?"

"I asked Fiona about it while you were recovering."

"And?"

"She thinks it might have something to do with that night in the attic..."

"Oh." I could feel myself blushing.

"Yeah." He glanced at me shyly.

"So does that mean that, as far as the Fae are concerned, I belong to you?"

"Not exactly. More like we belong to each other." He inched closer to me. "I think I could reverse it, if it bothers you."

"No," I said. "I think I'm okay with that." I reached for his hand. "As long as it's mutual."

He swept me up in his arms and took my breath away with his kiss.

If you enjoyed this book, please leave a review at your online bookseller of choice.

Don't miss the next book in the Modern Fae series, coming in Spring 2019!

To be the first to know about discounts, giveaways, sneak peeks, and behind the scenes book info, sign up for my newsletter at http://bit.ly/MagicForMortals.

ACKNOWLEDGEMENTS

This book wouldn't be what it is without the wonderful people who've helped me along the way.

The first draft of this novel was originally written during NaNoWriMo 2015. So, I want to thank the fine folks who organize and run National Novel Writing Month. I may never have taken the chance to write this without the encouragement of the NaNoWriMo community, including the writers in the Marin Region and my Night of Writing Dangerously table buddies: Team 50/50 Wombat Pajamas. Another huge thank you goes out to my UC Berkeley Extension professors, especially Mary Ann Koory for her Developing the Novel and her Mystery Fiction classes and her ongoing support of and interest in my writing career.

In addition to excellent teachers, I've been lucky enough to work with some great developmental editors at various stages in my writing process. Thank you, Naomi Hughes and Michelle Hazen, for your feedback and guidance.

Thank you to my amazing copy editor: Michelle Hope

555

from The Artful Editor. Never have I felt so embarrassed and appreciative at the same time. Any mistakes that remain are entirely my fault.

Thank you to my fantastic cover designer: Elizabeth Mackey. Your covers are magical, and I'm thrilled I get to work with you.

Lorna, Rowena, Anne, Kit, and Gail were some of the first people to read early drafts of this novel and provide me with feedback. I will forever be grateful for their critiques and encouragement, and all the tasty snacks we shared together while talking about our writing.

Thank you to my amazing beta readers: Kaitlin, Linden, Sharon, Kellie, Elizabeth, and Kilby. Knowing that you were eagerly awaiting the next section kept me on track and editing. Your questions and your super-reader abilities to spot plot holes and inconsistencies are invaluable.

Thank you to the Romance Writers of America (RWA) chapters whose contest judges provided critical feedback on first pages, especially: San Francisco's Heart to Heart Contest, and Kiss of Death's Daphne du Maurier Award.

Thank you to my SFA RWA chapter buddies. I wouldn't have had the courage and determination to publish this without your encouragement. Thank you for supporting me and pointing me toward resources I needed to figure out how to publish and market this series.

Thank you to friends and family who have always supported my writing: Merrilee and Uncle Tom, Aunt Lisa and Jeff, Aunt Lorraine, Cornett & Co., the Chaffins, the Olmettis, the Speeds, the Surbaughs, Scott and Lauren, Craig and Nancy, Megan H., Jen W., and Laura O.

Thank you to my mother-in-law and father-in-law who may still remember the four mile hike on Thanksgiving weekend when I mostly ignored everyone and started talking to myself while I worked through some sticky plot points in the first draft of this book.

Huge thanks to my mom, who is definitely my first and biggest fan, and to my husband, Greg, who never fails to push me, encourage me, and take care of dinner when I'm drafting or editing.

And, most importantly, thank YOU, dear reader! This book is incomplete without you, and I am forever grateful that you chose to spend time with me and the characters in this world.

ABOUT THE AUTHOR

Elizabeth Menozzi is an award-winning writer of science fiction and fantasy with romance. A former Midwestern girl with a bad case of wanderlust, she currently resides on Orcas Island with her husband. In her spare time she is a competitive swimmer, reluctant runner, and devourer of books. This is her first published novel.

You can follow her on Twitter (@emenozzi) and Instagram (emmenozzi), or contact her via her website at http://www.elizabethmenozzi.com/.

Made in the USA
Monee, IL
15 April 2021